Dragon Heart

BOOKS BY CECELIA HOLLAND

The Serpent Dreamer
The Witches' Kitchen
The Soul Thief
The Angel and the Sword
Lily Nevada
An Ordinary Woman
Railroad Schemes
Valley of the Kings
Jerusalem
Pacific Street
The Bear Flag
The Lords of Vaumartin
Pillar of the Sky
The Belt of Gold
The Sea Beggars
Home Ground
City of God

Two Ravens
Floating Worlds
Great Maria
The Death of Attila
The Earl
Antichrist
Until the Sun Falls
The Kings in Winter
Rakóssy
The Firedrake
Varanger
The High City
Kings of the North

FOR CHILDREN
The King's Road
Ghost on the Steppe

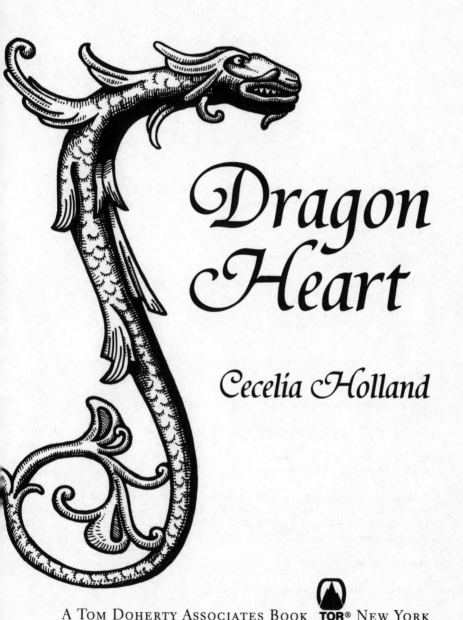

Dragon Heart

Cecelia Holland

A Tom Doherty Associates Book ■ **TOR**® New York

DRAGON HEART

A Tor Book
Published by Tom Doherty Associates, LLC
175 Fifth Avenue
New York, NY 10010

www.tor-forge.com

Tor® is a registered trademark of Tom Doherty Associates, LLC.

The Library of Congress Cataloging-in-Publication Data is available upon request.

ISBN 978-0-7653-3794-8 (hardcover)
ISBN 978-1-4668-3649-5 (e-book)

Tor books may be purchased for educational, business, or promotional use. For information on bulk purchases, please contact the Macmillan Corporate and Premium Sales Department at 1-800-221-7945, extension 5442, or write to specialmarkets@macmillan.com.

First Edition: September 2015

Printed in the United States of America

0 9 8 7 6 5 4 3 2 1

This book is dedicated to the 59 Angels who gave me back my hearing.

Dragon Heart

1

JEON COULD HEAR HIS SISTER SCREAMING ALL THE WAY FROM the other end of the cloister, and beside him the abbot was fumbling with a set of keys. Jeon wheeled on him.

"You've locked her up? How dare you lock her up!" He strode down the walkway toward the heavy door, which Tirza's wails pierced like knives through the wood.

"My lord, she is uncontrollable; she screams during prayers, she hits us—"

"She is a Princess of Castle Ocean." He tore the key from the monk's hand and thrust it into the lock. "You'll suffer for this, Abbot."

As Jeon turned the key in the lock the screaming stopped. He swung the door open, and there sat his sister, cross-legged on the cot, staring at him.

She burst into a huge smile and, stretching her arms out, leapt to her feet and ran to him, this funny tiny girl, with her wild red frizz of hair, her dusky skin, her huge blue eyes, who looked nothing like him but was his twin. He gathered her into his arms.

"My dear. My dear one."

She nuzzled him, clinging to him. She came only to his shoulder, slender as a twig, like a feather in his arms. Her hair smelled of the sea dew that flavored her bath. She wore only a long shift; he looked quickly around for other clothes, for attendants, and turned on the abbot again.

"This is an outrage."

"My lord, my lord." The abbot was bobbing up and down like a bird. "We did not know—we did not expect—"

Tirza was pulling away from Jeon, brushing her wild hair back with both hands. She gave him an intent look, and went straight out the door and through the hedge there onto the sunlit grass at the center of the cloister, and stood there, raising her hands and her face into the light and the air. Jeon said, "You mean, you didn't think we would care what happened to her." He went after his sister, now turning slowly around on the grass, her arms raised over her head. "Tirza, come along." He had to find her something to wear.

She came up to him, her eyes direct, and tugged on his cloak. "Ah," he said, and took it off, and she wrapped it around herself, her gaze never leaving his face. She gave a low, mushy growl. Her brilliant blue eyes rounded, asking something.

He had always understood her better than anybody, some shared mind. "Oh," he said. "Yes, we have to go home. Mother wants us all there. She is being married off again."

Tirza's whole face flared with temper. She shook her head at him.

"I'm afraid so. Another of the Emperor's brothers. Nobody likes him, not even Mother. And he has two sons of his own. Whom he has brought with him to Castle Ocean. You won't like them, either."

She shook her head at him again, she clenched her fist, and her mouth opened, and he put his hand over her mouth. "No, Tirza. Not to me."

She shuddered. Turning, she walked quickly away, and he caught up with her in a stride and took hold of her hand. Her fingers closed tight on his. They went on down the walkway, silent. At the door, he said, "I want to leave directly. I came overland, but there's an Imperial galley here that's on its way to Castle Ocean. That can take us home, and fairly quickly, too. The abbot has orders to pack your things. Didn't you have any women with you?"

She aimed a brief, flashing look at him, and he laughed. Six months in this place had not subdued her, and he was beginning to enjoy the idea of seeing her meet the new putative stepfather. Outside the cloister, Jeon's men waited by the wall with the horses. They bowed to him, and then also to Tirza, murmuring some greeting. Bedro was the closer of the two and bowing put him within reach, and she patted his head like a dog's.

Jeon left Bedro to collect her baggage, put her up behind his saddle, and with the other man riding in front of them to clear the way they went down through the market. Santomalo covered both banks of the river here, its rows of red-roofed houses rising up the gentle hills from the beach. The sun was high and the harbor glittered, full of ships. He pointed toward the galley drawn in against the long wharf. "That's the ship we're taking. They're trying to map the seacoast out to Cape of the Winds and then south, I think."

She was holding on to the back of his belt as they rode along; she leaned forward, looking toward the harbor. The street turned steep down into the market, a field of different-colored awnings, noisy and busy with people. Jeon's man called out and the crowd parted to let them through. Someone called out, "Monkey woman!" Jeon felt Tirza let go of his belt and swung his arm around behind him and gripped her fast. She leaned on him, snarling. They wound through the bazaar, past the rows of casks, the braided strings of onions and garlic, the bleating lambs in their withy pens. As they passed the lambs, Tirza bleated back. That she could do, make any noise but words. They were coming to the wharf.

"This is the Emperor's galley, remember," Jeon said lightly. "And the Emperor's captain." He reined up his horse on the bank beside the wharf, and she slid down to the ground, looking all around with her intense blue gaze. Jeon dismounted; his man came to collect the horse. There was no room for horses on the galley and these would go back overland. He was interested in the galley and glad to have a chance to sail on it, and he stood a moment running his eyes over it, seeing how it was built.

The galley was long and thin, with a high curled tail and a pointed head, laid against the wharf like a great wooden blade beside its sheath. The crew had gone off. No sails hung from the long diagonal yards and below the deck the oars were shipped inside the portholes, their leather sleeves like pursed lips. Down there, under the deck when the lips were plugged with oars and all the men were pulling at once, that space had to be a hot and airless hell. He stepped out onto the polished, honey-colored deck and turned to help his sister, whether she liked it or not.

The captain bustled importantly toward them. Like all the Imperial men, he put much effort into appearances. He took off his hat as he came, made a deep obeisance to Jeon, and faced Tirza.

"My lady, welcome. Whatever we can do to make your passage agreeable, you need only speak." He reached out for Tirza's hand and she drew back from his touch. With a gesture toward the foremast, he said, "You see we have made arrangements for your comfort." Still trying to grasp her hand, still bowing. Around the foot of the mast, several layers of light cloth hung suspended, enclosing a space hardly big enough to stand up in. She backed away from that, bumping into Jeon, and swatted at the captain's reaching hand. A string of barks and growls issued from her.

"My lady." The captain goggled at her, his arm dropping to his side.

Jeon said, "My sister is mute. She does not speak." To her, he said, "Go inside for now, Tirza." He had a firm grip on her arm; she was half-naked and he was determined to get her out of sight. She obeyed him, moved into the little silken room, and the veils fell between them.

SHE WAS NOT MUTE. SHE TALKED, BUT NOBODY UNDERSTOOD her. She had said Jeon's name, back at the cloister, and he had only frowned at her, uncomprehending, his own beloved name.

She sat on a cushion in this new, prettier cell, liking the way the sun shone through the veils of the walls. One was lavender colored and the light lay on her hands like a weightless wing. She thought over what he had told her, that they were forcing her mother to marry again.

They had tried this once before. Her mother had poisoned that one on their wedding night. She wondered why the Emperor did not take the point.

The chest with her things pushed in under the bottom edge of the silky wall before her. The same unseen hands whisked the veil quickly down again. It was a warm day, and she was comfortable enough in just the shift, but if she went out like this Jeon would make her come back inside. She unlatched the chest and got out a long dark gown. Through the wall she heard someone talking, close by, and then Jeon spoke. She pulled the gown on over her head, let the laces dangle, and went out onto the deck of the galley.

Jeon and the captain stood there in the beak. The captain had a long roll of parchment in his hands, and as she came up he spread it out before them on the rail where the gunwales came together.

She looked on curiously. The monks had had such parchments, which they marked carefully with black curling lines. This was not like that: this showed more of a picture. On the left-hand side was a busy clutter of zigzags, which she knew at once were the hills behind Santomalo; on the broad expanse there was a big cross in a circle, which meant the Empire.

To the west, the picture narrowed to a single feathery line, and that line soon vanished into nothing. On the far right side, another big upright zigzag.

The captain jabbed his finger at it, and said, "That is Cape of the Winds."

She understood now, and she almost laughed. They had set down this swarm of lines to mean the world, then. But they had left out everything that moved, the wind and the waves, light and the dark; they had turned the myriad shapes into one shape, as if they were the same forever, locked on to their parchment.

In the blank spaces, the maker had drawn little pictures, as if he could not bear the emptiness, a sword, a four-pointed star, a bird, a whale, a dragon.

The captain was saying, "You see the problem. None of this is charted." His hand swept from the busy edge across the blank space. His voice was stiff. "I'd like to wait for more ships, make up a fleet."

Jeon said, "Nothing ever was charted, until someone did it. Get a chart maker and take him along."

"I can't even find a man who will pilot us along this coast." Again the captain swept his hand over the chart. He looked up with a frown, toward where the line between the land and the sea swept away straight into the west. "And Cape of the Winds is famously treacherous. *Post Sanctum Malum malum*, they say."

"How did you get here?" Jeon asked.

"Down the river," the captain said. "That stream I know, every current and every rock and where to put in for the night. Not . . . this."

Her brother put his hand down on the middle of the parchment, as if he would seize it. "Then we will be the first."

"My lord. With all possible respect—"

"Let's go," Jeon said. He turned, saw her, and smiled at her. "I can't wait." He put out his hand to her. "Come, pretty sister; we shall walk along the deck together."

THE FIRST DAY, WITH THE WIND FAIR, THEY SAILED OUT OF the estuary of Santomalo and along the coast westward. On the leeward side they passed by a white beach covered with driftwood. In the evening they put into a little cove for the night and the whole crew went ashore, where they built a bonfire. Their shouts came faintly across the water to the ship. Jeon and Tirza sat on the deck, and he opened up his pack and got out their supper.

"This is another kind of invasion," Jeon said. "The ship, I mean. The damned Empire. The castle is full of soldiers. Luka will only go in and out of the castle by the seaways, so he doesn't have to pass by the guards at the door." Jeon put down his cup and took the flagon and filled it again. The sea breeze patted at them in little gusts. The moon was full, half-drowning the stars. Before them on a cloth the remains of their dinner: fish bones and tails, bread crusts, bits of cheese. Off on the shore the crew moved around their bonfire, settling down in the dark, like sleeping sea cattle. The long, narrow ship rocked gently against its anchor. Tirza was sitting next to him, her head tipped back toward the moon.

"Too bad we have no musicians," he said.

She sighed. She loved music; she let out a stream of noise that sounded a little like music.

"Anyway, Mother has refused, so far, to go to the altar, for all kinds of reasons, but mostly because she wanted all of us to be there. For a while Luka was gone, out to sea somewhere, you know how he is, but then he came home, and all she could do was claim that she could not marry until you were home, too."

Tirza gurgled, maybe a laugh. Jeon drank more wine, leaning on cushions. "I doubt this will make her like you any more, that she has to marry when you arrive."

She nudged him, and she did laugh. Between her and their mother much evil lay, which seemed to bother neither of them. He wondered, as he often did, what understandings Tirza had locked up behind the voice that would not work. He would never know what she thought, nor what she believed. Now she was looking away, the moonlight bright on her face, and babbling, perhaps meaning music. He felt a wash of loneliness, although he had her by the hand, as if he reached through a hole in the wall that surrounded her.

THIS IS BEAUTIFUL, TIRZA THOUGHT, AND SHIVERED.

They had been sailing west for days, now, every night putting in to sleep in some new place. This was the next new place. A wide, placid bay stretched out before them. The eastern edge rose into a long, dark line of hills, the shore curving deeply away beneath a palisade of sheer black rock, until it swung another arm out again into the sea. Shielded from the rough ocean, the water ran dark blue toward the beach, turned pale blue and green in the shallows, foamed white at the edge. Below the foot of the palisade the constant moving margin of surf separated the water from an arc of pale brown sand.

The crew had hauled down the great triangular sail. The galley stroked steadily in toward the land, the oars rumbling in their sockets. She leaned on the gunwale, looking down over the side. As they passed over the clear, green-blue water, she could see dark clumps in the depths: reefs and rocks. There was a reef directly below their boat now, the lumpy stone waving green with seaweed and alive with fish.

The broad bay was empty, desolate. On the shore, no huts showed, no smoke rose, there were no signs of fire pits or trash. No ships rode on the sheltered water, and no trails climbed the far green slopes.

Yet as they drew closer, all along the clean pale beach, in the driftwood, she could see the sun-bleached ribs and planks of boats. Some of these chunks of wood looked burnt. Down on the bottom in the clear blue depths, as the men rowed steadily across the bay, she saw a boxy stern and part of a thwart poking out of the sand. Nowhere was there a sign of a living man, except those newly come, but everywhere she saw shipwrecks.

She saw fish, also, everywhere, great schools of them. Their silver backs blended into the pale bottom and she found them first by their shadows on the sand. A seagull wheeled above them, screeching. She thought, for an instant, she caught a note of warning in its voice.

Jeon came up beside her. "Isn't this lovely?" He was still a moment, his face grim. "I hate that they are coming here."

She said nothing, thinking of the parchment and its lines. They would turn all this into lines, too, while she and Jeon, who should protect this place, did nothing. The captain strode up the ship, calling out orders. Three men ran up to the foremast, to take down the slantwise yard. Along the sides of the galley, all the oars but two rose dripping, cocked into the air, and withdrew through their ports into the hull. The galley glided through the calm water toward the beach, the front oars rising and falling in a slow rhythm.

She felt the boat under her quiver slightly.

The captain bellowed, "Steer, will you? What's wrong with you?" He went down amidships, cursing.

From the stern came a wail. The ship hit something under the water; Tirza staggered, and when the deck tipped steeply up she slammed down into the rail.

Jeon sprawled across the deck. She flung out an arm to catch him; he struck the mast and rolled out of her reach. The ship careened sideways. The captain staggered and came up against the mainmast, buckling her house of cloth around him. Tirza was holding tight to the rail with both hands; a sailor rushed past her and dove overboard. She twisted, looking for Jeon, and saw him huddled facedown under the stern rail.

She felt her grip on the gunwale slipping. She hung over the rail. A wash of salt water broke over her. She rocked back up again into the air, gasping. Below, the water was churning and leaping, thrashed to madness, and then up through the chaos came the dragon.

He was red as new blood, big as the ship. The enormous horned head reared up into the air, borne high on the long neck, and the shoulders thrust through the water. Tirza struggled to turn to go to Jeon; he still lay on the deck down below, wedged against the footing of the tiller, and she lunged toward him, and then the dragon's jaws parted and a gust of green flame erupted from its throat.

The fiery stream hit the deck of the ship and it burst into flame. From under the deck came the screams of the oarsmen trapped down there. Tirza stretched toward Jeon, veiled in the fire, and the dragon struck the ship and heeled it over, and this time it broke in half.

The stern lurched up, and Tirza fell overboard. She plunged deep into the water; in her ears the constant roaring faded to a muted hum. She came up a few yards from the blazing bow of the galley, the glare in her eyes, the heat beating on her face. The sea was steaming. In the wild thrashing waves she could not swim; she could barely keep herself afloat. She flailed out with her arms, trying to claw her way through the broken battering waves. Something struck her in the side and drove her under. She swam up, and her outstretched arm caught something solid and she clung to it and pulled herself up to the air. A moment later she realized she was clutching a dead body.

Even recoiling from it, she looked to see if it was Jeon. Then from just above her the huge red head drove down and took the corpse away, so close she saw her reflection in the fierce slits of its eyes.

She screamed, clawing backward. The beast loomed over her, enormous, its red scales streaming. She saw its head dart down beyond her again and rear up, a man clutched in its jaws. The sailor was alive, thrashing, his mouth open, and the dragon flipped him up into the air, so that he came down headfirst, and swallowed him whole. The huge maw swung around again. Away from her. She struggled in the furious water, trying to swim across the tow, but the crashing directionless waves carried her swiftly always closer to the dragon. Her ears were full of roaring and screaming. She could not breathe; salt water stung her nose. She saw the wedge-shaped red head rise again, another man in its teeth.

Then the surge of the water brought her directly against the dragon's side. Her fingers scraped over the slick red scales, trying to find a hold. Above her, along the beast's spine, rose a row of giant golden barbs, and she lunged up and caught one and held on.

The beast was snapping at some other swimmer. Clutching the spine, Tirza was borne higher up into the air. Below her she saw the bow of the ship but not the stern. Nothing of her brother. Below her, the water was full of men, some drowned, some screaming and waving their arms, and some trying to swim, and the dragon caught another, and another, its head darting here and there at the end of its long, supple neck. She wrapped her belt around the spinal barb, to stay on, the barb thick as a tree bough, polished smooth and sleek as gold; she was sick to her stomach; she could not breathe; she knew that Jeon was dead, that they were all dead. She would die next. The beast whirled and her head struck the barb hard enough to daze her. The sky reeled by her, and then abruptly the dragon was plunging down again into the sea.

She flung her head back, startled alert, and fought to untie her belt. The wet knot was solid. Just as the sea closed over her head she managed to draw in a deep lungful of air.

The sea rushed past her. The light faded. They were going down, steadily down. She looked up, and far over her head she saw a body floating limp in the shrinking patch of pale water. Then the dragon was swimming sideways, and the water was rushing in one direction like a river, through some deep, cold place.

The light vanished. In the pitch-darkness, surging along on the dragon's back, she could not imagine an end. She had to breathe. Her lungs hurt. The dark water rippled on her skin. Her arms were wrapped around the barb, her body flying along above the strong-swimming beast. She counted to herself. Surely something would happen. When she got to ten she counted again. Her lungs ached. She could see nothing. Strange lights burst in her eyes and were gone. Nausea rose in her throat. Then the dragon was swimming upward and above them was sunlit water.

She counted again, and at eight she burst into the light and the air.

Her whole body shuddered, taking in great gulps of breath. She clung to the barb, looking around her. They were in a lake, or a lagoon, surrounded by high cliffs, the water salt but calm. She realized she was inside the headland, that some passage beneath the sea cliff connected this lagoon to the sea. Ahead of her the golden barbs ran up the huge coiled neck of the dragon; it was swimming toward the beach, a strip of sand at the foot of a pleated black cliff.

She tore at her belt; with a leap of relief she saw the cloth had frayed almost apart in the wild ride, and with her fingers she ripped away the last fibers just as the dragon reached the shallow water. She plunged down the red-scaled side and ran up onto the sand.

The black cliff there rose impossibly high and steep. But its sheer face was runneled and creased, and she ducked into the nearest of these seams, back into a narrow darkening gorge that bent sharply to the left and then pinched into nothing, a cage of rock.

Far enough, she thought. She was only a few feet from the beach, but the opening was narrow and the beast couldn't reach her here, and the bend might shelter her from the flames. She crept cautiously up nearer the opening and peered around the corner, to see out.

The dragon had lain down right in front of her on the sand, its great head only about ten feet away. So it knew she was there. But it stretched out, relaxed, well fed, half-asleep. She leaned against the rock wall behind her and looked it over.

At ease, the beast sprawled with its neck coiled, its head

between its forepaws, arched claws outstretched, each claw as long as she was. The massive bulk of its body curled away, its tail half in the water still. The red arrow-shaped head lay half-turned toward her, the eyes closed. A glistening horn thrust up above each of its eyes, which were rimmed in gold, the wide, curled, oddly delicate nostrils also gold trimmed. The long red neck led back between the high, round ridge of shoulders with scales a yard across. Each scale was glossy red, gold edged, at the center a black boss. Below its barbed spine the scales overlapped in even horizontal rows, smaller with each row, red squares in golden outline. As they shrank, the black boss at the middle became smaller and fainter, the gold trim thinner; until the scales low on its sides were red alone.

She watched the dragon until the daylight was gone. Once, in its sleep, its jaws parted and gave a soft greenish burp and a little round stone rolled out. Still sleeping, its red tongue licked over its lips and it settled deeper on the sand.

The sun went down. In the night, she thought, she could escape and she edged closer to the beach. Just as she reached the mouth of the crevice the dragon's near eye opened, shining in the dark, fixed on her. Tirza scuttled back into the deep of the crevice, all her hair on end. She thought she heard a low growl behind her.

She wept; she wept for Jeon and even for the Imperial men, and for herself, because she knew she was lost. At last she slept a little. When she woke, it was morning and she was so hungry and thirsty that she went back to the mouth of the crevice.

The dragon was still there. It stood on its short, heavy legs, looking away from her. The sun blazed on its splendor, the glowing red scales, the curved golden barbs along its spine. Then the narrow-jawed head swung toward her, high above her on the long neck. Between its wide-set eyes was a disk of gold. Its eyes were big as washtubs, the black pupil a long vertical slice through the red silk of the iris, the haw at the inner corner like a fold of gold lace.

It gave a low roar, and the roar resolved into a voice so deep and huge she imagined she heard it not through her ears but the bones of her head. "Why don't you come out where I can eat you?"

"Please don't eat me," she said.

His eyes widened, looking startled. Her mouth fell open. He understood her. For a moment, they stared at each other. She took a step toward him.

"Why shouldn't I? You'll just die in there anyway." He gave a cold chuckle. "And by then you'd be too thin to bother digging for. Tell me what you'll give me, if I don't eat you."

She stood at the mouth of the crevice, and all the words crowded through her mind, everything she had ever said that nobody else had understood. But all she said was, "What do you want me to do?"

"Can you dance? Sing?"

"I—"

The dragon said, "Tell me a story."

A cold tingle went down her back. "A story," she said.

"If it's good enough, I won't eat you." The dragon settled himself down, curling his forelimbs under him like a cat, waiting.

Her heart thumped. She sifted quickly through all the stories she had ever heard; she knew at once that those stories of men would not satisfy the dragon, much less save her life.

He was waiting, patient, his jeweled eyes on her. She realized since he had begun speaking to her she had thought of him as "he." That gave her a wisp of an idea. She sat down in the mouth of the cave, folded her hands in her lap, and began, "Once there was an evil Queen. She was so evil everybody was afraid of her, except her youngest daughter." Tirza gave this Queen a round, angry face, a voice like a slap, remembering the last time she had seen her mother, remembering so well that her throat thickened and she almost stopped. She forced her mind cool. She sorted rapidly through the next possibilities. "And this Princess would not yield or bend. So the Queen hated her daughter, and decided to get rid of her. But she did not intend that the Princess could be free, to do as she pleased."

That was the real injustice. Tirza spent some time describing the beautiful daughter, so that she could plan the next part. The daughter looked a lot like her sister Casea, with her white skin, her black eyes, rather than like Tirza herself. The feel of the words in her mouth was delicious. The dragon was utterly silent, his eyes watching her steadily, his long lips curved in a slight lizard smile.

"So she shut the Princess into a tower by the sea, and set guards around her." The story was growing stronger in her mind, and she let her voice stride out confidently, telling of the tower, and the wild storms that rocked it, the sunlight that warmed it, and the birds that came to sing to the Princess in her window. "There she lived lonely, singing to the birds, and grew even more beautiful, but nobody ever saw her, except, now and then, her guards.

"But one day a Prince came by." She made the Prince like Jeon, honest and brave. Dead now, probably, dead in this monster's belly. Her voice trembled, but she brought herself back under control. She gave the Prince Jeon's red hair, which she saw amused the dragon, for the wrong reason. "The Prince heard the Princess singing, and climbed up the tower wall to her window. They fell in love at once, because she was beautiful and good and he was handsome and brave and good. But before he could carry her off, the guards burst in on them."

The dragon twitched, and she leaned toward him, intent, excited, knowing now she had him. "The guards drew their swords, and although the Prince tried to fight back, he had no weapon, and he was one against four. So they got him down quickly, and they sent for the Queen."

The dragon growled. Tirza kept her voice even and slow, rhythmic, speaking each word precisely over the rumble: this was the best part. "The Queen came at once, riding on the ocean waves, faster than any horse. She told the Prince, since he was such a lizard that he could scale a castle wall, he would become the greatest lizard. And she turned him into a dragon, and cast him into the sea."

The dragon lifted his head up and roared, not at her, but at the sky, and then quickly sank down again, his eyes blazing.

"But the Princess. What happened to her?"

Tirza was ready to run for the crevice, if this did not suit. She met the dragon eye to eye. "Her heart was broken. She fled from her mother and the tower—"

"Good."

"And now she wanders through the world looking for her Prince. Only her love can change him back. But every day she grows older, and every day, the dragon grows more like a dragon, and less like the Prince."

She was poised to run. But the dragon's eyes were shining. His long lips drew back from his dagger-teeth, and he nodded his head once. Turning, he bounded into the lagoon and disappeared in a whirling eddy.

She went cautiously out onto the open sand. From the cliff a little farther on a long spill of water fell, and she went there and quenched her thirst, all the while looking for some other way out of the lagoon. The towering black cliff enclosed it like a wall. She looked up, wondering if she could climb it, but she could see no path on the sheer face.

In the lagoon, too soon, the water churned and the dragon's head rose through the slosh of his passage and he swam to the

beach and strode up onto the sand. In his jaws he held a flopping green sea bass, which he flung down before her.

"Eat." The voice like speaking bronze.

She recoiled; the fish was still flopping, its desperate glistening eye on her. She cast around quickly for wood for a fire. "I need
to cook it—"

He growled. "You should eat your food alive. But wait." He
reared his head back and shot forth a bolt of flame, which blasted
around the fish for several seconds, until it lay utterly still.

She went warily up to it, knelt down, and touched the carcass.
Under the charred skin, the fish was nicely cooked. She peeled
back the skin and ate the hot flaky white meat. It tasted a little
sharp, but it was delicious.

The dragon was crouched there, his neck folded between his
shoulders, his head settled above his forepaws, watching her.
When she was done, and sitting there licking her fingers, he settled down around her, stretched his head out along his forepaws,
and swung his tail in a long curve, so she stood in the middle of
his coil. Half embrace, half prison. The great red eye blinked
once in a flash of gold. "Tell me another story."

AFTER THAT SHE COULD ROAM AS SHE PLEASED AROUND THE
lagoon, as long as she told the dragon stories whenever he asked.
She told him everything she knew about her family, weaving all
that together, how in the beginning the sea's youngest daughter,
Atla, came ashore at the tip of the land, where Cape of the Winds
jutted into the endless sea. Wise and kind and merry, she drew
every creature to her.

She lured even the monster Hafgavra, the Mist from the Sea,
who seized her with his many arms and carried her into his cave
above the battering tides and forced her to lie with him. After,
when he lay sated, she cut out his two hearts with a clamshell.

As he died, his body turned to black rock, and calling up all the creatures to help her, she built her castle of him. His enormous belly was the center of it, and his yawning mouth the hall, open to the sea. Of his many arms she raised four straight up as towers into the sky and wound the rest around as corridors through the rock. And there she lived, and there of the rape by Hafgavra she bore a son, the monster Atlarro, who became the first King of Castle Ocean.

Atlarro married a human woman, and their son, Lukala, had the guise of a man, but he kept the heart of the monster. And all after, his descendants had hair as red as Hafgavra's red heart's blood.

Of all this Tirza made stories. As the generations piled one on another, like the rocks of Castle Ocean, King followed on King, rescuing Princesses, punishing the wicked, battling monsters in the sea, chasing pirates, and defending his people, stories sprouting and intertwining, growing on one another. She fed all these stories to the dragon, except one.

That was the last part, the newest, how to the east the Empire was growing, spreading over the land, grinding out evil and death, until at last it reached the sea. Then her father, King Reymarro, called up all his friends and kinsmen to fight. But the Emperor lured them away from the ocean and in the mountains destroyed them.

There was no way to tell this well. She thought this story was not over yet.

One day ran after another. When the winter storms blew by and rain fell and the wind howled above the lagoon, the dragon made fires for her in her cave. He brought her fish, well cooked, and every day she told him stories. She loved the words, their feel in her mouth, their power over him, how they held him utterly rapt, all his strength and rage suspended on her breath. But the more stories she told, the more she longed for Jeon and Luka, Casea and her other sister Mervaly, and even for her mother, and for Castle Ocean on its cliff, where she belonged.

She was sitting in the sun one afternoon, thinking of Jeon and Luka, of her sisters, even of her mother, and tears began to roll down her cheeks.

The dragon said, "What's the matter? Why are you sad?"

"You ate my brother," she said bitterly. "I hate you."

He gave one of his throaty chuckles, unperturbed. "You eat the fish. You don't care about their brothers."

She cast off the thought of fish, which she had always eaten. "Do you have no family? No home but here? Where did you come from?"

He looked surprised. His huge eyes blazed red as the heart of a fire. "I was always here." But his stare shifted, and as much of a look of perplexity as she had ever seen came over his long reptile face. "I was always alone. Until you came. Now something has changed. I just realized this." He turned, and disappeared into the lagoon. She got up, and walked along the beach looking for something else to eat.

During the day he slept in the sun, or went down into the lagoon and was gone for a long while. She guessed he went out the tunnel under the cliff, to the open sea, and hunted. She wandered the beach, drinking from the waterfall, eating the berries that grew down the steep, rough wall of the cliff, and gathering sea lettuce, crabs, and clams. She worked out stories as she walked, saving bits and pieces when she could not make them whole. She thought of new words, and new patterns of words; she saw in her mind the pictures made of the words, and saved everything to tell to him.

When he came back, he always had a fish for her and cooked it with the fire of his breath; no matter what the fish—bass, tuna, or shark—the meat always had a faintly tart, spicy taste. If he had fed well he burped up lots of stones, some as big as her fist, most toe sized or smaller, crystals of red and blue and green. If he had eaten nothing or not enough, he complained and glowered at her and licked his lips at her and talked of eating her instead, his red eyes wicked, and his tongue flickering.

"I don't have to listen to you," she said, holding herself very straight. She turned back toward her crevice, where she could get away from him.

Behind her, the deep rumbling voice said, "If you try to escape I will definitely eat you."

She spun toward him. "But I want to go home. Someday, when I've done enough, you have to let me go home."

At that he gave off a burst of furious heat and exhaled a stream of green fire. She dodged him, and ran toward her safe place.

One huge forelimb came down directly in front of her, the great claws biting the sand. When she wheeled, his other paw stamped down, fencing her in.

"You can't leave!"

She put her hands over her ears, the roar shaking her whole body. The ground trembled under her. He was lying down, and his tail swung around, curling around her, not touching, but close. She lowered her hands. He was calm again, now that his great scaled bulk surrounded her. Only a few feet away the enormous eye shut and opened again. "Tell me a story."

So she had to escape. During the day, she searched through the seams and gullies worn into the cliff, hoping to find some way through the wall, but all the openings pinched out, or ended in falls of broken rock. Once in the shadows at the back of a defile she found a skeleton, still wearing tattered clothes—a cloak with fur trim, and pretty, rotten shoes, even rings on the finger bones.

The bones were undisturbed, laid out in a human shape inside the rags of cloth. Whoever this was, however he had gotten here, he had never even left the cave.

She had left the cave. She found herself a little proud of that.

She took one of the rings and slipped it on her finger, wondering who he had been. Somehow she had to fit this into a story. The ring was loose and cold, and finally she put it back on the bony finger she had taken it from.

One evening, after she told him about some adventures of the Prince as dragon, she turned to go back into the crevice, where she usually slept. Before she could reach the cliff he caught her lightly with his forepaw—the long, curved claws like tusks inches from her face—and tossed her backward. She stumbled off across the beach, wondering what she had done wrong. The other paw met her and sent her reeling. She whirled, frightened, her hands out, and he batted her around again. His head suspended over her watched her with a cold amusement. He was playing, she realized, in a haze of terror, not really hurting her, just enjoying his power. She caught hold of his scaly paw and held tight, and he stopped.

But he did not let her go. He reached down and took her between his long jaws, gently as a mother with an egg. Tirza lay, rigid, her breath stopped, between two sets of gigantic teeth, the long tongue curled around her. He lay down, stretched out, and carefully set her on the sand between his forelegs. He put his head down, so that she lay in the hollow under his throat, and went to sleep.

She lay stiff as a sword under him. Something new had happened and she had no notion what he might mean by this. What he might do next. Yet the cavern under his throat was warm, and she fell asleep after a while.

The next day, he dove into the lagoon and was gone and she

went back to the search, working her way steadily from one end of the cliff to the other, trying to find a way out. She went back through every crevice, tried to chimney up the sides, and crawled along the top of huge mounds of rubble. She found many openings back into the cliff, but always the space came to an end, the cliff pressed down on her, dark and cold.

She crept back out to the sunlit lagoon again. The beauty of it struck her, as it always did, the water clear and blue, grading darker toward the middle of the lagoon and paler in the ring of the shore, the tiny ripples of the waves, the cream-colored sand. The sky was cloudless. The cliff vaulted up hundreds of feet high, sheer as a wall of glass.

As she stood there, wondering what to do, the blue water began to churn, throwing off breaking waves, and the dragon's great head thrust up through the center of it, a white fish between his long jaws.

He saw her, and came to her, cast down the fish, and breathed on it with the harsh fire of his breath, and then, as usual, stood there watching her eat it. She was hungry and ate all the pale, flaky meat. Being close to him made her edgy. She had thought of a good story to tell him, with a long chase through a forest and the dragon's escape at the end. She could not look at him, afraid of what she might see brimming in the great red eyes.

He sat quietly throughout the story, as he always did. She had learned to feel the quality of his attention and she knew he was deeply involved in it. She brought it to an end, and stood.

His head moved, fast as a serpent, and he caught her between his jaws. He laid her down on her back between his forepaws. She lay so stiff her fists were clenched, looking up at the wedge-shaped head above her, and then he began to lick her all over.

His tongue was long and supple, silky smooth, longer than she was tall, so that sometimes he was licking her whole body all at once. She was afraid to move. He licked at her dress until it was bunched up under her armpits. His touch was soft, gentle, even tender, stroking over her breasts he paused an instant, his warm tongue over her, and against her will she gasped.

He said, in his deep, harsh voice, "It's only me, the Prince," and chuckled. He slid his tongue down her side and curled it over her legs.

She clutched her thighs together, but the tip of his tongue flicked between them, into the cleft of her body. She shut her eyes. She held her whole body tight, as if she could make an armor of her skin. Her strength was useless against him.

But nothing more happened. He slept, eventually, his head over her. She dozed fitfully, starting up from nightmares, her body licked in green fire.

In the morning he went off as usual and she searched desperately along the cliff face. At the waterfall she stood in the tumbling water, thinking of his tongue on her, wondering what else he would do.

Through the streaming water she looked back into the crevice in the rock and saw a way to climb up.

She stepped in behind the waterfall. The air was cool and damp, the rock wall of the hillside hung with long green weed. The gap where she stood closed up above her head, but just beyond, within reach it seemed of the very top, was a ledge, where a little twisted bramble sprouted.

She slid her hands over the smooth, mossy rock, found a place to hold on with her hands, and got her foot wedged into a crack. She began to climb. The wet green weed was soft and her toes clutched at it and her soles skidded across it. She found a handhold deeper into the crevice and pulled herself higher. That led her back into the waterfall, which slammed down on her shoulders, her head. She reached up, grabbed the bramble, and drew herself up, and the bramble pulled out and she fell hard down into the rocks.

She rolled over, her whole side throbbing, her hair plastered to her face. I can't do this, she thought. I can't do this. The water pounded her. She stood again, filthy and soaked, and looked up. Knowing better what to look for on the rock, she picked out a seam where she could put her fingers. A bulge below that where she might be able to get a foothold. She leaned up, bent her hands into the niche, and stretched her leg up and got her foot on the bulge, and pushed up, hard, lunging toward the top. With her free foot she scrabbled at the curve of the mossy wall, and for an instant got enough hold to lunge higher. Her head and shoulders burst up out of the waterfall and she stretched her arms across the ledge.

Her feet lost their grip. She was sliding back again. Her hands rasped helplessly over the bare rock of the ledge. She pumped her legs, and jamming one knee against the rock she got an unexpected purchase and lurched up and forward again and got most of herself onto the ledge.

Stretched on her belly on the warm stone, she closed her eyes. Her knee burnt with pain and her hands were numb. She wanted to rest, but she could not stay here, she was still too near the beach, and she got to all fours.

The ledge ran crosswise of the cliff, but up there, several body lengths above her, was another such shelf, bigger. She ran her eyes over the stone before her. From below the rock face looked blank, but now she could see the little fissures and edges and seams. She started cautiously, sliding one hand up above her over the rock, finding something to hold on to, moving each foot until she was sure of its grip.

A roar from below shook her. She nearly fell. Pressed against the stone, rigid with fear, she sobbed for breath.

"No! Come down! Come down now!"

Her heart was banging against her ribs. He could burn her here, cook her like a fish. She thrust her hand into a crevice of the rock, and with her feet paddling at the wall she dragged herself up. If she fell he'd kill her. In a rush she scrambled over sheer rock to the next ledge and crept out onto it. Panting, her whole body trembling, she could not move for a moment. The muscles in her calves jerked.

"Come down!" he shouted. "You're making me angry! Don't make me angry!"

She licked her lips. He might do anything now, if she went back. She got to her knees, her gaze sweeping the rock. There seemed no way up, except, to the right side, a nearly vertical gulley, a runoff channel, full of pebbles.

She began to creep up along it, her face to the cliff, her hands groping along. Under her feet the pebbles rolled and slipped and her ankle began to throb. Her arms felt heavy and limp as water and it took all her effort to reach up. Her body ached all over. Her face was inches from the black rock; her nose banged it, more painful each time.

"I'll never let you go!" he roared, and a wave of heat flared over her feet and legs. "I'll hunt you down until I find you." Her heels felt scalded. She smelled burnt hair. She could not go back now, ever.

Yet he had not killed her: she had gotten out of reach of the edge of his flame.

Below her he raged and bellowed up and down the beach, threatening and pleading with her and howling out blasts of green flames. Her dress was soaked with sweat, the late sun burning on her back. Her fingers bled so she could not grip the rock. She rested, pressed to the cliff face, panting. She dared not look down.

She found a toehold on the rock and pushed herself up, her

hands sliding up over the surface. The palisade wall changed abruptly from black rock to deep-packed dirt, hairy with roots. Nothing to hold on to, only loose dirt. She tasted dirt. She got one foot on the ridge where the rock ended, and pushed herself up. Slipped, and for a sickening moment was sliding; the rock ledge against her stomach stopped her hard. She hung there. She was too tired. Her legs wobbled under her. She leaned on the dirt, her eyes shut, her mind blank. Bent her knee, slid it blindly up onto the ridge, and pulled herself up. The dirt had fallen away here. Tilted inward. She leaned her back against the crevice, her hands numb.

It was hard to move again. She had dirt in her eyes. Stretching her arm up, she groped for a handhold, a root, anything. Her hand reached over the edge of the cliff into air and grass.

She clutched a handful of grass. The sun was going down. Behind her, the dragon gave up a despairing cry. She lurched upward, over the top of the cliff.

Her eyes that for hours had seen only rock a few inches from her nose now stretched their gaze across a broad meadow, an oak tree, a pond of water. She had escaped. She did not turn back even to look at him. She crawled up over the rim of the cliff into the grass and lay still and slept. All night, in her sleep, she heard him roaring.

SHE HAD NOTHING TO EAT, BUT THE SPRING HAD COME; THE meadow was full of mushrooms, and the trees of birds' nests and eggs. She walked a whole day inland, picking a way down a long ridge, and finally came to a path. She followed that much of the night, through a brilliant waxing moon, going steeply downhill, and toward dawn came on a heap of stones: a road marker.

Yet she saw no one else. The narrow, stony path tracked across an inland valley clogged with brambles and thickets of willow, and when the path climbed up high onto the next ridge she looked back and saw only mountains. She walked on, eating whatever she could find—roots, nuts, even flowers and grubs and crickets.

On the third day the little path climbed up to the high road, winding along the crest of a hill from north to south. She sat down under a spreading oak by the side of the great road, and after another day she saw some travelers coming toward her.

This was an ox-drawn cart, with two women riding in it, a man walking beside the ox, three boys with sticks herding along four or five sheep. Tirza sat up, eager. After days without words she wanted to talk again. When she told them who she was, they would take her home and she would reward them with stories. She began forming the stories in her mind, beginning with the dragon.

Turn by turn of the wheels they drew nearer, and when she could see their faces she stood up, waved her arms, and called out, "Help me—please help me!"

The cart stopped, all the people bunching together. A woman cried, "What is she?" The man with his staff stepped forward and called, "What do you want?"

She went toward them, her arms out to them. "I am a Princess of Castle Ocean, lost and alone. Take me home and you will be well rewarded."

In the frightened cluster of people one of the women screamed. The boys stooped to gather rocks. Even the ox recoiled from Tirza. The man called, "Get away! Get away!" and shook his staff at her.

Alarmed, she stopped, her arms falling to her sides. "No. You don't understand." In her own ears now she heard her voice as they heard it, no words, only growls and whistles and shrieks. A rock struck her on the arm.

"Get away! Witch! Demon! Get away!"

With a scream she turned and ran. Another rock flew by her head. Tears dribbled down her face; she had lost; she had lost; it was all gone. Their screeching voices behind her sounded fainter, farther. When she could hear them no more, she flung herself down in the wild grass and wept.

 2

THE SEA CAME OUT OF THE WEST FROM BEYOND THE WORLD'S
edge, and broke at last against the tip of the continent at Cape of
the Winds, and there on those jagged black rocks, with the sea
on three sides, stood Castle Ocean. Its five towers, its ramparts
braced up with tree trunks where the sea had eaten away the
base, its balconies and terraces and pinnacles, rose up like forms
of the natural rock, as if it had been there since the world began.
Even on calm days the surf crashed and beat endlessly around
the foot of it, and on this afternoon, with a storm coming in,
the wind screaming, the salt spray lashed up even as high as the
King's Tower, the tallest, where Marioza stood looking out the
window into the west.

The Queen of Castle Ocean loved such storms. Nothing ruled
this wind, this cloudy streaming uproar. Another rolling crackle
of thunder made her laugh. She laid her plump forearms on the
naked rock of the windowsill and thrust her head out to the air,
the sea's wild breath all around her, her hair already soaked.

Cousins of the King, her family had always lived in Castle Ocean. When she married Reymarro, she had only changed rooms. Here, in this place, was who she was. Now her King was gone, and she stood alone against this final enemy, who ruled everywhere but here.

She had never seen the Emperor, and yet she thought of him endlessly, how to resist him, how to defeat him, piece by piece, somehow. She would not submit. She could see no way to win, but that did not matter.

The treaty insisted she marry his brother. He had sent her one, with a wedding party, and she had killed him and sent the party back. This time he had sent soldiers. Also: another brother, another wedding, another ring, the shackle on her thumb, braided gold like rope. So far she had forestalled the ceremony, since a mother in mourning for her youngest daughter could not be expected to marry. She leaned farther into the tumbling air. Her face was soaked with the salt spray, mingled warm and cold. In her blood the connection with the sea ran like a salt and tidal memory.

"I have him now," Reymarro had said. "He's cornered up in the mountains. One last push and he's gone. You must keep my castle. When I come back I will bring you diamonds." He never came back. And now she was about to give her sacred charge to an ordinary man, without webs between his toes.

Behind her, the door opened and a page said, "Mistress, the noble Imperial Archduke Erdhart will see you now."

Ordering himself into her own room. Within the massive fortress of her flesh she gathered herself for combat. "Send him in."

He was already there, the Emperor's brother. Smooth, pale, his face always smiling. He seemed polished. His clothes were exact and his fine fair hair perfect. His hands were soft as a nun's, the nails trimmed to pink and white ovals; he held his hands together, stroking each other, below the constant smile of even teeth. She had turned from the window, although she still leaned with one arm on the sill. She brushed back her dripping, salty hair.

"Yes, my lord. You wish something?"

"My dear lady." He flexed toward her, not bowing, and got her hand and lifted it to his lips. He kissed, not her skin, but the gold ring. "You should not stand so in the storm. Where are your women? Let someone bring her a dry cloak!" The last in a voice aimed at her servants, in the next room.

Marioza said, "I am warm enough, sir. But thank you for your concern." She pulled against his grip, driving her nails sharp into his skin, and he lifted her fingers again to his lips and bit her knuckle. His eyes gleamed, as if he thought of pouncing on her. With a hard twist of her arm she got her hand free.

Behind her, in the doorway, Jeon said, "Mother."

Erdhart turned swiftly; wisely, he let none of her children behind him. He said, "Prince, we are in conference."

"No," Marioza said. "Come in, boy." To Erdhart she said, "I am still so glad to see him, sir, after I feared so long he was lost to me." She put out her hand to her boy, and let a tear fall. "As his poor sister is forever lost."

At that Jeon gave her a weighty look. He was tall and slim, as his father had been, his hair red as pomegranates.

Erdhart said, "Lady, this grief for your dear child becomes you, but I beg you to give thought to our impending marriage. There is much trouble in the land, and my Imperial brother wants a strong and forceful master here."

Jeon's head jerked back, and his face flamed. He said, "My brother Luka is the master here. He is the true King."

Erdhart bent his smile on Jeon. His pale hands clasped together before him. He said, "Dear Prince Jeon, whom I shall soon call Son, there is a paper in the Holy City that says otherwise."

Jeon bit his lips together so tight he seemed to have no mouth. Marioza knew he would not say what he had come to tell her while this man was here, and she was suddenly very eager to hear him. She went across the room to her bed, and sat down on it.

"Whatever that paper says, I am still Queen in my own bedroom. I will accompany you later, sir."

Erdhart's hands parted. She saw he was considering commanding her. Once she married him, he would see no barrier to being in her room whenever he wished. In her body also. Her knuckle throbbed where he had bitten her. She put this new hate in with all the others, like a quiver of arrows.

Jeon said, "My lord, my mother has dismissed you."

The Emperor's brother smiled at him, smooth as silk. "Then I shall take my leave. Lady, we shall dine." He turned back to the door, where now, out in the corridor, his two sons were waiting; he went out between them.

Jeon went to the door and slammed it and ran the bolt over it. "Mother, he is vile."

She put her hand over her knuckle, which was bleeding, and turned her gaze back to her window. The oncoming storm was lashing the sea white as far as she could see, the clouds boiling black, the wind full of grit. She said, "What is it? I saw how you looked at me."

"Mother—" He came up beside her. "I heard something today—from the north. A traveler, in the marketplace, come from the north, He was talking about a crazy woman roaming wild up there."

Marioza lifted her head, all her body suddenly thrilled with premonition. Her son fixed her with his eyes. "A woman who shouts and screams gibberish."

"Ah!" she cried, joyful. Then, almost at once, she saw the other side in this.

So did Jeon. He was taut as a harp string. He said, "Mother, what shall I do?"

"Ah," she said, again. "She has always been a bad omen to me, since she was born." She put her hand to her mouth, and licked her knuckle. Her daughter: in spite of all, Marioza's heart warmed, glad. Tirza was alive, alive. "Go find her. We must send her back to Santomalo, as soon as possible, but I would see her first."

He embraced her. "Mother. Thank you. Thank you." And went away, silly boy, to find the misbegotten child who was better off gone.

THE COAST RAN LONG OUT OF THE EAST TO CAPE OF THE Winds, and there beneath the black rocks of Castle Ocean turned sharp to the south. From the cape, a long jagged spur ran southward for over a mile, like a row of long teeth, which the local people called the Jawbone. Between this spur and the shore was a little bay, and in this shelter, halfway between sea and land, over long years the town of Undercastle had grown. The castle itself stood above the head of the bay, black as thorn against the clear blue sky, reaching halfway to the sun.

Jeon came out of a sea gate onto the beach and went on toward the town. He knew every stone of this place, every name and face, and that had begun to grate on him. The town's four fishing boats usually moored at the head of the bay, in the deep water there, but they were all gone, left when the tide went out. He came up to the edge of the town, where the potter was just opening her stall, and caught the first whiff of the bread baking in the ovens she shared with the baker. Under his feet the mixed black and white sand crunched. A lean dog followed him a few steps, looking hopeful, but Jeon hitched his pack up higher on his shoulder and ignored it and the dog veered off. At the foot of the trail up the cliff, several people were waiting to go up to work in the castle. They waved to him and he waved back. He knew they cared more about his red hair than they did about him.

The black rock of the cliff was pocked with caves and over the years people had hollowed these out into houses and stores and shops. The two biggest caves, well back into the cliff, held the brewery's vats and oasts. The brewery itself stood next door, dug far into the cliff, with a wooden porch built along the front. Slowing his steps, he looked for his brother, Luka. There was already a little crowd in the brewery and Jeon went on, not wanting to go in there among all those people.

Ahead, at the butchery, the beach widened, rising to a little prairie just inland. On this stretch of sand, an old cypress tree stood, a fat trunk like a bundle of barrels under a sparse prickly crown. A wooden bench encircled the trunk and Jeon saw his two older sisters sitting there.

He walked toward them. Someone from the town had brought a new baby out and Mervaly had it on her lap and was cooing at it, smoothing its little body with her hands, as if she molded it into shape. The remains of a christening feast littered his sister's skirt, the bench she sat on, the ground at her feet. Beside her Casea sat with her needle and a long strip of cloth over her knees, patterned in colored thread. When Jeon came up she gave him a quick, eager look.

"What did she say?" Casea crossed her long white hands over the fabric in her lap. Mervaly looked toward them, keen.

"I can go find her," Jeon said. "She says she'll have to go back to the monastery, but first she wants to see her."

Mervaly said, "I'll never let her go back to that place." She lifted the baby, kissed it, and held it out to the mother. They settled into a long discussion of naming. Casea threaded her needle with purple silk. A few red and white chickens had come over to peck at the crumbs on the ground. Jeon looked around the beach, at its widest here, fringed with shops and awnings. The weavery was shut, across the way, and the forge. Everybody knew there was a storm coming up, in spite of the blue sky. The butcher's boy Guz walked by, his tray suspended before him from his shoulders, hawking his father's meat pies.

In among all these familiar people, there walked a clutch of Imperial soldiers in their puffy striped doublets. The doublets looked soft, but Bedro, who had gotten into a fight with one of them, said underneath they were hard enough to break your hand. Jeon watched the soldiers; like all the Imperials they were big, square-shouldered men. Each of them carried a ten-foot pike, double bladed, leaning on it as if it were a walking stick.

The striped doublets made them stand out among the fishermen and farmers here like rocks in the soup. They stared at everybody, at everything, clutching their pikes, their helmets on their belts. They stayed in their little pack, always.

Jeon said, "Why do we have to let these hayheads here?"

"You know perfectly well," Casea said, busy with her needle, stitching a meandering line into the white cloth between her hands. "Because Papa got himself killed fighting on the wrong side." She glanced at him, at Mervaly, and across the common at the Imperial soldiers. "Which we should all take a lesson from."

Mervaly said, "Let Mother deal with this." She kissed the baby's mother and waved her off. They three sat alone under the cypress tree.

"Mother," Casea said, "has only gotten us into more trouble." She lifted her face to Jeon, her skin pale as eggshell, her wide black eyes like onyx. "Are you sure you can find Tirza? There's another storm coming after this one."

"I'll find her," he said, a little uneasy; Casea sometimes knew things. He looked away: the boy Timmon from the stable was leading Jeon's horse across the beach toward them. Across the way, one of the Imperials had turned to watch.

Mervaly's voice called Jeon back to his sisters. "Where exactly are you going? So I can tell Luka where to look, if you don't come back."

That nettled him: they treated him like a child sometimes, just because he was youngest. "East. I'll go inland, first; that's where this traveler saw her, on the high road." There was another way along the coast, but that was often impassable, especially in bad weather. That was the coast where the galley had been wrecked. He shuddered suddenly.

Casea said, "What are you afraid of?"

"I'm not afraid."

He knew what fear was. Of the wreck of the galley he remembered only the ship hitting the rock, or whatever it was, and heeling violently over. He had come back to himself sprawled on a piece of the deck, floating out to sea. He thought he remembered lightning flashes, the mountainous seas, so there must have been a storm. In his dreams there was lightning. Clinging to the deck, delirious with thirst, he had drifted a long while on the coastal current, until a fisherman picked him up, freezing and feverish. If they had found him a few hours later he would have been dead. He said, "I'll take the high road as far as Santomalo. Follow the coast back from there as much as I can."

Casea said, "What if we lost both of you, you know?" Her voice was gently chiding. She got up suddenly and kissed him. "Go on, Jeon; good luck." He took the reins from the stable boy, mounted his horse, and rode out of the village.

CASEA WATCHED JEON RIDE ACROSS THE BEACH TOWARD THE path up to the top of the cliff. As he went he passed by several

Imperial soldiers and one pointed at him, but nobody moved to follow him. At the foot of the trail Jeon stepped down from the saddle, and he and the horse walked on side by side. The Imperials wandered off along the beach.

Her eyes lingered on the long slope of the trail, remembering when her father the King had summoned his army here and led them off to the war, four years ago almost to the day.

Her father had been splendid on his charger. Her brother Luka, still a boy then, rode beside him, carrying the long banner on its staff. The army marching after had moved up that path all day long, everybody cheering and weeping.

When Luka brought the survivors back, after the massacre in the mountains, there was only weeping.

She saw a pattern in this, as she saw patterns in everything. She lowered her eyes; without any thought from her, the needle was making tiny precise stitches across the linen.

Jeon had been too young to go to war, a quiet, watching kind of boy. She looked for him on the cliff; he was almost to the top now. "He's different," she said. "What happened to him?"

Mervaly sat with her hands in her lap, her gaze turning toward the cliff. She said, "He's gotten older. And everything is different."

Jeon led his horse over the rim of the cliff and disappeared. The more Casea imagined it, the more she was sure he would come back. He would bring Tirza back. Casea's heart lifted; she made a tiny blue star at the top of her work. Blue was Jeon's color.

Off across the common suddenly a shriek went up. Mervaly stood, and Casea raised her head to see. Leanara, the baker, was the one screaming; she was leaning over the counter of her stall, throwing something at one of the Imperials crowded in front of her.

All around the beach, people were turning to look. Mervaly was already halfway there. Casea stuffed her needlework into her apron pocket and followed her sister across to the stall, where several people were gathering; they stood back to give Mervaly room.

Leanara was shapeless, floury as a loaf, her head almost bald beneath her headcloth, which was always coming loose and hung down now over her ear. She shouted, "I can't use that. He has no tally stick!" She thrust out one arm, pointing at the Imperials, standing in their clump in front of her stall.

The other people around them were watching attentively, Casea saw. Aken the butcher was there, and Lumilla, the brewer's widow, stood across the way, her elbows cocked and her fists on her hips. Mervaly bent and picked up something from the dirt.

"What is this?" She held it out toward the Imperials.

The tallest of them came forward, a big, square man like them all, fair skinned and rosy cheeked, straw haired and blue-eyed. Casea noticed on the front of his striped doublet was some insignia the others did not wear. He recognized the princesses: he bowed, his head bobbing, and Mervaly said impatiently, "Well?" and he straightened upright.

"That's all I have, Princess. It's good money. What do I need to have to buy something in this place?"

Mervaly glanced down at her palm. "Who are you?"

"I am Master Sergeant Pal Dawd, Princess. I mean no trouble." He put out his hand for the money. "We'll go." In the pack behind him a soldier grunted, angry. Pal Dawd turned his head and the man quieted.

Mervaly took the bit of metal between her thumb and forefinger and looked it over. Casea went closer to see. It was round, with a little wreathed head on one side, a gate or a house or something else square on the other. Mervaly held it out to Leanara.

"It's pretty. Keep it. It may come to be useful. Give him the bread."

Leanara pressed her lips together, not liking this, but from the crowd a sigh went up, and Lumilla lowered her hands to her sides.

Mervaly waggled the coin under Leanara's nose. "Do it."

Leanara said, "Or they will just take it." She thrust the loaf at the soldier and held out her hand to Mervaly for the coin.

Casea stepped back, looking over the Imperial men. The tall one was dividing the loaf among them and that made them content. Leanara was right: the soldiers were easy enough now, but that could change. The new men in the castle were not so easy, and they wanted more than a loaf of bread. Mervaly turned to walk back to the cypress tree.

"I'm going home," Casea said. "I'll see you at supper." She patted her apron, to make sure of her work, and started off up the beach toward the rock below the castle.

THE BREAD WAS DELICIOUS, AND NOW MAYBE THEY COULD buy ale. Pal Dawd fingered his purse, fat with Imperial silver pennies, good everywhere in the world, and now perhaps even here. The merry Princess had gone back to her bench by the tree. He nodded to the other men.

"Let's try this again."

His corporal, Marwin, said, "I think these people need a lesson."

Dawd elbowed him. "Remember what the Archduke said— no trouble." Dawd led his men over toward the broad porch of the brewery.

The town fascinated him, so much different from an Imperial town with its ordered streets and square buildings; here the wooden porches and steps and little shops seemed to be spilling out of the cliff, like overflow from hidden places. On the porch of the brewery several old men were sitting on benches, cans of drink already in their hands. They watched him with piercing

eyes, and the lanky woman who ran the place came to the top of
the steps.

Dawd stopped, held up a penny, and said, "How much for a
cup?"

The woman gave a little shake of her head, frowning. She
came down and took the coin from him, and, like the Princess,
turned it over and studied it. She shook her head again. She said,
"Well, I'll take it, since they say so. One cup each."

Dawd said, unthinking, "One per cup?" and she turned quickly
and smiled.

"Yes," she said, and he saw he had cheated himself: she would
have taken one penny for all of them. But already the men were
moving toward the keg on the porch and she was taking down
cups from her rack. As he went up among them she thrust her
hand out. He dropped six more pennies into it, and she gave
him ale.

It was good ale, too, and he drank deep. But being cheated still
rankled him.

THEY WERE ALL MONSTERS, THE ARCHDUKE ERDHART
thought, looking around the hall. They wore human faces to
beguile the world, but the truth about them always showed
through. Knowing that made it easier to plan what he had to do.
He placed his hands together before him and thought this all
over.

The two Princesses sat on his left side, beyond their mother.
They were beautiful, Mervaly round and bubbling, Casea qui-
eter, slender, pale, both with the hair of the family, the red of late
oak leaves, the red of poison. Mervaly was always laughing, an
unseemly merriment, no decorum in that woman, no sense of her
rightful place. He would deal with that.

Casea had already formed all the objects around her into

straight lines; now she was arranging them by size. While he watched she lifted her eyes and stared at him. For a moment she seemed not to see him at all, only some other object she had to put in order.

He would deal with that, too. He would deal with all of them. He laid his hands together in front of him, palm on palm, admiring the flicker of the ruby on his long white forefinger. Marioza would have to yield, in time. Make him King here, by the law as well as conquest. His brother had insisted on that: bind them with the laws, until no one there can draw so much as a free breath.

Under that, the unspoken: fail me once more, Erdhart, and you'll never see the Holy City again.

He did not mean to fail. This ocean kingdom was small, weak, with no army, and he would bring it under him as he brought its Queen under him. Then he would have a place to advance himself within the Empire, force his way back into his brother's councils, even . . . aspire . . . He stopped thinking about that. Not yet. He watched the red light against his white skin, charmed.

There was, certainly, little to like about Castle Ocean itself, and he would have to move to a better place, once he was truly King. Inland, out of reach of the sea. He moved his gaze around the hall again, long and low as a cave, which was probably how it had begun, a wretched cave, the walls and ceiling of solid rock. Even the great winged chair he sat on was carved from the rock; he shifted his weight, uncomfortable on the hard, uneven seat.

Before him the great room opened up onto a broad terrace that overhung the sea. Now with the rain beating down from the west they had sealed that end of the room behind a wooden barrier, but the wind still swirled around, fluttering all the rush lights. Several fires burned in the hearths around the room, and he had to admit it was warm enough, but the light was very strange, like being underwater.

He frowned down at the rest of the court, seated at the inferior tables. His own officers sat nearest him; he had always insisted on this. Below, at the far side of the hall, were the local people— the kinsmen of the King, some such designation. Old men and women, of no consequence. Some lived in the castle, some in the town, and they did nothing but gobble food. They barely acknowledged even that he was there, stared through him, never spoke. Once he was married to the Queen, he would send all them out, to feed themselves. Leave them here, when he moved inland.

A servant had brought him wine, which he did not drink. Instead, after he had seen Marioza, on his right, take several sips of her cup, he exchanged his cup for hers. Her long, colorless eyes slanted toward him and the massy bundle of her body trembled with silent laughing. When they were married he would make her weep and beg in his arms, plead for mercy. For all this fearsome look, she was only a woman. He turned away, thinking of the wedding night.

Let it come. Let it come.

"My lords! Glory to the Empire!" The herald with his red tunic and high black boots swaggered up from his station by the door, rapped his ribboned staff on the floor several times, and called out, "Enter the Imperial Princes, the High Lords Oto Erdhartsson and Broga Erdhartsson. All bow. All!" He banged down his staff again. Erdhart smiled, pleased: his own court, at least, acted properly.

And after him came Erdhart's two sons. Tall and stout, with the bearing of true Princes, dressed gorgeously in silver lace and purple silk, bright swords swinging from their hips, they were the finest men in the hall. Half the people around the table stood, bowing, recognizing the golden blood when they saw it. Oto, the elder, came up before his father, swept off his plumed hat, and performed an elaborate obeisance, one leg thrust forward, his arms spread out past his knees.

Mervaly laughed. Oto, without hesitation, turned and performed for her the same bow, perhaps even more elaborate. "My lady Princess." But then he faced Erdhart. "My lord, we have tidings from the east, for your ears alone."

Erdhart shifted, indecisive. He thought he knew what this was, a closely held, important thing, but he could not order everybody else out, surely not Marioza, who was watching keenly beside him, and who would not leave. And she must not know of it. But if he got up and left, to hear it somewhere private, he appeared smaller. Before he could find some third way through this, the door crashed open and another man strode into the hall, unheralded, and came straight up the room.

He was taller than either of Erdhart's sons. His hair was red as carnelian. His long green shirt glittered with salt. He carried no weapon, only a game bag by a strap over his shoulder. The two men who followed on his heels were just as shabby. But suddenly everybody else around the table was standing up, except for Erdhart and Marioza. The newcomer walked up past Oto and Broga as if they were not there and bowed his head to Marioza.

"Welcome, my son," Marioza said. "Did you come in through the storm?"

Luka waved that off. "It's hardly raining yet. I have brought you a wedding present." From the game bag he took a casket.

Oto murmured, moving closer. Erdhart leaned forward. Marioza put out one hand and tipped up the lid of the box.

"Ah." She turned the box around, into the torchlight, and tumbled out the heap of sea jewels, coral, pearls, nacre, serpentine, and chrysoprase. "What beauties." She picked up a bit of green serpentine and licked it, and admired the gleaming surface. Revolted at this gross behavior, Erdhart tapped his fingers on the arm of his chair.

Luka was taking something else from his game bag.

"For my sisters."

This was a little owlet, still in down, blinking in the bright light. Mervaly cooed and held out her cupped hands; Casea was smiling at Luka. "Thank you." Mervaly held the little bird against her cheek, and it pecked at her. "She's cold," Casea said. Mervaly at once tucked the owlet into the ample bosom of her dress.

Luka said, "I have heard something about Tirza. Is she truly found? Is that where Jeon is?"

Erdhart sat forward again, intent. Marioza said, "We have some hopes."

Erdhart said, "What is this? The freemartin isn't dead after all?"

Luka glanced at him, as if he had just noticed him. "That is my seat," he said. "The high seat."

Oto stepped forward, his hand on the hilt of his sword, and his voice rang, "Treat the Archduke Erdhart with respect, sir, and sit where you belong."

Luka wheeled around toward him. Marioza said sharply, "Stand, Luka. I will not permit it."

Luka snorted, looking at her over his shoulder, so his back was to Erdhart. "Then I will take my leave of you, Mother. I will not sit lower than my rightful place." He strode off, walking straight between Oto and Broga, so he brushed each of them as he went by. Broga started after him and Erdhart said, "Wait. Sit; we will talk later." He wanted no fighting, with the wedding suddenly within his grasp. He turned to Marioza.

"What news is this? The girl is found?"

"We are very hopeful, sir. The sea has been kind to us again." She had always assigned Jeon's survival to the goodwill of the sea.

Erdhart swelled, triumphant. "Then we shall marry at once."

He moved his foot, under the table, and ground his heel into the toe of her shoe. She said nothing, did nothing, although he saw the blood leave her cheek.

"I suppose we must." But her voice shook.

The servants were moving around them, and a great platter of fish slid onto the table, dishes of fruit, of bread. Erdhart's page came up to serve him. "Attend my lady first." Left to herself, she would dig her own hands into the food, like a slave. The girls were already crumbling cheese in their fingers. The page laid a slab of salmon on Marioza's plate. Erdhart watched her carefully, and when she ate at once and avidly of the fish he nodded to the page to fill his own plate.

"We should send Luka to court in the Holy City. Let him learn proper address, how to bear himself, how to fight. He lacks the manners of a Prince." This would also remove an important obstacle to Erdhart's progress. He picked at the succulent pink meat before him.

Marioza gave a throaty laugh. "If you find him so biddable, my lord, I beg you, propose it to him." She turned to share some mirth with her daughters.

It passed through Erdhart's mind that perhaps something poisonous to man might not hurt such as these he was marrying into. But he would not starve. Carefully he began to put the salmon into his mouth, a little at a time.

Lord Oto Erdhartsson considered himself to be two men: the courtier—polished, elegant, impenetrable—and the inner man—where all his thoughts could be hidden well from the world. He paced impatiently up and down the little bare waiting

room; they had sent out the guard and the pages. His brother
had gone to kneel down at the little prie-dieu in the corner of
the room; now he signed himself and rose.

"We should make a chapel here. Bring the truth of God here
to this place."

Oto said, "In time, probably. You may have charge of that."
Broga understood nothing about this, the great fool, drunk on
God. Oto swung his arms as he walked, impatient; he disliked
waiting. It came into his mind that his father might have gotten
lost on the way here.

The castle baffled Oto. He had lived here now, off and on, for
almost six months, and he still could not find his way around.
This room where he stood now, this entire tower, in fact, was
different from the rest, made of grey worked stone; here, he felt
sure. He had worked out the way from his apartments here to the
cave-heart of the whole place, where stairs went up and down and
through a heavy doorway the great hall faced the sea. Oto could
confidently go from the hall to his father's apartments in another
tower, but he was constantly finding corridors and doors along
the way that he had not seen before. He had sent out two
men to map the castle for him. They were gone for two days
and, when they came back, said they would go no farther down,
although the tunnels and shafts continued down, and they could
hear the sound of the sea below. They each made a map, but the
maps did not agree. The third man Oto sent did not come back
at all.

Broga said, "Papa is here," and the door grated open. A page
came in and, after him, the Archduke.

"At last." Oto gave Erdhart the grandest of bows. In fact, Oto
thought the old man was doing this all wrong and often wished
he could tell him so, straight to his face, but he kept that inside
the shining case of himself.

His father said, "Yes, you may rise." With a glance he sent out the man behind him and, the door shut, he faced his sons.

"Well? What is this you have to tell me? Has there been a message from the Holy City? Is he sending more men?"

They both spoke at once, "No, not that, but—" and Broga fell still and Oto went on.

"Nothing so momentous, sir, but a good thing. We have found the place for the new fortress you spoke of—on the coast, east of here. It controls the coast road and there's a lot of rock around to build with. There's a fine little harbor with a good approach, and it's only five days away."

"Excellent. You've kept this secret."

"Oh, yes," Broga said. "When we came in, we told everybody we had been off to hunt in the mountains."

Erdhart folded his hands together, smiling. "We shall need to send most of the men down there. But now she must marry me, and the need to keep them all here is over, I think. Take three squadrons. They can build the fortress." His hands stroked and fondled each other, his habit when he was pleased. Oto spent a moment enjoying his contempt for anybody so easily read. At the same time Oto kept his face perfectly smooth, respectful, filial.

Broga said, "My lord, who shall command this?"

"Well," Erdhart said, and for a moment his voice hung there, between them both, ripe with possibility. Then he faced Oto. "You shall oversee this. Do it properly. It will not be an easy task."

Oto bowed. "My lord, I am gratified."

"Of course if I need you, you must come at once."

"My lord," Oto said.

Broga said, "Papa, give me a task to do. Test me, also."

Erdhart smiled on him, clapped him on the back. "You shall always find your challenges, my boy. I waste no worry over you."

He slapped Broga's back again and nodded to Oto. "You must leave at once. Keep me constantly advised."

"Of course," said Oto, hating him.

"Very well, then. You've done well; I am pleased with you." Erdhart went to the door and Oto moved swiftly to hold it open for him, but it was Broga who got Erdhart's damned smile. The old man left.

Oto said, "Three squadrons." Sixty men. That was more than the cohort Erdhart would have under him here. And a castle of his own, if he could build it properly. The ground was unstable there, but the fort did not have to be large. Once they could bring ships here from the east it would be vital.

Broga said, "I will plan my chapel." He picked up his hat from the table. "Good day, Brother." Going out, he left the door open, and Oto followed him, hoping he remembered the way back to the hall.

3

ALL THROUGH THE STORM, JEON FOLLOWED THE HIGH ROAD
east, going all the way to Santomalo, but did not find his sister.
He heard about her; even with the rain pounding and the wind
blowing he met a traveler, a lone tinker, who carried rumors with
his pots and pans and even claimed he had seen her, shrieking
and howling from the trees. All the while looking eagerly at
Jeon's purse. When he asked the tinker what she looked like he
could not remember. Jeon paid him nothing.

Santomalo was busy, smelly, crowded, and Tirza was not there.
Jeon rode west again, this time taking the way along the beach
until the impassible sea cliffs forced him up onto the marine
terrace above. Out here, with the mountains rising just inland
and the high road well beyond that, the land was empty of people.
The rain ended and the sun shone on a brilliant green world. The
road he followed was hardly more than a goat track, pounded
deep into the ground, rushing with the runoff of the storm, and on
all the brush around him the flowers were opening. He saw no

travelers, no goats or cattle, only wild things, the bees in the flowers, the birds in the sky.

After a hundred miles following along the foot of the mountains the road dropped down again to the coast and he went west along the shelving beach. Sea cattle flopped and barked on the offshore rocks, and the surf broke over long black reefs like rows of teeth, gashing the constant white slosh of the waves. Above the high-tide line the wind had blown the sand up into billowing dunes. Grey bones of driftwood poked up out of the matted sea-weed and shells that covered the wave slope. A flock of seagulls clamored into the air as he came, rising away from a half-eaten seal carcass. The tide was coming in. Out to sea, another storm blurred the western horizon.

Where a stream ran down into the sea and its banks made a wide, sheltered place, he came on a fishing village too small to have a name. He stopped to water his horse at the well.

He wondered what he should do next—where else he could look for her. He was running out of food and he was tired of sleeping on the ground. He might never find her. He might never go home again but wander, always, looking for her. The four little huts of the village were quiet, everybody gone, only a few old people sleeping in the sun. He had to ask someone, and he was thinking of waking one of these elders when two boys ran into the common around the well, shouting.

"They've caught the witch. Come on!"

He reached his horse in a single step, bounded into the saddle, and galloped inland, back the way the boys had come, up the stream; he heard screaming and shouts ahead. Thickets of willow and brambles closed down around him, but the path was deep and wide and he followed the racket ahead of him. People were running after him from the village—the two boys, the elders.

"Burn the witch!"

Up ahead the trail came out on a clearing. At the stream bank an enormous old tree rose, something dark huddled in its branches. Beneath the leafy crown several people stood, shouting up, and one cocked his arm back and threw a rock. Another was poking a rake into the branches and two women in aprons were heaping brush against the trunk of the tree. On the path right in front of Jeon, another man knelt in the dust, lighting a torch with his tinderbox.

Jeon charged his horse straight over the man with the tinderbox, knocking him flat, and rushed the mob under the tree. There were six or seven of them, all on foot. Jeon had no time to draw his sword and anyway he was no good with a sword, but he was good with a horse. He ran down one woman, wheeled the horse around on its hocks, and chased another, who ran shrieking out toward the path. Now he managed to get his sword out of the sheath. Under the tree the man with the rake was set, ready to fight, and beside him another man flung a rock, but when Jeon launched the horse at them, the sword high, they whirled and fled. All the others were already running. The horse was enjoying this and fought against stopping, and when Jeon wrestled it down by the tree it reared and neighed and clashed the air with its hooves.

"Tirza!" Jeon shouted. He backed the snorting horse underneath the branches.

She slid down out of the tree to the ground. She was filthy, her hair matted and full of burrs and leaves, her face black with dirt, out of which her blue eyes shone startlingly clear and bright. He ran his sword back into its sheath. The villagers stood around them at a good distance, wary. A surge of power filled him. He had saved his sister. He glared around him at the crowd, suddenly longing for them to jump forward and take him on. None of them moved. He reached down his arm for her, drew her up behind him on the horse, and rode away.

THEY WENT FAR DOWN THE BEACH UNTIL JEON FOUND A LITTLE overhang of rock where they could sit out of the wind. He built them a fire and divided the last of his food between them. She sat in the firelight with her back to the rock cliff, her knees drawn to her chest, her arms crossed on top, and her chin on her wrist. She was thinner than he had ever seen her. Above her hollow cheeks her eyes seemed to float in her face, haunted. But when he turned to her, she burst into the broadest smile he had ever seen.

He put one hand on her arm, and she came to him and hugged him again, muttering gibberish. He held her tight, grateful for this love, known from the womb. She settled back again, smiling at him, and he said, "Where were you, all this time? Just wandering around?"

She made sounds; she twitched from side to side, something urgent, which she could not tell him; her hands moved in the air. Her face crinkled up, baffled, and she shrugged, and set one hand in her lap and with the other made the circling gesture he knew meant, "And you?"

"Back at home, most of the time. Until I heard about you." He shrugged. "Then looking for you. I don't remember anything about the shipwreck. All I remember is the storm, the lightning. Then floating a long way."

He wiped his jaw with his hand, still burdened with the memory, like something ahead, an ambush. He was clenching his teeth. She shook her head at him, her face puckered with worry.

He said, "I was so thirsty I drank seawater. When they found me I was raving. I still have horrible dreams."

She shook her head at him. Her eyes filled with tears. She made those shapes in the air again, uttering senseless noises.

"It's all right," he said. He did not have to know. They would go home now. Good beds, food, wine, the family around, the common life. "Casea and Mervaly will help me keep you out of Santomalo. Mother loves you; she wants you back, whatever she says. And we need help against Erdhart."

At that, Tirza pushed away from him and sat there straight upright, the rags of her clothes hanging around her like molting. She said something, a low growl, staring off into the woods. He gave a little shake of his head. She was angry about something, not Erdhart and not Mother. The old longing gripped him, to understand her, hear her voice. Yet she was here now, he had found her, and he had saved her, when no one else had really thought he would, and he sat smiling into the fire, enjoying that.

JUST BEFORE SHE FELL ASLEEP, SHE THOUGHT, THEY WILL send me back to Santomalo.

She fell into a fitful sleep, into a dark, obscure place, moving and shifting around her. She seemed to be standing on a shore, looking up at a hillside layered with the red roofs and awnings of a town. At the top a white ledge of a building was the monastery. The sun was rising, away to the side of her. Behind her, people were screaming. Then a roar began that turned her bones to ice.

She burst with sweat. She could not move. A man ran by her, up the hill, and another, and then some women, looking back as they ran, but she was stuck in her place. A flickering baleful light, darker than the sunrise, shone all around her. The smoke burned her nostrils. The shrieking people ran by her and from above them the dragon struck and caught them in his teeth. She saw them sticking out between his jaws, their legs waving. He strode past her, the light glowing on his scales. He let out a blast of his breath and the houses before her burst into flame.

People ran ahead of him and he was eating them as he climbed the hill. His long head swung from side to side, but he did not see her. He caught running people and gobbled them up, and burned their houses. When he saw her he would eat her too. The flames roared up around her, their crackle deafening. She could not run. She was so hot she could not breathe.

Then something seized her by the arms. She opened her eyes, and saw Jeon's face above her, his hands on her arms, shaking her awake.

"Tirza, what is it?"

Panting, she stared into his face, the dream melting away into the deeps of her mind. She sat up, shaking, soaked with sweat. He held out a cup to her, full of fresh, clear water, and she drank. The water spread through her, cool in her chest.

He said, "I have bad dreams, too, sometimes." He hugged her. "It's all right. It will go away."

She shook her head again. He did not understand: it would not go away. It was only coming closer. She wanted to tell him everything, to make him remember, so he would help her, but she could not.

The dragon was coming after her. That was what the dream meant. They would go home now, and she would have to face her mother. And she could not tell them. And they would lock her away again, and let the dragon eat her.

THEY FOLLOWED THE COAST WEST, WHICH WAS SLOW GOING; the tide had washed out long stretches of the road and they often had to wait for the sea to relent and let them pass. Jeon's pack of food was empty, but Tirza was adept at catching crabs and digging up clams. Jeon realized she had been living so for the whole long time she had been lost. They chewed seaweed and drank from streams. One morning, crossing a narrow little beach toward a cliff, Tirza went running off ahead of him around the bend.

A moment later she reappeared, running back, and three men in striped doublets, with pikes, raced around the foot of the cliff after her.

Jeon galloped up to his sister, and she ran into the shelter of the horse. The three Imperial pikemen surrounded them. One seized the bridle of the horse. Another soldier thrust the tip of the pike up into Jeon's face.

"Off the horse!"

Tirza clung to his stirrup, a seed between millstones, and he reached one hand down and gripped her shoulder fast. The soldiers were reaching for him. The pike jabbed at him. He shouted, "I am Prince Jeon of Castle Ocean, and if you don't stand back, I will see the Archduke—"

"Stop!" one soldier shouted. "Stand back!" In unison, the other two stepped back, lowering their pikes to their sides. The helmet stared at Jeon a moment and said, "Yes, that's one of them. Look at the hair." He bowed to Jeon, very deep. "My lord Prince, I plead your pardon; we did not recognize you, come here so alone and without ceremony."

Tirza growled at him. Jeon still had one arm stretched down to her and she pulled herself up behind him on the horse. She pointed on ahead. Jeon lifted his reins, and the helmet moved, abruptly, and got in front of him, blocking the way. The two pikes came up beside him.

"It's well we did meet you, though; my lord Prince, you must turn back. The way ahead is not passable."

Jeon lowered his hand to the pommel of his saddle, crossed the other hand over it, and stared at him. Behind him Tirza was grumbling and fussing, and she pushed him; she wanted him to go forward, to strut his way through this, as Luka would. Make them let him pass in his own country. He saw something else. Erdhart's name had backed them up the first time, but now the men were willing to stand against him, so whatever was going on that they did not want him to see was Erdhart's business.

"Very well," Jeon said.

Tirza squawked like a goose and battered his shoulders with her fists. The soldier before him broke into a wide, relieved smile. Jeon turned the horse around. None of them followed him. He rode back down the beach until the shore bent around again, carrying him and Tirza out of sight of the Imperials, and reined in. She whacked him again from behind and he twisted around and caught her wrist.

"Stop hitting me," he said. "Look—there's a way up this cliff to the top. I can see what's going on from there. You stay here with the horse and wait."

Her eyes widened, understanding, and she looked at the cliff, and at once she leapt off and ran to climb it. Jeon laughed. He loosened the saddle girth and slipped the bit out of the horse's mouth so it could graze, and went after her.

"Be careful," her brother said. "Don't let them see you."

He and Tirza lay flat on the grassy brow of the cliff and crawled up to the edge. She put her head down on the ground a moment, the sun warm on her back, and spread her arms out. The distant boom of the surf sounded in her ears. She felt like never moving. After the long aloneness she had Jeon back again and soon would be home, deep in the middle of her family. Beside her, Jeon muttered something.

"There are a lot of them here."

She crept to the edge of the cliff and peered down through the stalky grass. She had already seen this, from down there on the beach. Below them the cliff had fallen away in a long crumple, forming a bowl of higher ground behind the beach. On the raw, dark earth at the bottom, the striped men moved like beetles, digging and hauling rocks, and laying rocks together. Already they had covered the toe of the slide with a neat crisscross of stone lines. She nudged Jeon, and turned her palm up, asking.

He cupped his hand around his mouth, shielding his voice, even here. "I think they're going to build some kind of wall. Maybe a fortress. You see how they can watch anybody moving down the road from here. And the cove here is sheltered enough for a couple of ships, if the wind doesn't blow too foul."

She looked down again. She remembered the sea captain's chart: they were casting their net over more of the world. The men down there were too far away to make out faces; they swarmed around in constant movement, their black and white bodies sharp against the dark earth. She thought there were at least thirty people here, maybe twice thirty. Beyond the toe of the slide, down the beach, there was a mess of sticks and tents. She thought she saw smoke rising. A camp. That was where they lived, all these men. From that direction a man on a horse was jogging up toward the workers.

Jeon said, "That's Oto." His voice was suddenly hard, like a blade. "Erdhart's son."

Jeon gnashed these names between his teeth. She glanced at him, startled at the raw anger in him. She could not remember that in him before. Now he was pushing himself back from the cliff.

"Luka will want to know all of this. Come on. We have to go back east up the coast and circle around inland to the high road—they picked this place well. It blocks the whole coast trail." His voice was still tight with purpose. She went on down the hillside, to where they had left the horse, and they rode off down the beach.

OTO STARED AWAY TOWARD THE FAR END OF THE SHORE, WHERE the high cliff came down almost into the ocean. "There was just the one?"

The soldier at his stirrup said, "Well, except for the girl. Should I have brought him in? You said—"

"No, no, you did well, keeping him away." Oto put his hands on his saddlebow, thinking of Jeon. "A mere boy, this Prince, not tall, thin, no beard yet."

"Yes. He had a girl with him."

"So you said."

"She had red hair, too."

"Well, well."

He gathered his reins. Swiftly he ran this through his mind. Clearly Jeon had found the missing Princess. Oto's father would marry at once. Oto would be stuck down here, piling up rocks, while Erdhart took Castle Ocean into his hands, gave out power and privileges. Oto's fingers curled around the reins. He had to be there when all this happened. He could not let Broga seize all the benefits. Oto looked around the new fort, which only that morning he had been so pleased with. Now the long, straight walls, the beginning of the tower, all swarming with workers, looked like nothing more than a prison.

"Go," he said to the soldier. "Make sure they have gone back." He reached into his saddle pouch for the map, so he could decide the quickest way back to Castle Ocean.

JEON AND TIRZA RODE TWO DAYS EASTWARD ALONG THE coast to where a track up the cliff led inland. A few miles from the sea, they came on the highland track, winding through the brushy meadows and low hills below the first wind-bent line of the forest, down into the west toward Cape of the Winds. After more days, the road led them down through a saddle in the hills, and ahead they could see the thin black towers of Castle Ocean against the horizon.

At first all they saw was the tops of towers. As they rode on through the day, the black bulk of the castle appeared, crouched above the sea. Birds circled it. The air was hazy with the spume of the surf beneath it. The new tower, eastmost of the five, looked false, with its squat shape, its grey stone quarried from the hills. The gate was of the same stuff; some early King had built them, to keep people out of the castle while seeming to let them in.

The road led up to the cliff's edge, short of the gate, and turned to run down to the south. A bridge arched across the gap between the cliff and the castle gate. Riding along behind Jeon, her hand on his belt, Tirza leaned out to look, and saw people moving on it, those same black and white bodies that had swarmed over the half-begun fort.

They weren't coming away, or going in, but standing there on the bridge, and they all had the long sticks in their hands, the blades jutting up higher than their heads. She said, "What is this?" and heard the incomprehensible mutter that came out.

Jeon's head turned toward her. "Erdhart's men. They patrol the bridge day and night." He pointed off across the cliff-top meadow. "They have a camp over there."

She laughed. Then that was useless. But she wished her brother had taken another way, down by the beach, so they could have avoided this. Pace by pace, the horse carried them on up the arch of the bridge, past narrow-eyed strangers with pale hair and padded striped chests, toward the big gatehouse, toward her mother, toward whatever happened next.

*　*　*

Marioza could hear them laughing, out in the hall, long before they burst in the door, Mervaly and Casea like bells pealing and Tirza higher, wilder, and then they crashed into the room. Mervaly's lavender gown billowed around her when she stopped, and she reached to draw Casea back out of the way. Between them, the youngest of them all stood, skinny and shabby and dirty faced, staring at her mother.

Marioza felt a violent surge of love. She stretched her arms out, and Tirza came up to her and she gathered her to the warmth of her bosom. The girl was stiff in her mother's arms, wary, as always. Scrawny as a sick chicken. Marioza touched Tirza's hair. "Ah, my little. I am glad you are home. We'll fatten you up and make you glad again." She let the girl go, and Tirza backed up a foot and stood, her wide blue eyes fixed on her mother.

Mervaly came up beside her, a hand on her shoulder. "Mother, she's here now. You heard what Jeon said. You must never send her back to Santomalo." Tirza looked up at Mervaly, and put her hand on Mervaly's hand.

Marioza sat back. The glow of motherliness was ebbing away. And now she would have to marry Erdhart. There was nothing to be done but go through with it all. Yet she was still glad to see Tirza, and smiled at her, and nodded. "I think we must abide each other. No more tricks, hah."

Tirza suddenly smiled back. This made her prettier, but not much. The blue eyes blazed with that fierce stare, as if she could speak through looking, force the words from her mind to her mother's without the use of voice. She made a little awkward bow to Marioza. Tirza was a full year older than when Marioza had seen her last, a young woman now, but still all angles, like a sawtooth.

Something else had changed in her, something deeper.

"Tirza!"

Luka strode in the door; he slapped Mervaly on the behind,

and gave Casea a quick kiss, all the while heading toward Tirza, as she was turning to meet him. Reaching her, he gathered her up with a shout and tossed her into the air and caught her. "You're back! How did you do that? 'Zeyes, don't you wish she could tell us." He hugged her, their red heads together. Tirza, Marioza saw, hugged him back, burrowing her face into his shoulder. Through the door behind him came Jeon and then, to Marioza's surprise, Erdhart himself, his younger boy on his heels. Luka set Tirza down on her feet.

"You're so thin. Look at you. Somebody clean her up. Mervaly—"

"She's just arrived, Luka; they've been traveling for months."

"So," Erdhart said. He was standing by the door. He looked, as always, polished like a gemstone. He was smiling, as always. "The freemartin has returned."

They had all fallen still at the first sound of his voice, their heads swiveled to look at him behind them. Marioza said, "This is my daughter Tirza."

He laid his gaze briefly on the girl before him. He gave a harrumph, half laugh and half sneer. His attention turned to Marioza.

"Then we shall be married tomorrow." He passed his smile around the room, his eyes glittering. "We shall all rejoice." He inclined his head to Marioza, and left.

She grunted. Before her, Tirza swung around toward her again, and their eyes met. Mervaly was bending over her sister, saying, "Come on; we'll give you a good bath." Tirza let her sisters lead her away.

Alone, save for the servants, Marioza sat staring into nothing. In the morning she would marry Erdhart. She could not bear that. His touch was awful to her already, when he only took her hand. She thought of Reymarro. They had married by their fathers' arrangement, but from the first kiss she had loved him. He would have told her what to do. He would never have lost his castle to them in the first place, if he had stayed here. But they had lured him away from the ocean, and then they had killed him.

She would not endure this. She would not let Erdhart have this. She shut her eyes, to let the boom of the surf, far below the window, pour into her mind.

THE SISTERS ALL LIVED IN THE ROOM AT THE TOP OF THE south tower, which had a big window looking out over the bay. Since she was a child Mervaly had loved birds, lured them in with treats and singing, rescued them from cats and boys and the weather, mended broken wings and legs. Most of them left eventually, but many came back and forth through the window, and so the room was always full of their chirruping and whirring.

When the sisters came in the door, the seagull on the windowsill squawked and the chitter-chatter rose to a merry screech, all the wings flapping. Through this noisy welcome Tirza followed Mervaly through the room toward the window. There were fewer birds than usual: the seagull, who never left, and an old raven, the four swallows with their nests up under the eave, an owl, and in one corner of the hearth a petrel, very sick, all its feathers staring.

A serving girl with a broom stood back to let them pass, smiled at Tirza, and bobbed a little bow. She was tall and skinny and Tirza thought once she must have been a stork. Mervaly's big wooden tub sat by the window. Tirza stood tamely while her sisters peeled off her clothes, lifted her, and plopped her into the hot water.

"Aah!" She gave up her breath at the shock. The warmth soaked into her, and her sisters' hands stroked her, scrubbing away the dirt on her body, on her hands and face, between her toes. She let them handle her, her eyes shut, all her body blissful.

Mervaly sat her up and washed her hair, tugging and pulling, and she didn't even mind that. They dried her off, put on her a clean shift of Casea's, far too big, wrapped a scarf around her waist to keep it on, and then sat her on the bed so that Mervaly could brush her hair.

Casea leaned toward her, took one of Tirza's hands, and opened it up, running her fingers over the palm. "Oh, poor thing," she said. "Look at her poor hands, Mervaly."

"I saw them while I was washing them," said Mervaly. "She's lived by her hands." Mervaly's arms dropped down around Tirza and drew her back against her softness. "What a marvel you are. To have done that."

Casea said, "Tell us about the shipwreck."

Tirza made motions like the boiling sea, and brought the dragon up with both hands. But her sisters knew it was a shipwreck, and so they did not understand. She howled once, frustrated, and Mervaly hugged her.

"It was awful, I know."

You do not know. Tirza got up and walked away across the room, looking at the birds.

Behind her, Casea said, "Mother has to find a way to put this wedding off."

"He is such a toad. Did you see how he looked at Tirza? What he called her? Freemartin! We have to do something. I won't let that happen, her marrying him."

"Leave it to Mother," Casea said. "Whatever she decides we'll all go along with."

Tirza did not want to hear all this. It was delicious to be clean, to be dry and fed and safe again, a sister again. The fluttering and cooing of the birds was delicious. The swallows up under the ceiling were whispering together. On a wall perch, in a basket full of straw, the owl sat, her new feathers prickling up through the down. Tirza put out her hand cautiously toward her. She would not think about the rest of this. The owlet put out her beak, as if to kiss Tirza's finger. She laughed.

There was a sharp knock on the door. She turned.

The page opened it, and Marioza came in, alone. She wore a long embroidered nightdress, a cloak over it, and her hair in a braid down her back. She swept her gaze over her daughters, fixed her eyes on Mervaly, and said, "Please, leave me alone with Tirza."

Tirza gave a start. Here came what she was afraid of. She cast a begging glance at Mervaly and Casea, but they both dipped their knees and went off through the door to the hall. Tirza pressed her lips together; she turned her eyes on her mother, high above her. Marioza was watching her steadily, and now she sighed.

"So, girl."

Tirza said, "Mama." It came out a growl. She locked her hands in front of her.

Marioza stood before her like a piece of the rock, immovable. She sighed again, and frowned, and then said, "This must be done. I have never told you this. I am the cause of all this between us. When you were born, I cursed you."

Tirza felt that like a stone striking her; she let her hands fall to her sides, and her mouth opened. Nothing came out. She felt a lump rising in her throat. Marioza went on, looking away, toward the wall of birds.

"You came by surprise. You were four hours at least after Jeon was born, a big, lusty boy, bellowing like a bull calf. I was lying in the bed, and there was a shiver in my loins and out you came, little wizened thing there between my legs. And I picked you up and held you up before me—"

Marioza stopped, and her gaze came back to Tirza's. Tears coursed down Marioza's cheeks. "In your eyes, I saw my doom. And now you have proven it."

Tirza said, "I didn't mean to." A jumble of clicks and whistles. She clenched her jaws. All this time, she had thought something was wrong with her.

"So I pinched your lips together. 'Whatever you know, you can tell no one.' As if that mattered. I pushed you off, sent you away. But it has still happened."

She held out her hands to Tirza, palms up. "I wish I had not done it. I wish I had been braver. But I have failed. I lost Reymarro; I have lost his castle. Tomorrow I marry his murderer's brother."

Tirza could not move; her mother seemed to be dropping away, smaller and smaller, into an abyss. She blinked. Marioza stood before her, solid, still.

Her mother spoke again. "I laid a curse on you. I cannot remove that. So I am giving you another curse. Keep faith. That's all. Keep faith." She turned, and walked out the door.

CURLED UP IN THE BIG BED IN BETWEEN HER SISTERS, TIRZA could not sleep. Since she escaped from the dragon, she had slept in ditches, under rocks, in the high grass, cold and hungry. Now she had deep featherbeds under her, white pillows. She was where she belonged. She was warm and clean and comforted, and yet her mind would not rest.

Like birds circling, her mother's words went around and around in Tirza's mind: I cursed you. Her own mother had made this happen to her. And now a new curse.

Keep faith. With whom, to what? And why was it a curse?

Her mother's voice, speaking words. Tirza shut her eyes. On her side, with Mervaly against her back and Casea before her, she drew her body close, and began to tell herself a story about a Princess, who was cursed with keeping faith. But Tirza slept almost at once, and the story disappeared.

In her sleep she imagined that someone was caressing her, tender, gentle as music, all over. She turned to see who it was, and above her was the huge red eye of the dragon.

JEON AND LUKA WENT DOWN INTO THE TOWN, NOT BOTHER-ing to go out by the gate where Erdhart had his guards but down a long, steep passage that often opened up just outside the great hall. For a long while the way was dark and they went along carefully, but then the passage leveled out and they came into a wide, high-ceilinged room of six or seven walls of different lengths. A green lamp hung from the high ceiling, giving only a faint light that fell in veils toward the shadowy floor. All around the irregular room, set in the walls, were niches, and in each of the niches a body lay. Jeon made a bow to them before he went by, and after; the old ones had always awed him.

Luka did nothing, frowning, but went on through to the sea gate, below, where they had to wade because the tide was in.

The evening was coming and the beach before the shops was full of people packing up and going home. Trollo, the piper boy, had made up a puppet show, over by the cypress tree, and a crowd of children still lingered there, watching him take down his stage. A shepherd, a lamb on his shoulder, was herding three ewes along toward the grass on the high end of the beach.

Luka led the way to the brewery, with its broad, open porch stretched along the foot of the cliff. Lumilla, the brewster, had taken in the kegs off the porch, and the open deck was empty. Jeon followed Luka through the door into the smoky, ill-lit cliff room, full of people waiting for Lumilla to feed them supper. When Luka came in, they all called out to him. As usual the people were mostly women. Since the massacre in the mountains, men had been in short supply in Undercastle.

At the back of the room was a stair cut into the rock, and the two brothers went up and through a corridor to another, smaller room. One wall of this was open to the air, and the evening light filled the space. Lumilla's daughter followed them in, wiped off the table, and moved another chair to it. She was a big, muscular girl, tawny as a lioness. Her name was Amillee. She gave Luka a broad smile.

"Your customary, my lord?" Leaning over the table to pick up a stray dish, she gave him a good look down her dress. Luka sat down, grinning. Jeon took the other chair. Amillee hardly even glanced at him; she gave a waggle of her hips and went back into the stairwell.

Luka watched her go. Jeon said, "Is she—are you—" and felt the heat rise into his face.

His brother laughed at him. Luka leaned his forearms on the table, and said, "So tell me more about this work you saw them doing up the coast, when you went to get Tirza. Where was it?"

"About half a day west of the Black Reeks. An old landslide comes down, there's a cove, some offshore rocks."

"Just east of Pelican Head."

"I guess so," Jeon said, uncertain. Nobody else knew the coast as well as Luka.

His brother said, "What do you think they're doing there?"

"They're trying to build some kind of fort. But they're doing it on the toe of the slide, so I don't see how big they can make it. There's a lot of rock, but the ground is still settling."

"The beach there is worse; the sand sweats there. But it's a very good position."

Amillee came back with a pitcher and two cups. Luka said, "My brother is likely hungry—Jeon, do you want something to eat?"

"I'll bring something," she said, and went out again. Luka poured a cup of ale and leaned on the table. Jeon drained his cup; the fragrance made his head pulse.

"How any men are there?"

"Maybe sixty. Oto was there."

"Ah, yes. I've seen him coming and going; he always says he's going to hunt, but he never comes back with game." Luka drank. "I thought there were fewer soldiers here, but they're always moving; it's hard to keep track."

"What are we going to do about Mother?"

"Us? Nothing. Let Mother deal with Erdhart."

"But we can't let her send Tirza back to Santomalo."

Amillee came in again with a plate of bread, cheese, and sausages. She took the pitcher, now empty, smiled at Luka, and left. Luka watched her go.

"Nobody is going to Santomalo. It burnt to the ground, a long month ago."

"What?" Jeon said. His mind flew back to the red roofs, the awnings of the market. That must have happened soon after he was there, searching for Tirza.

"Somebody came in from the sea and torched the place. Slavers. Everybody not burnt up they carried off."

"What are you going to do?" Jeon broke off a chunk of bread, but now he had no appetite.

"Me? Nothing. Santomalo is an Imperial town."

"What is Erdhart doing?"

"A lot, and very little. He sends out patrols, every day, to the high road. That makes it hard to figure how many men he has, but I'm thinking somewhere around forty. They make up their squadrons in twenties. And he's put a guard on the big gate and won't let anybody in and out without purpose. He wants to tax everybody, even the people in the hills, and to do that he has to know who everybody is. So far he can't even find out how many people are in Undercastle." Luka flashed a smile. "He's waiting for messages from the Holy City. I'm thinking the galley that wrecked under you and Tirza was bringing him messages. Nobody here talks to him. Travelers come and go without him even seeming to notice. I knew about what happened at Santomalo long before he did. Something he said once makes me think they will try to bring a fleet here sometime this summer."

Jeon chewed and swallowed. All the while he had searched for Tirza he had thought of none of this, how the Empire was settling in around them. He said, "What do you think Mother is going to do?"

Luka gave a snort of laughter. "Erdhart is marrying his grave." He lifted the cup. "To Marioza, Queen of Castle Ocean!" And drank.

LUMILLA SAW HER DAUGHTER COME DOWN FROM THE BACK room, the pitcher in her hand, and followed her over to the taps. She waited until Amillee had filled the jug again, and then Lumilla got between her and the way back to the stairs.

"What are you doing? Or, I should say, why are you doing it?"

"I don't know what you're talking about."

"We have other custom than him! Listen to me." Lumilla put her lips close to her daughter's ear. "I love Luka. If not for him, after what happened in the mountains, there would be no men left in this town at all. But you keep your place with him."

"My place," Amillee said, with a flirt of her hips. "Like your place with Aken? You think I don't know about that?"

"Bah," Lumilla said, unperturbed. Everybody knew about her and Aken. Her husband had died with Reymarro and she was a lusty woman: nobody could expect her to do otherwise. "He lives next door to me. He is my kind. Do you imagine you'll live up there in the castle, someday? Is that it?"

Amillee shrugged one round shoulder. "I don't see why I—"

Lumilla pushed her back toward the taps. "You're wasting your time. They are not like us. They are half ghost, and half something I don't even want to think about, and we are just people."

"Let me by," Amillee said. She held the jug before her like a ram and moved. Lumilla stood where she was, blocking the way, long enough to show she could keep Amillee there if she really wanted to, and then stepped aside. Amillee went by her with a swish of her long skirt and back up the stair.

LATE THAT NIGHT, OTO ERDHARTSSON RODE ALONE OVER THE bridge to the gate of Castle Ocean. The guards admitted him into the gate yard with many bows and welcomes, which he liked, but then he saw his father's herald coming out the door into the main tower. This he did not like. He gave his exhausted horse to the nearest soldier, and tramped up the stair.

The herald bustled around him, with flourishes of his hands and his head bobbing up and down. "My lord, your father commands you to him."

Oto could not refuse, but he stood a moment, staring down at the herald, until the man cringed. "Lead me there," Oto said loftily, and the herald hurried away ahead of him, into the big, round room where all the stairs began, and up.

Erdhart was sitting in a corner of his room; he tended now always to keep his back to the wall. Oto went across to the broad table by the window, where wine waited in jugs, and nodded to the servant there to pour him a cup. Erdhart watched him steadily, his face dark with temper. Oto ignored this until he had his cup, and then drank. When he went up before his father he sat down without waiting for permission, and his father flared at him.

"You should have red hair. You are acquiring their manners. Why have you come back without orders?"

"One of them turned up at the new fort," Oto said. He planned to call it Otosberg, but he was not yet that sure of himself.

"Ah." Erdhart lifted his head, alarmed, and Oto smiled at him, pleased, a step ahead.

"Rest assured. He saw nothing. We shunted him properly off. He had a girl with him. I formed a certain conclusion. So I came. When is the wedding?"

He drank more wine. Erdhart cast a quick glance at the servant, who came at once for his cup.

"Tomorrow. The prize is almost in my hands. When the Queen is mine, the whole of Castle Ocean is mine." He shifted his weight. "Everything is done by the law; there is no undoing it." The ring in his voice sounded false. He was quaking like a rabbit in a field of foxes. Oto wondered where Broga was: probably praying, the fool. He clenched his jaw: his father was playing this too softly. These people needed to be bitted and bridled and ridden hard.

If it had been Oto's command that would have been done immediately, when they first got here, with the body of Marioza's last husband still warm in its coffin. Only the Emperor's nice concern with law stood in the way of it. This family had no army anymore, only fishermen and shepherds. Oto hated Luka, the way he strutted around, the way everybody bowed and cringed around him, but he had never even seen Luka carry a sword. The younger brother was nothing, barely out of his wet pants. The only other one who mattered was Mervaly, and Oto wanted to throw Mervaly down on the nearest bed and bury himself in all that soft, sweet flesh, stuff her laughing mouth with his flesh, own her entirely. The idea made his head swim a moment, delirious. The others he would only kill, but Mervaly he would marry.

The servant came back with the cup, and Erdhart stopped to drink. He needed both hands to hold the cup.

He went on, "This is where my brother Ruddich failed. He let his guard down, when she seemed to marry him, and she tricked him. I intend to keep this going my way. Before the wedding, you will personally go through the chamber where I am to bed her, make sure there is nothing concealed, no weapon, no vial, nothing. The ceremony and the feast will be in the hall. You will personally inspect every inch of that room also. And then, during the ceremony, during the feasting, you will station a man to watch each of the Queen's children, each of her servants, ready to draw dagger and do death at the slightest sign of evil intent."

At this Oto smiled again. "Yes," he said. He could imagine a wide variety of signs of evil intent, especially once his father was wedded and bedded and the kingdom was theirs. Erdhart emptied his cup and beckoned to the servant again.

"Put someone in the kitchen. A couple of men. Make sure the cooks taste everything."

"Yes, Father."

"Keep a guard constantly in the bedchamber."

"Yes, Father."

He held his voice rigid against the drip of condescension. He was the man to rule here. It was an injustice that his father would be King here, when Oto was already doing most of the work. And Erdhart, lifting his cup with his trembling hands, looked like an old man, feeble, in the way. Oto rose, and without taking leave, he went out to find his own chambers.

 4

THEY DIDN'T EVEN HAVE A CHURCH HERE, ERDHART THOUGHT, and Broga's chapel was still just an idea. So the Imperial Archduke came out to marry on the open terrace of the castle, in the sunlight, with the broad sea stretching out over the horizon, as if to call the brute forces of the world to witness. They might as well have held torches and made him walk between, or sacrificed a horse.

Erdhart had brought his own priest with him, to wrap this all up tight with the right words, a short bald man who stood there now with his book open in his hands. Afterward they would feast here, probably throwing bones into the sea.

Today the ocean was placid, looking blue and soft as a baby's blanket, only a low rumble down there far below the edge of the terrace. Erdhart went up to stand before the priest, aware of the crowded hall around him. The gathered family took up one side of the room, packed together, cousins and aunts in the back, in the front a row of redheads. His men fit more easily into the other side. Between them were the banquet tables, already set with cups and knives.

Then the main door opened. The room hushed at once, everyone turned to watch, and Marioza appeared.

Down the length of the room she smiled at him. She came slowly up the center of the hall, splendid in a dark gown trimmed with pearls, gold in a scaly wreath around her neck, gold in loops hanging from her ears. He thrilled a little. She was a fine woman, her bloodred hair curling lushly over her white shoulders, her great eyes shining above the slant of her cheekbones. She reached him, and compliantly, she lowered herself down onto her knees, her head bowed, and held out her hand to him.

From her children there went up a sharp gasp of disbelief. Erdhart himself was startled at her submission; at once he thought of a trap, but their shocked faces reassured him. They thought she was yielding to him. This was going well, then. He took her by the hand, and lifted her to her feet. That meant she was taller than he was, but she bowed her head, docile.

The priest said the words. Among the children a constant little mutter ran, a stirring. They had not expected this. This was part of no plan. Erdhart began to think that he had won.

He would not weaken, though. Ruddich had weakened, had taken the cup, at the last minute, died at her feet.

When Erdhart led her to the bedding, it would not be in her chambers, not with her servants, but in his, with his men all around. He would strip her down with his own hands, make sure she carried no weapons, no poisons. Then, only then, let her near his body.

Next to him now, her warm, abundant body.

The head table was put back in place, and they sat there, and shared a cup. He kicked her once, to see what she would do, and she only stooped a little and lifted her eyes toward him, brimming with tears. High color rose in her cheeks. The servant put a stew of lobster before them in a single dish, and he took a bit on his fork and held it to Marioza, and she accepted it between her lips.

He reached for the wine; she had already drained it. The servant leaned past him and filled the cup again. Music began, pipes, a drum. Two rows of people formed down the open space before them, the men on one side, the women on the other, crossing the room from the doors almost to the sea. At the shadowy end of the double row Luka danced with the freemartin, tiny as a child. The others clapped, the pipes shrilled, and the drum pattered. Luka and the little Goblin danced toward each other, and caught hands. They whirled around each other. The Goblin threw her head back and laughed a hideous cackle. They whirled together in the middle and Luka lifted her up off her feet, eye level with him, and kissed her forehead. Then again setting her down he led her in another spin, moving down between the rows into the sunlight. Again they came together and kissed, spun around, and kissed, and backed up each to one side and began clapping, and another couple pranced and bounded in the middle.

"Charming," Erdhart said. The drink had muddled his head a little. He saw the dancers as smears of color. He ate more of the lobster. Sliding his hand under the table, he laid it on Marioza's thigh, and she gave a start. He moved his fingers higher, inward, between her legs, pushing the cloth down, rubbing her there. She sat soft and yielding, her head down, and after a moment shifted her legs apart so he could reach the folds of her body more easily.

His head reeled. Soon he would be there. But now, all the

dancers were clapping and they were staring up at him and Marioza.

"Dance! The King and Queen must dance! Make the marriage lucky and fruitful; dance!"

He sat a moment, startled. This seemed beneath his dignity. But she was rising, smiling at him, her hand out. He took her hand, thinking of the kisses. Her hand in his tightened, warm. He thought he could smell the excitement of her flesh. They went down and took their place at the head of the dance. Everybody, all through the room, was clapping. He watched her feet, and moved forward, caught her hands, and they spun around each other, and came together, and their lips met.

The heat of her mouth stirred him all the way to his loins. They parted at once, and whirled around again, the room thundering with applause. He leaned toward her again, and their mouths met, and her tongue slipped between his lips.

He gasped, his member throbbing in his codpiece. He spun her, and this time, when they kissed, he caught her against him; he pressed himself against her from mouth to thighs, his hands on her backside. The whole room whooped. She clung to him. For an instant, face-to-face, he saw the glitter in her eyes, and a sudden cold alarm flooded him. When he tried to pull back, the floor seemed to tip under him. He lost his balance, and staggered, and with his hands gripped in hers, her red hair flying, Marioza whirled them both toward the lip of the terrace and danced with him out onto the empty air.

LUKA TURNED ON HIS HEEL; BACK BY THE WALL A PIKEMAN stood, slack jawed, staring at the terrace, and Luka leapt at him, snatched the pike out of his hands, and sank the butt end deep into the man's belly. "Jeon!" Luka bounded onto the table, kicking the wedding hams out of the way, and bolted toward the door. Somebody screamed, "Stop him!" but most of the crowd was rushing the other way, toward the sunlight, where the King and Queen had just disappeared over the edge.

In the open doorway a soldier faced him, his pike across his body like a shield, and Luka at full stride jumped on him, feet to his chest, smashed him down, fell himself, staggered up off the body, and dashed out.

That passage was there again, the one opening up on the right, this time a stairway. He plunged into it, going down three steps at a time. Someone was coming after him and he wheeled, the pike ready. Down the dim steps his brother rushed toward him, his face white, his eyes shocked white. Luka reached out, and he and Jeon locked their arms a moment. Then without a word Luka turned and raced on, Jeon on his heels, down the twisting, steepening stairwell, toward the sound of the sea.

OTO SAW HIS FATHER DISAPPEAR INTO THE AIR AND A WILD triumph filled him. The shrieking crowd rushed by him, going to gawk over the edge of the terrace, but Oto stood silent, stone hard, collecting himself.

This was the opening; this was what he needed.

Too late, he saw Luka racing away out the door and shouted but could not stop him. Oto went up through the crowd to the front of the terrace. Broga, the besotted fool, was on his knees at the edge, screaming, "Papa!" All around in the stunned crowd women were weeping. The priest was praying in a loud voice and another language. Nobody moved, except Oto. The soldiers were mixed into the crowd and he went around to them one at a time, shaking them by the shoulder and giving them orders. Seeing Mervaly and her sisters standing at the far side of the terrace, he went straight at them, six men at his back.

They made no effort to escape. Mervaly had her arms around the other girls and they were all sobbing. For a moment he could not get them to pay heed to him, so he could order them locked up in their room, but once he had Mervaly's attention she obeyed him. The freemartin was jabbering nonsense at him, and the other girls took her by the hands and led her away. The cousins and aunts had vanished while he was confronting Mervaly. Tears streaming down his face, Broga rushed up.

"I'm going down to find Papa. He's down there somewhere."

"Go," Oto said, and waved him away. Slobbering, Broga raced off. Oto turned to the priest. "I am King now. I will be crowned at once."

The priest's eyes popped. He said, "My lord, I don't know the rite—"

"Make one up. There has to be some authority here. I am the only one. I shall be King. Tomorrow." He raised his arms to the rest of the soldiers, and led them off to find the missing red-haired Princes.

IN A HIGH-PITCHED, RAGGED VOICE, MERVALY SAID, "I shouldn't have let him order us around. I live here. This is my place, not theirs." She strode around the room like a small storm, so that the birds on their perches rose up and flapped their wings.

Casea wept. "There's nothing we can do. Nothing good, anyway." She sat down on the bed, put her face in her hands, and gave herself up to her grief. Mother, Mother, she thought. Mother, why did you leave us like this?

Before her she saw the whole of her family coming apart, like a fabric unraveling, all the threads apart, and all the patterns gone.

Across the room, behind the bed, Tirza was creeping along the wall. Even she was crying. At the same time, with both hands, she was groping along the stones of the wall. Casea knew what she was looking for, and presently saw her find it, saw her fingers push gently at what seemed like solid stone, and open the seam, and slip into it. Slowly the wall closed behind her.

Casea thought, Even that, even that, will make things worse. She folded her arms around herself a moment, trying to sort this all out, and finally went for her needlework, to keep her hands busy.

THERE WAS NO WAY STRAIGHT DOWN THE CLIFF FROM THE castle terrace; Broga had to go miles around, along the flat grassy meadow at the top of the cliff to the angling narrow trail down to the beach, and then up the beach to the foot of the beetling rock where the castle stood. At full tide the waves beat against the sheer cliff face as high as the edge of the terrace, but now the tide was going out, draining from the jagged seams of rock along the beach.

A white cloud of birds screamed and flew upward at his approach. Beneath them they left Erdhart, lying there on his back below the terrace. Broga gave a cry, and splashed out through the last of the tide. His father had fallen onto the rocks, his body sprawled, the subsiding water around him stained with blood. Over his chest and face the crabs were already crawling.

Broga charged in through the ankle-deep water, and stamped and kicked at the crabs until all had scuttled off or lay crushed in the rocks. He sank down beside the ruin of his father. In the cups of their sockets Erdhart's eyes were bloody slicks. The gulls and crabs had already opened wounds on his face. His hair flooded on an eddy. The side of his skull dented inward. Broga put out his hand, to form the head back into shape, and the matter squished under his fingers. He doubled over, wracked with grief.

The three soldiers he had brought stood at the edge of the water. He forced himself calm. Someone would pay for this. He would make someone suffer for this. He straightened to his feet, and caught the sergeant's eye.

"Go find me a stretcher, a litter, some way we can carry him back to the castle."

"Yes, my lord." With a salute the sergeant led his men back toward the village.

Broga turned his eyes again to his father's body; his heart beat unsteadily, a cauldron in his breast. He looked around for the other one, the woman who had done this, who was here, too, somewhere.

He would trample her into something not even crabs would eat.

The rocks came up through the sand like the ragged edges of baskets, holding pots of water. He searched around where Erdhart lay, but she was not there. Broga went wider, all along the foot of the cliff, out to the retreating edge of the sea. She was not there.

He growled, aching with frustration. She was here somewhere. He searched again, all along the rocks and sand, everywhere. He found nothing. The soldiers came back, with a litter they had made of poles and cloth, and two mules.

He stood watching as they lifted his father carefully up. The sergeant did most of the work, directing the others, folding the broken body together, arms across the chest, leg over leg. He stretched a cloak on the ground and they lifted Erdhart onto it, wrapping the cloak tight around him, so that nothing spilled. They carried the litter off toward the mules.

The rocks where Erdhart had lain were bloody, and clumped with awful stuff. Through the water something gleamed. Broga stooped, and took up a piece of gold. A ring. He held it up into the sun. By the twist of the gold he knew it: not his father's but Marioza's ring. Broga stood again, and looked all around him, among the rocks, the puddles, the distant surf, but there was nothing left of her, except the ring that had pledged her to Erdhart.

Abruptly in Broga's mind's eye he imagined her carried off by gulls. Spreading wings and flying away. Turning into a great fish. His belly clenched. He could not see what this meant. Convulsively he flung the ring away. The soldiers had rigged the litter between the mules in tandem, and were waiting for him. He tramped by them with a curt wave and led them off the long way up to the castle.

At the castle's big main gate, four of his own men saluted him. The walk had calmed him and he stood to one side and watched without a shiver as the others carried in his father's body. He said to the sergeant, "Go lay it in the hall, in state, as befits a King." But he hung back when the litter went on.

To the guard on the gate, he said, "Has my brother caught the Princes?"

The guard cleared his throat and glanced at the other men. "No, my lord. We were just talking about that, my lord. Nobody can find them."

Broga looked around him at the gate yard. There was no other way out of the castle. "If they haven't tried to get through this way then they're hiding somewhere in this infernal place. What about the women?"

"They're locked up, my lord. I heard that myself from the tower guard."

"Where is my brother?" Broga loved to see Oto getting something wrong. But first there was Erdhart, and Broga said, "Stand a continual watch, here, then; they will have to show up here sometime. Seize them then and send to me," and went into the castle to care for his father.

* * *

Pal Dawd, who had come here as sergeant of the Archduke Erdhart's guard, was having some difficulty deciding who
his officer was. Both of the Erdhartssons kept giving him orders,
although Oto was to be crowned King, and perhaps that would
solve it.

On Broga's order Dawd and his corporal Marwin laid out
Erdhart on the stone table in the hall. Dawd sent the corporal
up to the lord's chamber for his best cloak, and to find servants
and water to wash the body. Broga was pacing around and around
the terrace room like an ox driving a millstone.

"I want a railing built across that open edge. Maybe we can
block it up entirely." His voice rasped. "But first I'll throw every
one of the children off the edge. Let them feel what my father
felt." Broga flung himself down on his knees beside the corpse.
"Oh, God. Take him into Your pure bosom; let him find Your
perfect peace."

Marwin came back with the cloak, a fine brocaded cloth with
fur and gold, but no servant had appeared with water. The body
was filthy. Dawd went out to the next room, the big, round antechamber where all the stairs began, and looked for someone to
help but there were only soldiers. Finally he beckoned over a
couple of grunts and took them into the hall.

Broga was still praying, fervent, his fists clutched to his face.
Dawd pointed the two men at the corpse. "Get water and wash
him."

Marwin came over to Dawd, his eyes sharp, and made a gesture
with his head toward the corner. Dawd glanced at Broga, who
was wholly bound up in his mourning, and followed Marwin over
to the wall.

"You know," Marwin said, his voice eager, "this is all coming
apart, here."

"Sssh," Dawd said. Marwin faced him; over the other man's

shoulder Dawd could see Broga and he looked for signs he was listening. Hunched into his prayer, Broga did not move, except his shoulders, which trembled. The men washing the body were making enough noise to cover a whisper. Still Dawd moved off along the wall, toward the front of the terrace.

Marwin pursued him. "Did you hear what they said, back there? They can't find the Princes. And Oto wants to be King. But who's to say? And these people hate us."

"What are you saying?"

"I'm just asking you, that's all."

Dawd looked out toward the sea. In the blazing late sun the sea was rising, its surface breaking into whitecaps, the long combers crashing over the shore rocks. A cormorant teetered on the wind near the edge of the terrace, so close he could see the black disk of its eye. The death of Erdhart weighed on him, the Emperor's brother, a man of the golden blood. They had come here thinking this tour of duty would be easy. Dawd remembered looking forward to this.

He had been born and raised in the Holy City, far to the east of here, where the water was a placid lake. He became a soldier because there was nothing else to do, for a lowborn man, except shoveling dirt. He was a good soldier; he understood his orders and obeyed them perfectly and he kept himself ready to fight. He had spent some time in the hard wars in the south, where the Empire was increasing over the savage desert tribes, and the move here, with the House of Erdhart, had been a promotion, even a chance to settle down.

"Do we follow Oto?" Marwin said. His voice dropped to a murmur. "Broga is the better man."

Dawd wheeled on him. "We're Imperial soldiers. We do as we're told."

Marwin snapped up straight as a plumb line. "Yes, of course." Without moving his head, he shifted his eyes, not far enough to see Broga, far enough to indicate him. "I never had any doubt of you, sir." He cocked up his forearm, his palm turned out, saluting. "Thank you for justifying my faith in you. Glory to the Empire!"

Dawd growled at him. "Glory," he said, and flapped his hand, returning the salute. He gave another glance at the ocean, and went over to the body again. Naked, still damp, the corpse's skin had a ghastly greenish tinge. He helped the men slide Erdhart onto the beautiful cloak and lay him out on the table. Marwin went up again to the royal chamber for Erdhart's sword. Through it all, Broga prayed. Dawd went out to find a servant, remembered, and got one of the many idle soldiers to find him some candles. The soldier came back, eventually, with lamps, and they put them at Erdhart's head and feet.

Dawd's hands were shaking; he felt the coldness of the corpse under his fingertips even when he lit the lamps. He sent Marwin away and put the other two soldiers to standing guard. The ocean was booming under the terrace, the tide rising, Dawd thought, the water reaching out again for Erdhart, and he shivered, and he went out of the room.

In the big, round antechamber beyond, where all the stairs began, the idle soldiers had begun a game of bones. Dawd stood a moment wondering what to do next, and then, off on his right hand, at the foot of a staircase, he saw the littlest girl, the one everybody called the Goblin, half the size of anybody else, with her mop of frizzy red hair and her enormous blue eyes.

So even the girls were not really locked away. He went toward her, and for a moment she did not move; she stared at him with those piercing eyes, and then went off up the steps behind her.

Dawd followed. On the next landing, ten steps up, she gave him a long look and then went into another passageway that led, not up, but off sideways through the wall.

He stopped, his gut contracting. He had not seen that long, narrow way before. He did not come here often and yet he was sure it had not been there before. But she was standing just inside, watching him. He went cautiously toward her.

At the very threshold of the passage, with the girl almost within arm's length, he put his foot out, half-expecting to meet solid, if invisible, rock. His foot went on beyond the threshold and came down on the floor. The girl went back another step. He crept after her.

"Come, now. Come to me. I won't hurt you." If he caught her, he could get her back into the bedroom and Oto and Broga never had to know she had escaped. She watched him a moment, and stepped backward, and behind her in the gloom the corridor bent and she disappeared around the corner.

Abruptly a light glowed on the rough black rock of the passage wall. She was just there, just beyond that turn, and she had lit a lamp. Dawd went a few steps on, going well to the right, so he could see around the corner before he reached it.

The light retreated as he moved. When he saw her again she was standing in the middle of the narrow way, one hand on the rock, the lamp in the other. The passage was narrowing with each step, and behind her, he saw, it ended in a blank wall. He had her trapped.

He said, "Come, now. I won't hurt you. I'll just take you back to your sisters." This was the one who could not talk, and he wondered, briefly, if she was deaf also, but he had seen others talk to her. He crept on cautiously toward her, to keep from frightening her, crouching to make himself smaller, whispering, "I won't hurt you. I want to help you." And she turned toward the blank wall and was gone, and the lamp with her.

He stood in utter darkness, a black like nothing.

He was only a few feet from the staircase back down to the antechamber. He put out his hand, feeling for the wall, and his fingertips grazed the rock. Turning, he groped his way along, going back the way he had come in. When the corridor turned he would see light. He kept one hand on the wall always, so he would not lose his way.

The corridor did not turn. Under his feet it began to go downward. A sudden gust of damp, salty air blew into his face. He stopped. As if the rock closed around him he suddenly could not breathe.

Under his hand, the solid rock was warm, like flesh. It does not know me, he thought. I am inside and it does not know me.

He struggled not to scream. His legs were watery. He turned, and felt his way back along the wall. He began holding his breath, to keep the darkness out. He thought he felt the rock move, drawing closer, closing in around him.

Help me, he thought. Please help me. Not knowing who he called on.

He realized he had shut his eyes; he opened them again, and saw the rock wall before him, faintly lit.

He whirled around, sobbing with relief. The corridor rose up away from him, turning to the left, and a light bobbed steadily toward him. As he stood there, shaking, the tall girl, the Princess Casea, came around the corner toward him, a lamp in her hand.

She said, "What are you doing here? Come with me."

She stretched out her hand to him, and he took it; the strength in her fingers surprised him. She led him back around the corner, and there was the stair landing, ahead of him.

"Oh," he said. "I should have just kept on."

She gave him a long, strange look. She said, "I have saved you. You must come when I call you." She blew out the lamp and went away across the hall. Dawd stood in the hall, panting, wondering what had just happened to him.

OTO STOOD STILL, LETTING HIS MAN PUT ON HIS DOUBLET and arrange the pleats over the puffed breast. He said, "I've had a proclamation written up. Nothing particularly difficult. I'll send the herald down to read it in the marketplace. Then the day after tomorrow, we shall have the coronation." He admired his embroidered sleeve, gold and green.

Broga made a sound in his chest. Oto said, "Do you object?"

"I think we should find the Princes first," Broga said.

"Oh, we'll have them by then." Oto watched the man arrange the ruffles of his sleeves. "Once they see what's happening, these people will give us no trouble." At the moment, the main trouble they were giving was that all the native servants had disappeared. He was having to allot the work of the castle to his own men. He thought of sending for some of the men stationed down at the new fort to help out.

Broga said, "The Princes did not go out by the gate. But nobody can find them anywhere. How do you explain this?"

Oto frowned, and turned his eyes at the sergeant, standing by the door. This particular sergeant, whose name Oto could not remember, had served his father. Erdhart had trusted him, and he did seem more competent and intelligent than the rest. Oto said, "Why haven't you turned them up? Can't you search the place?"

The sergeant's square, fair-skinned face turned ruddy over the cheekbones. "I've searched, my lord. But they live here."

"What does that mean? Are they still in the castle?"

The sergeant shook his head. "My lord." His whole face was

red now. Maybe after all he was just as stupid as the ordinary run of soldiers. Oto shrugged off the annoying memory of the men he had sent to map the place who had never found the end of it.

Broga said, "Catch them. Keep watch on the kitchen, especially; they must eat."

Oto glared at him. "I give the orders." He nodded to the sergeant. "Do your job. Find them. Go make sure of the Princesses."

The sergeant blinked at him. "Yes, my lord." He saluted. "Glory to the Empire."

"Glory," Broga and Oto said in unison.

Oto faced his brother again. It came to Oto that Broga was showing a selfish interest in all this; certainly he was plotting. Another reason Oto should proclaim himself King as soon as possible. He would send a copy of the proclamation to the Holy City. He nodded. "You have something to do, I'm sure?"

His brother stared at Oto a moment. "Yes, in fact," he said. "The funeral of our father." He turned on his heel and walked out of the room.

THE LONG, STEEP PASSAGEWAY LED TIRZA OUT TO THE STAIR between the two rows of dwellings dug into the cliff. Below her was the beach, with its shops and stalls, and just to the south the broad common with the cypress tree. Only the local fishing ships floated on the blue water of the bay. She saw this with a little start of disappointment. Jeon had told her a ship had come from the south while she was gone; there had been strangers, new gewgaws, music, clothes.

The marketplace was full of people, moving like busy fish along the edges of the market, the shops and stalls. She knew them all. A red hat went by below her: that was Trollo, the piper boy, in the sack over his shoulder the balls and boxes he used in his juggles. She remembered the bright metal hats the Imperial men had worn, when she had seen them up the coast. She went down the steps; in the cliff houses as she passed, the women looked up from their soups and their brooms and smiled.

They liked her here. She was not ugly here. Nobody stared, or threw stones at her. The children who ran in a flood along the beach, screaming, who struggled along after their parents with buckets and baskets, did not come to harass her. She went by a makeshift stall rigged up on the beach, its slab of a counter stacked up with cheeses wrapped in cloth: a shepherd from inland, likely. Then Leanara's bakery, the oven door wide, the old woman bent over with her shovel to take out her round loaves. Her apprentice Suan leaned idle on the counter. They would give bread to Tirza if she only held out her hand. The aroma of the fresh baking made her stomach rumble. In the sail shop next door, cut into the wall of the cliff, the two sailmakers were arguing in ascending voices.

Before the men all died in the mountains the great porch of the brewery had been their place alone, but now among the few men left the women filled the benches and tables, so it was just as crowded. They made her shy; she had seen too much of packs of people. Wary, she went up the side of the steps, and people fell still to watch her. She felt all their eyes on her. Their silence. But they were moving, also, even bowing a little, and she went through their midst to the door.

The cave room beyond was also full of people, eating at the long tables, and they too quieted when they saw her, and bowed. She crossed to the steps and went up to Luka's room.

She came in behind a row of backs, one of them Jeon's, but beyond them Luka sat on a chair, facing her, and he saw her at once. "There's my sister. I knew you would come." He put out his arm and she went to him through the others and he hugged her against him. "Mervaly, Casea—they're safe?"

She nodded, looking into his eyes; she put her hands together in a ring, and set them on top of his head.

The room erupted in a jubilant roar. Jeon stood up, thrusting his arms over his head. Huge Aken, the butcher, leaned toward her and pounded her heartily on the back, and beside him Lumilla and her daughter and the three other townspeople began to call out, "King Luka! King!"

He looked down at her, smiling.

"You're a good girl, Tirza." He stood up.

They all quieted at once. Luka said, "We won't get through this by yelling. We need weapons. Jeon, you have a bow."

"Yes."

"The rest of us need blades. Spears. Whatever we can make or find, and quickly." He turned to Tirza. "Go on, now; leave this to us. You're a good girl."

She backed up, startled. He was sending her away. They bent together, all of them, shutting her out. He was appointing this one to go there and that one to go somewhere else. He was giving no work to her. She went to the door and left again.

The sun was high and hot, but the marketplace was still crowded. On the brewery porch Trollo was playing his pipe, and two little barefoot girls had come to dance. Tirza stood nearby, to listen, the music like speech without words. A dozen women waited around Leanara's stall for the oven to open again, their hands full of dishes to be baked. Tirza wandered back toward the common. At the weavery the long counter was stacked high with cloth and wool. The sheep fair would not be long past. Maybe that was why the ship from the south had come up. She put her hand on a skein of dark wool. One of the weaver sisters came over, blinking, eager, and Tirza went away; she had no use for that. She thought of her mother, who had cursed her to be always separate. But then where the row of stalls turned toward the beach the boy

Timmon with his water cask offered her a cup and she drank. At another stall a woman handed Tirza mutton on a bit of old bread. She went to the cypress tree and sat on the bench to eat.

She watched the brewery, back on the north beach, wondering what Luka would do. People went up constantly onto the porch, came back, went down. As they passed each other their heads turned and they spoke to each other. Whenever these proper people met, this was what they did first: build this little common porch of words. This was what she lacked, this connection. The way to make it. She turned away from the brewery, looking toward the bay, the water blue in the sunlight, the curl of foam at its lip. Trollo's music reached her faintly on the wind.

At the high corner of her vision something fluttered; she raised her gaze to the cliff top, at the head of the path to the town. Up there a man in a striped tunic held a long bright ribbon of cloth. After a moment he started down the path and behind him came another, very gaudy man, with a long staff, and then more striped tunics, all stepping at the same time. No one in the town seemed to notice them. They came zigzagging down the path, two by two, walked out onto the sand, and lined themselves up in two rows. The man with the banner went out in front of them, and beside him a man with a horn blew a blast.

Tirza stood up and trotted closer. Around the marketplace everybody was turning around.

Between the horn blower and the banner man, the gaudy herald strode forward. Tirza had seen him before, in the castle, attending Erdhart; he walked with a strut, and carried a staff. He had a short cape with heavy, glinting trim, high-topped black boots, a hat with an enormous feather secured on the crown through a jewel. Behind him the twelve Imperial soldiers with their pikes stood like a striped wall and the banner fluttered on the breeze in from the sea. In front of all of them, the herald banged his staff on the ground, and nodded at the soldier with the horn.

The horn blared again, a cold screech like a rip through the air. The herald began to shout. He had a huge, carrying voice, and his words pitched into the silence like weights.

"After what has happened to our master the Archduke Erdhart we can but grieve, and yet the demands of polity require us to take measures. And so tomorrow the High Lord and Archduke Oto will take the crown of Castle Ocean on his head."

Tirza twitched all over and her jaw dropped open. She cast a quick look around her for her brothers, nowhere in sight. All the people in the marketplace were drifting up closer, looking at one another, and murmuring. She went forward toward the front of the crowd.

The horn shrieked again. Again everybody else stood still, silent. The hard, evil voice went on, "After the coronation, the King will come down to receive the homage of his people. At this time he will accept gifts of you, and be assured the manner and the value of the gift will recommend you to him for your advancement."

Tirza stooped, her fingers scrabbling at the ground, and tore a rock out of the hard surface. Running forward a few steps, she flung it at the herald.

"Here is a gift!"

She heard her own voice rising, a tuneless bird-like shriek, just before the roar of the crowd drowned everything. The herald shrank back under a barrage of stones and dirt and food. The first volley splattered Imperials behind him, but then they lowered their pikes point forward and charged.

Tirza ran for the shelter of the cypress tree. The butcher's boy Mika was already there, picking up rocks. Panting, she wheeled to look back.

In the common the crowd swirled and screamed around the

orderly row of the pikemen, pelting them with showers of stones and dirt and shit. The pikemen strode straight ahead in their tight double rank while the town dogs barked and charged and nipped at their heels. Before this charge the crowd broke and scrambled away to either side, and from the shops, the houses, more people were rushing out to see what was happening. The crowd swelled, three times as many now as the pikemen.

Back there in the abandoned dust at the head of the common, a pile of gaudy rags lay half-buried in stones and dirt.

The rank of Imperial soldiers, their striped tunics filthy, had reached almost to the far end of the common. The crowd had wheeled around out of their way, and once they passed closed again behind them. Tirza saw Luka out in front of everybody, a fish gaff in one hand, shouting. She could not pick his voice from the general roar. The soldiers turned and marched back, toward the crowd, still in their double row.

A horn blew, and the pikemen stopped. At a shout from one of them, three pikemen in the front row moved two steps forward and in the row behind three moved two steps back. The remaining men wheeled neatly around, all together, into the spaces, so that they formed a square of bodies.

The horn blew again, and the square moved quickly forward. The mob of townspeople swirled around before them, and the Imperials all at once lowered their pikes down flat and charged into the midst of the mob.

Tirza ran toward the fighting, looking for her brothers. Screaming like gulls, the townspeople were reeling back out of the way of the pikes. They fell back to either side of the common and kept throwing anything they could put their hands on. Mika with his shirttail full of rocks ran by her, going toward his father. Out there in the open, away from the fighting, somebody was thrashing on the ground—Leanara, the baker. Tirza ran to her and knelt down.

The old woman clutched her belly, where the red blood was gushing through her floury apron. Tirza laid a hand on her face, and felt the life go out of Leanara.

She sat back on her heels, her heart pounding. Blood all over her dress now. An unbearable heat rose up through her, for this death, for all the deaths. Keep faith, she thought. Keep faith. Bounding up, she chased after the crowd, looking for stones as she ran.

BROGA STOOD AT THE SIDE OF THE GRAVE, STARING DOWN AT his father's body; he could not bear to lift the shovel in his hands. The priest had finished reading the holy words and was watching Broga expectantly. He signed himself and prayed again, asking, once again, for the greatness to be Erdhart's son, and behind him somebody screamed.

He lifted his head, annoyed. This graveyard was on the top of the cliff, well back from the edge, almost to the high road, but, still, someone was running toward him from the direction of the beach. He had seen the herald and some soldiers go down there; in fact, he had made a point of bringing Erdhart here to his grave just as Oto sent his proclamation down. But Broga could not be drawn away now. He gripped the shovel, composing himself, and drew it back to stab into the pile of dirt.

"They're fighting!" the oncoming runner screamed. "On the beach. Somebody's dead!"

The shovel stopped in Broga's hands, halfway through the motion. Abruptly he tossed it down and said, "Send for my brother." The groom brought Broga's horse at a trot, and he swung into the saddle.

"My lord," the priest said.

"Bury him," Broga said, and galloped toward the cliff.

* * *

OTO WATCHED FROM THE TOP OF THE CLIFF. THE TWELVE soldiers were crushed in the center of the great mob of people; there was no hope for them. He said, "We have forty-eight men left, and our own guards. I knew we shouldn't have sent all those men down to the new fort."

He glanced over his shoulder. Broga was watching the mob surge along the beach, the square of Imperials trapped in their midst.

"God have mercy on them." Broga signed himself. "Give me the order to rescue them."

"You couldn't get there in time. They're dead men. What we need now is to restore calm. Heed me. Down south, there's a good way onto the beach from the cliff. Isn't there? Summon up the army. Take half of them down there, come around onto the beach, and attack the town from the south. I'll start down from here, with my guard. We'll get them between us."

"We can't leave those men down there—"

"We can't waste more men," Oto said. "Obey orders. Go down and circle them; we'll crush them between us. In fact, you take all the army; just leave me my guard. You need the weight of numbers." Down there, the Imperial square had disappeared under a wave of people.

Broga said, "Very well. For once, I think I agree with you. This is a good plan." He gave him a crisp salute. "Glory to the Empire. God be with us."

"Oh," Oto said, "most certainly."

Broga was already reining his horse around. He loved to fight. He had already brought the soldiers out of camp and assembled them in their ranks in the meadow behind them, just short of the graveyard. Broga's voice sounded, and the horn blew, and with precision the men marched forward toward the high road. As they reached it the horn blew again and they moved flawlessly from their ranks of eight into two files. The horsemen of Broga's guard ranged up on the inland side of the road, their banner floating above them. At another toot from the horn they all marched away down the path along the edge of the terrace.

Under his breath Oto said, "Maybe you'll find the good end down there, too." Then he turned to look down at the beach again, where, to his astonishment, the little knot of Imperial soldiers was escaping from the mob.

5

A STONE'S THROW FROM TIRZA, THE PIKEMEN HAD STOPPED, holding their tight square, all facing out, their pikes leveled before them. In the hollow center of the formation lay two men who could not stand. The crowd was jeering and howling and raining down filth on them, but nobody wanted to charge the pikes. Trollo over there was holding a gashed arm, and several of the women were sitting down. Tirza could see big Aken, the butcher, going around the crowd, talking to people.

The leader of the pikemen, the tall one with the horn, called out something lost in the din; his men began to edge along, still in their square, dragging the wounded with them. Tirza stood up, rocks in each hand.

"Wait." Her brother Luka was there beside her, carrying the fish gaff in one hand and a pike in the other.

She stood where she was, wondering what he wanted to do. He said nothing more, only watched the pikemen in their orderly retreat toward the path, and she realized he was letting them go.

Everybody saw this. All around them, the crowd was whooping, cheering themselves, slapping backs, declaring victory. The circle of pikemen reached the foot of the path and began its awkward two-by-two ascent. Jeering and whooping, people came out on the roofs of the porches, on the ledges of the cliff rooms, throwing insults and garbage.

His eyes on Luka, Jeon walked across the common; his face was drawn. He had his bow on his shoulder and arrows in his hand. Tirza reached out toward him, but he ignored her; he went straight to Luka.

"Let me shoot, before they're out of range."

"No."

Jeon went red as cow meat, and exploded in a yell. "Why are you not killing them? They killed us!"

Still watching the pikemen, Luka said, "I don't want any more death than there has to be." He switched his gaze to Jeon. "They would do that. Harry beaten men. I am not like them." His head swiveled again, turning his eyes back to the path.

Jeon's face was locked in a snarl and Tirza's skin prickled up at the fury in him. She put her hand on his arm. He turned toward her with a jerk, his face set. That look startled her, and she stepped back.

Then a smile softened him.

"You led them, out there," he said. "While we talked you did, Tirza." He slung an arm around her and hugged her.

Luka said, "There. See?" He pointed to the top of the cliff.

Tirza saw what he saw. At the top of the cliff, more soldiers stood looking down at them. The men Luka had allowed to escape rushed up the path to join them. As they gathered together, the mass of striped doublets drew back again, out of sight behind the rise of the cliff.

Luka turned abruptly, looking around him, saw Amillee, the

brewster's daughter, and beckoned to her. When she came up, he said, "Get some of the women together; fill up some buckets with slippery stuff. Fish guts, latrine slop, oil, anything. Quick." He straightened, his gaze going back toward the cliff. He was already planning something else, Tirza saw, with a thrill of admiration. She hopped in place, and he noticed her again.

"Tirza," he said, and went to one knee, face-to-face with her. "Jeon is right; you led this. I love you all the more for that. Now I need your help again. This is not over. I want you to get back into the castle, to Mervaly and Casea, and all of you do what you can there."

She nodded. Her cheeks flamed with excitement. He needed her help. She was part of this. Turning, she raced away toward the rocks below the castle; behind her he was calling for Jeon.

Oto saw no reason to be courteous with these men, who had just been humiliated down there on the beach: he stared into the sergeant's face until the man dropped his eyes, and said, "You put up no more fight than that? You are an Imperial soldier, and you let a flock of peasants beat you?"

The sergeant gnawed his lips, his face reddening and his shoulders round. A great bruise was spreading over his cheek and one sleeve of his doublet was gone, exposing the steel rim of the armhole of his breastplate. Behind him his men were squatting on the ground around the two wounded. One of those was groaning, so he was well enough, but the other looked dead. Oto brought his gaze back to the sergeant.

"I need more of you than this. His Majesty the Emperor expects more of you." Oto stepped back. "Let's see if you can force your way back down again, and redeem yourselves."

The sergeant jerked upright. "My lord—"

Oto walked back to the top of the path. "Get some bows up

here. Let's make them hop a little." At the bottom of the path, on the beach, the townspeople swarmed like insects. Two women with buckets were climbing up the path. He wondered if they were within bowshot: he wanted to skewer them. As he watched they emptied their buckets onto the walkway and another woman hauled a bucket in each hand up toward them.

"Glory to the Empire."

He turned; the sergeant had brought two of the soldiers, armed with bows. Oto stepped back smartly, his hands tucked behind him, to see how they did. "Shoot anything on the path."

The sergeant cleared his throat, gave him a quick look, and nodded to the bowman. They knelt, drew their bows, and shot. The arrows sailed off into the lower air; Oto could not see where any of them went, but one of the women with the buckets slipped and went down. Oto was unsure if an arrow had struck her or if she had simply fallen on the path. A moment later another of the women got her by the arm and half-carried her down to the beach. The next volley of arrows sailed away. At the foot of the path, the crowd stood watching him, unafraid, so the arrows were not reaching them.

He lifted his head and looked off down the cliff, the way his brother had gone. Oto could see Broga's little army far down there, not each man, but the whole, moving along beneath a white puff of dust. He studied the path down the cliff again. Perhaps he should revise his thinking. Broga would get down there and harry the people. They could only escape by coming up this way. Then the narrowness and steepness of the path, and whatever they had spread on it to confound him, would work against them. Oto saw no reason to go into a bottleneck if he could simply stopper the bottle. He had the castle, and the women, which in the end would matter most.

He turned to the sergeant again, his voice crisp. "Yet I fear you would not be up to the task."

"My lord," the sergeant said. His face was taut. "We live only to serve the Emperor. We will do what you order."

"I hope so. Now I am saying we should post a watch here, and take these hurt men back to the castle." He glanced over his shoulder again; now he could see only the faintest trace of Broga's dust. "Form up. I have orders to give." The sergeant unhooked his horn from his belt and put it to his lips, and the little band of men made neat, even lines before Oto. He clasped his hands behind his back, surveyed them critically a moment, and began.

TIRZA WAS LEANING OUT THE WINDOW BESIDE THE SEAGULL, avoiding its numerous droppings. From here she could see the flat top of the cliff south of the castle and she was watching the Imperials divide up into parts. One part, the bigger, was going off to the south, but the other waited at the top of the path down the cliff. Maybe they would attack again. The angle of the cliff top cut off the near part of the beach from sight, and she could see nothing of what was happening there. Her skin crawled; she imagined leaping from the window, flying down, fighting beside her brothers.

Mervaly said, "We have to do something. Luka expects us to help. Oto and Broga are both gone, and a lot of their men. We could shut the gate on them." She glanced at their door. "Is there a guard out there?"

Casea put her ear to the wood. "Yes. Only one, though." She tugged on the latch; the string was on the far side of the wall.

Mervaly said, "They must have taken nearly all their men away. This is our only chance."

Tirza looked out the window again. Faintly she heard a horn blow. The pack of striped doublets at the top of the cliff was not moving down the path to join battle. They were lined up, not facing down but this way. They were coming back to the castle. Her back tingled.

Casea went over to the bed and picked up the water jug. "Make the guard come in here. I'll hit him and we can lock him in. Otherwise, if we leave, he's behind us."

Mervaly was watching out the window beside Tirza. She said, "No. Oto is coming back. There's no time. Hurry. Tirza, find the way."

THE TOWNSPEOPLE WERE CHEERING AND HUGGING ONE AN-other and slapping hands and chests, already drunk with their victory, and Lumilla had her swampers dragging a keg out into the middle of the beach. Soon they would be beyond the reach of orders. Luka moved backward down the beach, until his heels were pressing into damp sand. He could see much of the top of the cliff from here, enough to see a little band of riders and men on foot trudging toward the bridge into the castle.

Jeon said, "They are giving up."

"No," Luka said. There should have been many more Imperials in that march, if all of them were going back to the castle. Oto had many more men than that. "This is just a false fire. The rest of them went south. They're going to come down onto the beach somewhere and try to attack us from that side." He turned to Jeon. "Just be quiet, for once?" Although Jeon had said nothing. "We have to gather everybody up again. Men, women, anybody who will come who can carry a weapon. We have to meet them where we have some advantage. Hurry, before they tap the kegs." He clapped Jeon on the shoulder. "Here's where we can break the Empire. Let's go."

 6

Her sisters behind her, Tirza went at a run down the passage, which led into the empty antechamber. On the landward side the big, round room opened out to the gate yard and she went out to the stoop there, where three steps led down to the paved yard.

It was empty, all the soldiers gone. All this yard was made of dressed stone, not really part of the castle; the grey walls were like round arms encircling the space between this stair and the gate itself, a massive lintel on great square columns, where the hanging spikes of the portcullis showed at the top like a row of teeth.

Out the gate, across the bridge, she could see, down on the road, the little knot of Imperial men coming toward them. Oto, riding his horse, was leading them. On the bridge one lone soldier lounged against the stone railing, his back to her, his pike tilted in the crook of his arm. She ran across the inner yard to the winch that lowered the portcullis. Her sisters were only a step behind her. From the drum of the winch a stout chain led up to the top of the gate; Mervaly caught hold of it, taut as an iron bar.

"Help me!"

On the side of the winch the capstan bar stood up from a little wheel with teeth, which moved the drum; a chuck of wood was jammed into the top tooth. Tirza beat at it with her hand. Bracing herself against the wall, Casea hauled at the capstan bar. Mervaly went to help her, and the little wheel clicked reluctantly one notch tighter. Tirza knocked the chuck flying.

The little wheel spun, chattering, and the chain began to roll off. At the same moment a yell went up from beyond the gate. Tirza skittered backward, looking out there, through the shadow of the gateway. The Imperial from the bridge was running toward them. She looked up into the top of the gate: even with the chain loose, the portcullis hung a moment, stuck in its long rest. She turned and looked wildly around, saw the capstan bar lying on the pavement, and caught it up in both hands. The Imperial charged off the bridge toward them. With a rattle the iron grating began to travel down its tracks. As it clattered down, the soldier dove under it, landing on his hands and knees just inside the gate, and Tirza ran to him, and whacked him across the back with the capstan bar so he went facedown, his pike flying across the pavement.

The great spikes of the portcullis banged into the paved threshold of the gate. She swung back that way. Mervaly called out sharply behind her. Out through the dark grid of the portcullis Tirza could see Oto on his horse galloping up to the bridge, his men hurrying after. She shouted triumphantly at him through the bars.

Casea shouted, "Tirza, get away from there; you'll be hurt!"

Out there, Oto reined in, his fancy sleeves flapping, turned, and bellowed. His men rushed panting up behind him, into the outer yard, and at the wild swinging of his arm they charged the portcullis. One had a bow. An arm snaked through a square of the grid, grabbing for her, and she smashed it with the bar. The man with the bow had an arrow nocked, and Oto rode into him and knocked him down.

"No! You idiot! I need them alive!"

Tirza heard that, and rushed toward the portcullis, to hammer them. Behind her, Mervaly screamed, "Look out! He's getting up!" and Tirza stopped and whipped around.

The soldier she had struck down was struggling onto his knees. She had not killed him, she saw, disappointed. Mervaly had seized the fallen pike, and she jabbed at him with the point.

Still on his knees, he caught hold of the pikestaff and tore it from her grip. Mervaly sprang back. Tirza rushed at the kneeling soldier and swung the capstan bar at his head, and he thrust up the pike between them and with the haft knocked the bar flying from her hand.

"Tirza! Come on!" Casea cried. "There's more of them!"

Out the door from the castle another striped doublet flew— the guard they had left at their bedroom door. He bounded down the steps and ran for the capstan bar. The first pikeman had lurched to his feet, was brandishing his pike at Mervaly, in front of him, who backed away, her hands spread. Casea was pulling on Tirza's sleeve.

"Run! Run!"

The portcullis grated, its chains squealing. The man with the capstan bar had reached the winch, was hauling the grid up. The rest of Oto's men were charging through before the spikes were hardly off the ground. Casea screamed Tirza's name again and grabbed her arm. Mervaly was already running for the stair. Tirza raced after her on Casea's heels, up the stairs into the castle, and into the antechamber, and into the wall.

٭ ٭ ٭

"HOW DID THEY GET OUT? YOU WERE STANDING GUARD OVER them, at the only door! You let them out!"

"My lord, I never knew—They didn't come out the door, I swear—"

"They flew out the window? Keep hold of him, Sergeant!"

Dawd had the guard by the arm. They stamped up the narrow, uneven stairs to the women's room, and Oto flung open the door.

All around the walls the birds began to flap and beat their wings, and a seagull lifted away off the windowsill. The men all pushed into the room, and Dawd let go of the guard's arm and went to stand by the door, out of the way. The women were gone, of course. Oto turned toward the guard, who was still babbling behind him. Oto's face was like a shard of flint. He said, "You let this happen."

"My lord, I swear, I never—"

"Throw him out the window."

"No!" The guard went to his knees. "My lord, please—" Dawd stood rigid, but the two other men with him stepped forward, lifted the guard up, carried him to the window, and pitched him out, his wail disappearing after him.

Oto locked his hands into fists. "I must have those women." A raven cawed and flew at him and he ducked and the raven sailed out the window after the body.

Dawd was motionless; his breath had followed the raven. Oto paced by him, circling the room, and then on his heel spun toward Dawd.

"He was lying. How did they get out? Except that he let them out."

"Yes, sir," Dawd said.

He knew how they escaped, but he could not tell this; he thought of her coming with her light to save him, and he could not betray her. If Oto would even have believed it. Dawd watched the lordling pace around the room. He could see Oto's problem very well: Broga was gone to a great victory, and when he returned, Oto would have no leverage at all, without the women in his keeping.

The birds all around the room rustled and murmured, their eyes glinting. Another flew out the window. Oto, looking around at them, was abruptly calm, his eyes moving up to the ceiling.

"Well, now," he said. "I have an idea. Get some rope."

ALL AFTERNOON, LUKA LED THE TOWNSPEOPLE DOWN THE beach, a loose pack of fifty-odd, mostly women. He looked them over as they went; he expected a few to drop out, but none did. Each of them carried something, a shovel, an axe, and many had made packs of their shawls, or had baskets on their arms, to bring food. Lumilla, walking alongside her daughter, was frowning as she walked, her face set. Osa the potter's widow sang some of the time, and a few of the others with her. Up in front, Aken marched along, still wearing his bloody apron, the great block of his body in his striped shirt like a moving tree trunk. The fisherman Freo, beside him, looked like a wisp.

They came to Sinking Cove. Here the coast bent inward, cupping a beach of fine, dark sand littered with driftwood and seaweed. The water was pale blue far out beyond the surf line, the shallows studded with jagged black rocks like rings of teeth that broke the surge of the waves. Luka sent the people off to the high side of the beach, to rest and eat. With Jeon and the butcher Aken and some others Luka walked around the beach awhile, watching the sea.

"Where's the tide?" Luka said.

"Full high, by the drift." That was Freo, who did a lot of clamming here.

"Good. Build a wall here. Use all this driftwood. It doesn't have to be solid, just enough to slow a horse. Down to the tide's edge."

Jeon fingered his bow. He thought this would be much easier if Luka had killed all those other soldiers, back when he had them at his mercy. The cliff loomed up over them. On that highland, if Luka was right, thirty or forty Imperial pikemen were marching along. Up ahead, Jeon knew, a creek inlet through the cliff made an easy way down to the water's edge.

They would charge all at once. Many of them had horses. But the beach here was narrow; that might slow them down. Jeon gave a look around at the townspeople—more numbers than the soldiers. He wished more of them were men. They had gone to help Luka and Aken build the wall, piling up driftwood, hooking the bare grey branches around one another, jamming pieces into the crotches of other pieces. Aken made a rude joke and they all laughed.

Luka went around talking to people, helping with the wall, giving orders, and Jeon trailed after him, waiting to be told what to do. The tide was sliding away down the beach. To the south, against the blue sky above the beach, a faint brown haze rose into the air.

The ebb of the tide had left a bare stretch of sand below the end of the wall, but when Aken and his boy started out to build the wall down to fill it Luka stopped them.

"No. Leave that." He put out his arm and held Aken back.

"Papa, help me." The boy had run on ahead, into the wave, and when the wave pulled back he was stuck in the wet sand. Luka reached out, got his hand, and helped him pull free.

"See? Just build down to here." Luka pointed to the end of his wall.

He walked up behind the wall, and gathered the women

together, hugging them each by turn, Lumilla, Amillee, Osa, the three sisters from the weavery, Suan the baker's apprentice, the cobbler's widow, and the fishermen's widows and their daughters. "My sisters, you are brave. You make me glad and proud. Show me your weapons."

They stood around him with their shovels and paddles and forks. He made sure each of them had something useful. "This will be hard, now, and they will come at you heaviest. You must all stay together, arm to arm. Fight together. One of you can't throw a man. Three of you can. Stay together; help each other." He turned to Jeon.

"Go up on the cliff, where you can cover that end of the wall. Be careful. Have you got enough arrows?"

"No," Jeon said, who had twenty arrows. "But who does?" His voice sounded squeaky. He put his arm around Luka, and Luka embraced him, solid and strong. Jeon turned and went up toward the cliff.

The landward end of Luka's wall came up against the toe of an old slide. Twenty feet above the beach the slumping head of the slide had formed a ledge. He put the bow on his back, and climbed up onto the narrow shelf of dirt.

From this height, he could see much better. The tide was ebbing faster, leaving behind a widening stretch of flat sand.

The wind drove a fine ripple over it. A sheet of water covered it, as if the sand were sweating. His heart leapt. This happened in certain places all along the coast, and now he understood what Luka was doing. Down there, the brown haze was getting closer. Jeon unsheathed his bow.

EVEN AFTER THE LONG WALK UP THE BEACH AMILLEE WAS SO jittery her legs quivered. She stood by the driftwood wall, looking ahead, where their enemies would appear. Luka and two other men were rolling a big stump up into the wall; she went to help them. When the stump was solidly in place Luka took her by the arm.

"Stay in the middle of the line. Keep everybody together. Where's your weapon?"

"I left it so I could help you."

"Never let go of it. Go get it."

She ran back for the long staff she had brought, and took it to him. He took hold of it and moved her hands along it.

"Hold it like this, one hand here, the other here, your fingers going the same way—yes. Now how do you fight?"

She let go with one hand, swung the staff around point first, and lunged with it. Around them a cheer went up: people were watching. He got her arm again and took the bar away.

"No. Don't poke. You're finished if you poke. Hold it as I showed you. Use it like this."

He held the staff across his body, and thrust it forward broadside. "Osa, come at me."

Osa had a spade; she lifted it over her shoulder and rushed at him, and he took a step and brought the staff up crosswise between them. "Hit me, Osa! Come on, hit me!"

Osa whacked at him and he met the spade on his staff and slipped it off; she swung the spade around full wide, and again he got the staff across its path and knocked it aside.

"Like that." He put the staff into Amillee's hands. "All of you." He turned to the other people, went in among them, putting their weapons right in their hands.

Upon the cliff, his little brother Jeon called out, "They're coming, Luka!"

Amillee clutched the staff. Her stomach gathered into a knot. They were all moving now, up to the wall. The wall looked so little, so stupid. Her feet wouldn't move. She might die. She forced herself forward, up to the wall, only as high as her waist, and saw the horses coming down the beach toward her, the crowd of pikes like a little forest, and her with only a stick in her hand.

Osa stood beside her, shoulder to shoulder. Lumilla on the other side. All together, they waited, and Amillee felt the sweat running down her back. She wanted to shut her eyes. She gripped the staff, waiting.

BROGA REINED UP A MOMENT, THE EIGHT HORSEMEN OF HIS guard around him, and waved to the pikemen, on foot, to stop them also. They had come to the edge of a crescent-shaped cove, and there, on the far side, was a clot of wood and bodies.

He grunted. The cliff here was high and steep, and where the enemy was gathered, the beach pinched down to a narrow approach like a funnel. He turned to the rider just behind him, whom he knew to be farsighted.

"What do you make of this?"

The guardsman saluted him smartly. He said, "My lord, it looks like a lot of the townspeople. It's mostly women, sir. They've got some barricade up."

Broga made another growling sound in his chest. These people should not have been here; Oto should have been battling them in the town, so Broga could come up behind them. The thought came to him that maybe they had beaten Oto.

Broga did not believe that, but here he was, facing them, his brother nowhere.

Broga looked from side to side. On the ocean side, clearly, there was no chance for an ambush. The cliff side above most of the cove was bare wind-blasted rock, broken only by the crease of an old landslide. He faced forward again.

"My lord," said the long-sighted guardsman. "There's an archer on the cliff, there above where the rest are. Just one, though."

Broga stared, his hands on his saddlebow, trying to focus on that part of the cliff, and saw something move. A seagull glided over his head, the shadow across the ground ahead of him, and hovered there, as if it watched him. Spying. Broga's scalp prickled up. Then he straightened, pleased.

"Look, they've made a mistake. They built their little wall down when the tide was high, and now it's going out." His voice was velvety with satisfaction. He beckoned to the soldier commanding the pikemen.

"I want you in two columns. We'll march straight along that beach, there. Five strides from those people up there, charge. They won't move; they have a wall up. Your men go straight at the wall. They're women. They can't stand against you. I will lead my guard to circle around and take them from behind. It will be over in a moment. Glory to the Empire!"

"Glory to the Empire." The soldier saluted him, wheeled, and went to order his men.

They started off along the curve of the beach, jogging along the crusty dark sand. One hand up, Broga kept his horsemen back, letting the pikemen get well out in front, to draw the ragtag mob of the townspeople off to defend. So they were doing. As the Imperials came closer everybody on the wall rushed toward the middle. Now he could see the skirts, the aprons, the round faces of the women. This would be easy. After, he would let the men have some fun with the women. He reined in, his guards behind him. The two columns trotted forward. A horn blew, and they broke into a run at the wall, their long blades swinging down level.

A scream rose, and then a chorus of them, shrieks and cries. The soldiers were climbing up onto the wall. Broga swung his arm down, and led his horsemen at a gallop down onto the wet sand, to cut around the end of the wall and finish these people off.

* * *

AMILLEE GRIPPED HER STAFF, HER BREATH STUCK IN HER lungs, facing like an incoming wave a glistening spread of blades, aimed all at her. She screamed. They were all screaming. The first pike thrust across the top of their wall, and Amillee shrank back away from the wall.

On her left Suan lunged into her place and got the handle of her shovel under the pike. Lumilla leaned in from the other side to help her. They filled up Amillee's space. There was no room for her now. Suan staggered back, blood spurting from the side of her face. Now there was a hole. Amillee longed to run, to get away, but she had to fill that space. She had to get back up there. She held the staff across her body and forced her legs to move on up again, into the pack of the women, beside her mother.

Lumilla had managed to get hold of a pike. She stood on wide-spread feet, Aken on her far side, fending off the blows of an iron-hatted pikeman. From the side another blade flashed toward her, slantwise across Amillee's vision, and she lashed out with the staff in her hands. She could not let them hurt her mother. Amillee clubbed the pike down, the way Luka had shown her. Another thrust at her and from the other side Lumilla's pike thrust past Amillee and the Imperial man recoiled, and Osa lurched up and hacked at him. Osa banged into Amillee, knocking her sideways; Lumilla like a wall held her up. Across the driftwood another iron hat swam into her focus, a yellow beard, a red mouth, above the glinting edge of the blade, and then an arrow smacked him in the face and he fell.

Keep on. She tried to keep her staff in some rhythm with Lumilla's pike. A blow struck Amillee's arm; she wasn't sure if it came from an Imperial or one of her own people. A sharp pain sliced through her shoulder. She could not do this anymore. She kept on doing it. She gasped for breath, her mother beside her, blood all over her now.

* * *

AS THEY BROKE FROM THEIR TROT INTO A RUN, THE PIKEMEN came into range of Jeon's bow. He fired an arrow, saw it hit, and that man stagger, but Jeon's next shot missed, and the third ticked off a helmet. The cliff pushed the soldiers together, kept them from hitting the wall all at once, but when the first few smashed into the driftwood the whole ramshackle thing seemed to buckle. In the center the townspeople shrank back from the layers of blades. The narrow front of the wedge of pikemen crowded over the wall after them. Gritting his teeth, he shot arrows steadily into that pack of striped doublets. Luka ran up the wall, leapt onto a stump, swinging his arm to urge his people on. The pikes before him swung at once toward him and he stood lashing out at them with his fishing gaff. The townspeople stiffened; the women pushed back into the center of the wall, and stood.

But Broga's horsemen had held back. Now, Jeon saw, they were charging.

He drew the bow, but they were far out of range, galloping down two by two onto the damp sand, to get around the end of the wall. Jeon stood up. Broga led them, his horse three lengths ahead of the rest. From this high place Jeon could see the whole beach—how, as the horses galloped onto the damp stretch just above the surf, the sand suddenly blanched, all the water on the surface drawn inward like a breath, and with the next long stride Broga's horse sank down into the beach all the way to its chest.

Broga hurtled off. His horse flopped over, thrashing up gouts of the sand, driving itself deeper. Six of the horses behind him, going too fast to stop, floundered into the waterlogged beach around him. All the sand was rippling; as the horses scrambled for footing they churned it to a morass. Broga's horse had drowned, only its hindquarter showing.

The last two riders had skidded to a stop before they went in and sat uncertainly in their saddles watching. One took a brass horn from his saddlebow and blew a long, plaintive call on it. The other man leapt off his horse and dashed out onto the sloppy sand toward Broga and was gobbled up to his crotch. The horn blew again, frantic, and again.

Broga had hit the ground sprawled on his back. Now he struggled to get up and his legs disappeared. He bellowed, lunging helplessly toward the dry sand only a few yards away, and fell deeper into the grip of the beach. One of the other trapped riders crawled out of his saddle and plunged in up to his waist. His horse tried to rear up and one hoof lashed out and struck him so hard his helmet flew off and he sagged down bonelessly into the sand. The others sat where they were, looking wildly around. The riderless horse had fallen back into the sand, but now it clawed its forehand up out of the grip of the beach again and ramped forward, toward Broga. Broga flung his arms up to protect his head.

He was not sinking anymore, just buried to his armpits, his hands raised above his head. His feet had reached the bottom of the loose sand. Jeon fired an arrow at him; the range was way long and the arrow jittered into the surf. Below him, a bellow went up that stood every hair on his body on end.

The Imperial pikemen were retreating. The townspeople were swarming over the driftwood wall, and the Imperials were backing up. They stood shoulder to shoulder, their pikes leveled before them, but they were edging their way down toward their commander. The horn blew again, calling them, and they broke into an awkward trot. Jeon slung his bow on his back and started down off the ledge.

AMILLEE SHRIEKED. THEY WERE RUNNING, THEY WERE running away—she scrambled up over the trampled crushed driftwood heap in front of her. She thought of her mother and turned as Lumilla, panting, struggled up beside her. All around them the rest of the townspeople had come over the wall, jeering, waving their arms over their heads. Amillee ran a few steps after the soldiers.

"Run away, babies—run!"

Her voice was lost in the yelling of the others; the soldiers were backing away down the sand, and nobody got near the tips of the pikes aimed straight at them. Amillee bent, found a stone, threw it. "Babies!" Lumilla was laughing. Amillee threw her arms around her and danced.

"We won! We won!"

The pikemen had moved down the beach almost to the edge of the damp sand. The horn blew again, a brassy crow call, piercing even the yells and screeches of the crowd. The pikemen stopped and wheeled neatly into a single rank, facing the crowd behind the fence of their leveled blades. The crowd hooted and threw rocks and bits of driftwood.

Abruptly they all stopped. Luka was walking out into the space between them and the Imperials. Amillee let out a cheer that emptied her lungs, part of a deafening roar that rose from the rest of the people. Luka raised a hand to them, gestured to them to sit, to rest; he gave them a broad smile, and thrust up his fist over his head, and they cheered him again. He turned toward the soldiers, standing there motionless. Amillee sat where she was, beside Lumilla, all her people around her, her eyes fixed on Luka, her prince of the sea, who had made her a hero.

LUKA STOOD SILENT A MOMENT, LOOKING OVER THE MEN BE-fore him. He could see beyond the pikemen to where Broga was stuck in the sand. Two men were trying to reach him, but the distance was too far.

"Broga!" Luka called. "Give up, and I'll help you get out of there."

Broga was trying to force his way through the wet sand, but the more he struggled the harder it gripped him. He gave a breathless yell.

"Hold them off, Commander—I'm getting out by myself—"

The two men trying to rescue him joined hands, and one stepped cautiously out onto the sand, stretching his forward arm toward Broga. The sand took him up to the knee. He crept out another step, this leg going in to midthigh, and the man behind him sank to his knees; Broga strained and pawed the air and their fingertips glanced together.

"You're outnumbered!" Luka called. "Now you've got your backs to the sea, with the tide turning. Lay down your arms. I can get you out of this."

Just behind Luka, Jeon said under his breath, "Leave him there."

"No!" Broga shouted. "Get a rope."

A wave rolled up the beach and splashed around Broga's head. Luka was smiling; he said nothing. He cast a quick glance behind him. His brother was there, with his bow, scowling at him. On the dry sandy slope beyond, the army of Undercastle was setting up camp. Everybody had something to eat. Lumilla had brought ale in a skin bag and was filling everybody's cup. Suan the baker's apprentice had blood all over her face and one of the weavery sisters was helping her clean herself up. Aken's boy Mika sat slumped by his father, one arm slack. Mika's face was black-and-blue, his eye swelling shut. Luka wondered if anybody had died.

He turned to glare at Broga again. Another wave came up, and for a long moment Broga's head disappeared into the rolling, sand-filled foamy surf. Behind him a horse neighed and another of the trapped men yelled, "Help!" Broga's sodden head emerged from the wave, his mouth gulping for air.

"We can wait," Luka said, and sat down on his heels.

7

TIRZA WALKED SLOWLY AROUND THE CHAMBER, LOOKING AT each of the niches. Most of the people in them were sleeping. Her great-grandfather Obro lay on his back, his eyes open, looking up. He did not notice her. She imagined he was thinking about some deep past, more real to him than now. She wondered what could matter to him, who had been dead a hundred years.

Maybe it was all the same; maybe that was what death was, the end of time, and it all ran together, the same.

Behind her, by the lamp, Casea said, "If they can't find us, they can't use us against Luka. I say we go on out to the town and hide there."

Mervaly said, "We should find out what's going on first." She looked around at the chamber. "It's so annoying being boxed in like this."

Tirza's stomach growled. She was more concerned now with finding something to eat. She went on around the room, slowly, looking into each face: her mother would be here, somewhere, if not in this room, another.

"My birds," Mervaly said. "And this is our home. Papa left this in our care. It would be like killing him again." Tirza came closer, and her sister reached out and took her by the sleeve. "What do you think?"

Tirza shrugged; she had no idea what to do now. She patted her stomach.

"Yes," Casea said, "we have to find something to eat. And it will be cold here tonight." She was getting up. "But they'll be looking for us." She nodded heavily to Mervaly. "So we have to be careful. Stay in the walls. Don't go back to our room, whatever you do. Stay out of reach."

Up in a high chamber of the old tower, long unused, stuffed with discarded gear, Tirza found shawls and fur robes, and she went and brought Mervaly to help her carry them. On the way back to their hideout, they came to the big, round room where all the towers met, which was full of Imperial men. The only hidden passage moved along the edge, just inside the wall. The voices of the Imperial men came humming through the rock.

The passage forked, one side going down and the other opening onto the stairway up to the south tower, where the sisters had lived. Tirza went straight toward the downward way, but Mervaly stopped, and dumped her load of furs onto the floor. "You go ahead; I want to see about something."

Her arms full of musty sea otter, Tirza wheeled and stared at her. Tirza's first thought was that someone would hear them and the second that Mervaly was making a mistake, and she shook her head hard at her.

"Don't argue with me," Mervaly said. "Go back. I'll be right there."

Tirza said, "No, don't. Please."

"Ssssh! You sound like a bear." Mervaly pushed her away. "I'm your oldest sister. Do as I say." She backed up a step, toward the open stairway behind her. Tirza stood motionless, watching. Mervaly went quickly around the corner and up into the tower, out of sight.

IT WOULD ONLY TAKE A FEW MOMENTS. SHE WOULD FEED THE birds and bid them fly away. Otherwise they would wait for her; they would suffer. Mervaly slid through the wall into her room.

The seagull rose off the sill, screaming at her, flapping its wings, circled her head, and all around the other birds screeched and fluttered, a deafening cacophony, a mad glitter of eyes. The owlet even woke to screech at her. She laughed. She imagined what had happened when the Imperials burst in, how the birds would have greeted that. She crossed the room toward the bin where she kept their food in crocks, saying, "You must all go, at once; we are—" And one step before she reached the bin, her foot struck against something on the floor and a net fell from the ceiling all around her.

The birds hushed at once. Too late, she saw they had been trying to warn her. She twisted around, toward the wall, thinking surely Tirza had not abandoned her, had followed her, would save her now. And there Tirza was, in the stone, but even then the door burst open, three soldiers rushed in, and Tirza vanished.

CASEA HAD FOUND BREAD AND CHEESE AND A EWER OF WINE, and they sat together in the room of the dead, wrapped in the old fur robes and picking morosely at the food. The lamp spread its steady green light around them. It was probably still night but perhaps not. Tirza was worn down and wanted to sleep and she leaned on Casea, who put her arm around her.

"We have to find Mervaly," Casea said. "We can't just leave her with them."

Tirza yawned. She wondered where Mervaly was; remembering the net falling on her made Tirza shudder. She was more afraid of Oto now, who had done that, and she hated him.

"But we have to be careful. We can't let them catch us all," Casea said. "I wish I knew what Luka is doing."

Tirza straightened up, awake again, thinking of Jeon also. She said, "They will come back." Her voice made groans and barks.

Casea said, "I think one of us should go to find him." She hugged Tirza against her. "And the other go keep watch on Mervaly, somehow."

Tirza moved her head a little, where it rested on Casea's shoulder, nestling in. She saw the edge of a story, how a Princess became an outlaw and rescued her two sisters. But Tirza could only tell it to herself; Casea was out of reach, and Casea had already made up her mind.

"I'll go find Luka," Casea said. "You find Mervaly." She began to settle herself in the rugs of fur, holding Tirza against her, so when they were both lying down Tirza was in Casea's arms. "After we get some sleep."

Tirza stiffened, resisting that; she had the story now, even if it was different. But Casea stroked Tirza's face again. "Sleep. Sleep." Tirza yawned, and shut her eyes.

WHEN TIRZA WOKE, CASEA WAS ALREADY ON HER FEET, SHAKing out her crumpled skirts. "It's daylight now," Casea said, although Tirza did not see how she knew that. "I'm going to find Luka. You must look for Mervaly and stay near her." Casea raked her thick red hair back, and tied it in a knot at the nape of her neck. "But don't get caught." She bent, and placed a kiss on

Tirza's forehead. "Be careful. I'll come right back." She went off across the chamber, and disappeared into the wall.

Tirza folded her legs up and wrapped her arms around them. She wished she knew what to do. In the niches all around her the old ones slumbered, or stared, or smiled to themselves; not one of them would do anything to help her.

She bit her teeth together, angry. There had to be a way to make them help her. If she knew the right words, surely she could summon them. She struggled to imagine them bound to her will, an army of the dead. Maybe if she made a story about them she would discover what she needed to know to command them.

Her mind slipped, reversing that. They had come first. They had always been here. Maybe they were making up a story about her.

That bothered her and she pushed it away. Now she did not want them to help her. Suddenly she felt better. She got up and began to look for Mervaly.

THE LONG WIND OFF THE SEA RAKED THE GRASS BACK ON THE top of the cliff. Dawd grounded his pike and stared down the path toward Undercastle. The sun was well up now, but the beach was still in shadow; from high up here, he could see the whole town, and the quiet startled him.

"Where are they? It's full daylight; they should be busy down there."

Marwin took a long drink from his water skin. "Inside. Hiding." He slapped the cork into the skin's mouth.

"Then where is the Lord Broga?"

"Out there, somewhere." The corporal waved a hand vaguely to the south. "He'll be here soon, and these bumpkins will never know what hit them." He chuckled, and stretched. "Still, now that I'm off duty, I would like to go down to that alehouse."

"Go back to the castle." Dawd was searching the beach with his eyes. The place was quiet, the four boats drawn up on the shore, the space empty where usually the awnings of the shops flapped. But there came an old woman trudging up from the stream, hauling a bucket, and some small children were playing near the cypress. They were certainly not hiding. And Broga had left almost a day ago: he should have shown up by now. Then, from the near end of the beach, from the shadow of the castle, a woman walked along the sand.

Dawd knew her at once, her way of walking, the carriage of her head, the color of her abundant hair. He glanced around at Marwin, who was packing up his gear. His squadron was already lined up on the road to the castle, waiting for him. Dawd moved, drawing the attention of his men away from the beach, and began to give orders, so they would not see the Princess Casea, sauntering off along the edge of the surf.

It struck him this was disloyalty, probably even treason of some kind. He could not do otherwise. Betraying her was worse. The uneasy feeling in his belly deepened into a sour gripe. He was a soldier. He was supposed to obey orders. He went in among his men to tell them where to stand, what to do, who could not decide himself where he stood or what he should do.

TIRZA COULD NOT FIND MERVALY. IN THE GREAT HALL TIRZA saw no one except a few men trying to build a wall across the edge of the terrace. The birds were still flying in and out of the window of the sisters' room at the top of the south tower, but she saw no sign that Mervaly had been there since the net fell on her. Tirza went in and tipped over the jars of food, so that the birds could eat when they willed.

She went up and down the walls until there was nowhere left to look except the new tower.

She avoided the new tower, with its smell of stone dust and its blank walls. She had always hated it. Where its stair rose from the round antechamber, a fingertip's width of a gap opened between the living rock and the quarried grey stone of the tower, another mark that it didn't really belong. She was afraid to go up there; all its space was fixed and there was nowhere to hide. She crept into the wall in the big, round antechamber, and watched Oto for a while. The Imperial man spent almost all his time in the new tower, even to eat there. The antechamber was always full of soldiers, coming and going, and she could not see a way to get up into his chambers. She was sure that Mervaly was there. Tirza went around the castle, gathering up all the knives she could find, and hid them in the walls, every point aimed at that room where Oto was. Then she went out to the Jawbone and waited.

MERVALY SAT WITH HER ARMS FOLDED OVER HER CHEST, staring at Oto; she said nothing. She had said nothing much since they had brought her here, tangled in the rope net, and dropped her at his feet. He said, "My brother is vengeful. Only I can save you from his wrath, when he comes back. With Luka out of the way, you and your brother and sisters will be meat in his hands."

Her expression never changed; her eyes never wavered. She said nothing. Oto walked off around the room, swinging his arms. He decided on a shift in tone. Wheeling, he faced her across the room, one hand out, imploring.

"You do not know that I care about you. Deeply. I have watched you—learned to admire you. Give me the honor of defending you. You cannot know the danger you are in, and your two young—"

Outside, a horn blasted. He jerked up straighter, his head swiveling; that was the gate. He leapt to the window and leaned out to see the road.

"Broga," he said. He could see only a dark swarm moving along the road, but that was certainly his brother, coming back in triumph, marching like a King. Oto had no time left; he had to make do with what was actually here. "Guards! To me!" He stared back at Mervaly. "For this next part, lady, you don't have to speak. Let's go."

HE WAS READY FOR BROGA RIDING AT THE HEAD OF A VICTO-rious army. He was not ready for what he saw as they came nearer.

The Imperial soldiers walked in the midst of the crowd, foot-sore and weary, their striped doublets filthy, their heads bare and their hands empty. All around them the townspeople swarmed, singing, arm in arm, brandishing the pikes, wearing the helmets. Whatever had happened, it was clear who had won.

And who had lost. Oto picked out his brother, Broga, trudg-ing in their midst, head down, beaten, the lout, well beaten. Oto covered his face with his hand a moment, to mask his pleasure at this.

As the great unruly crowd reached the land end of the bridge, all but a few of the townspeople swung off to the meadow on the cliff where the soldiers had their camp, shoving their ex-hausted prisoners along with them. The dozen leaders strode up toward the castle. Oto glanced back into the outer gateway. There stood Mervaly, in a white lace dress, her hands clasped together before her, a guard on either arm. Oto gave her a friendly smile and moved a step to the side, so that she could see more clearly. He faced the bridge again. There had to be some-thing he could make of this.

First Luka walked toward him, with a long hooked pole over his shoulder. After him came his little brother and, to Oto's amazement, his tall sister Casea. Then Broga Erdhartsson, his hands bound, a collar around his neck.

Broga's horse paced along behind him, a brawny girl in the saddle, holding the rope to Broga's collar. Oto surged with fury, that an Imperial high lord, a man of the golden blood, was treated so, but also delight, that his brother had failed so miserably.

Broga was covered all over with a patina of sand, in his clothes and beard and hair, crusted on his skin. He was staring at the ground, his shoulders hunched. Oto went forward now, out onto the hump of the bridge, to meet Luka in the bright sunlight.

He did not let Luka speak first. Oto bowed, and said, "I don't know how you've done it, but you've beaten us. You have my fullest admiration."

Luka had brought the butt of his fishing hook down to the ground, and he leaned on it. He looked Oto up and down, and said, "Tell me why I should not command you to take all these and go."

Oto gave him another bow, to give himself time to assess this: Luka was not actually demanding that he surrender. "I have your castle," he said, "and your sister."

Luka said amiably, "I have your brother and your army."

Oto straightened, meeting the other man's clear green eyes. He had misjudged Luka; he made himself see that—no fool, this one. Oto nodded his head. "You are a master of the craft of war. How you defeated trained soldiers with this"—he veered away from calling them a rabble—"I shall need to hear at length." He took in a deep breath, seeing a way forward. "But let me warn you. Do not lose in the peace what you have gained in the war."

"Ah," Luka said. Behind him, his brother, Jeon, gave a violent twitch.

"There is still the Emperor," said Oto. "I can help you with him."

"The Emperor! He can give up any thought of Castle Ocean. He will never hold Castle Ocean."

Oto spread his hands, smiling, nodding. "Yet his reach is very long, and he forgets nothing. Let me help you. You are the King, by right and by battle. But I can be of use to you—working things out with the Emperor. Because, you know, otherwise—" His voice flattened a little, edged. "It will all happen, all over again."

Their eyes met. For a moment Luka was silent; Oto thought, He will kill me, or I will have him.

Luka said, "Let me think about this." He looked over Oto's shoulder, toward the gateway, and smiled. "I see my sister, and I will greet her."

"At once," said Oto. "Let us all come into the castle together, give up quarreling, and be friends." He stretched out his hand. "I give you my word of honor."

Luka gave a low laugh; his gaze was piercing. He let Oto shake his hand, and went on down the bridge toward the gate. Mervaly was coming toward him, her arms out. Oto turned, and faced Broga, standing there, scowling. The rope still led from his collar to the girl on the horse behind him.

Broga said, "Bah. You grovel."

Oto reached out and untied the leash from the collar; he tossed the rope at the girl on the horse. Eagerly he turned back to Broga.

"You seem quite wretched. How did he manage to destroy you like this?"

Broga's face was red as a coxcomb under the grime of sand, his lips twisting back from his teeth. "I'll kill him." He wrenched at his arms; his hands were still tied behind him.

"Well, you didn't." Oto smiled. His gaze flicked from side to side, making sure no one overheard him. The girl with the horse had gone. All the red Princes and Princesses had gone into the castle. Drawing his knife, he went behind Broga to slit his bonds. As he did he spoke into his brother's ear.

"Your way failed. I am in command here. Do as I will." His voice fell to a hiss. "Keep your hands off them. Our time will come."

Broga snarled something. Head down, he plowed across the gate yard toward the castle; Oto followed him.

 8

LUKA WALKED UP THE MAIN STEPS INTO THE CASTLE, AND IN the dark corridor Jeon came up close behind him, his voice a harsh whisper.

"Why did you let them back in here? Do you really think they have given up?"

Luka kept walking. "I'd rather have them here, where I can see them, than off somewhere making trouble." He gave his brother half a glance. "Consider them hostages."

Jeon snorted. Luka went ahead of him toward the hall; beyond the open doors the sun was blazing into the room from the ocean side, and the great roaring of the surf reached his ears. Luka was enjoying his victory and had no intention of worrying now. He thought Jeon did not see this well: there was no ignoring the Emperor, far away, and yet always there.

"Then kill them," Jeon snarled at Luka. "We can do this. Come out of the walls. They would have no defense."

"Am I to use my castle to do murder?"

In the hall, the light was different, and he stopped and looked around. A wall, knee-high, made of squared-off stone fitted together, bounded the rim of the terrace. Luka laughed; they thought they would stop Erdhart going over a second time. "I'll knock that down. Tomorrow. Hafgavra has to breathe." Luka spread his arms out, looking around, here for the first time in his kingly hall.

He went across the great room, to the high table, and his King's seat, carved out of the black rock. He turned, and sat, and could not keep the broad smile from his face. Through the door on his right hand the hall was filling up with people, and each one stopped as he came in and bowed to Luka. The old ones were appearing around the lower tables. He was glad to see them, although he knew that what they bowed to was the King's seat and not the phantom on it. That thought amused him, and he laughed again. That was what he had to live up to.

The servants had not yet come back. Most lived in Undercastle, which was still celebrating. Therefore, Oto's Imperials in their striped doublets were attending the tables. Oto walked in through the big doors and stopped, his gaze on Luka, his face stiffly smiling, the courtier's face he wore like a mask. He was splendidly dressed in tissue of red and gold. Beside him Broga, well tidied up and packed into the same colors, hung back also, looking elsewhere. Oto bowed to Luka with many flourishes and mouthed some phrases. Broga simply lowered his head, his eyes still directed away. They crossed to the far end of the high table.

Now Mervaly and Casea walked down the room toward Luka, and as she came Mervaly, trailing veils of lace, danced this way and that. Casea in a dark gown was like her solemn shadow. Mervaly swept him a lavish courtesy.

"Luka, my brother, well seen, well honored, I salute you."

Casea bent her knee also, and came around the end of the table to his right side, and kissed him. "Thank you. You saved us."

He knew that they had expected him to fail, to lose to Broga, to deliver them all into the Empire. They would have more faith in him now. The two girls sat on his right side at the table, and Jeon appeared on Luka's left, the place of the King's brother. A soldier brought a goosenecked pitcher and poured their wine.

Luka took his cup in his hand, and stood, and at once the whole room hushed. Dozens of people here now. He had waited a long time to do this, and he swelled with the pleasure and the power. He lifted the cup and said, "Remember Reymarro, King of Castle Ocean, who gave his life for us. Hail, Reymarro!"

Everybody shouted, even the old ones, and drank. Only the two Erdhartssons stood silent in the uproar, their heads bowed. Luka sat down again. That was well done, but he would not see Reymarro here among them until his body lay within the castle walls.

His body would be bones, now, if anything at all was left.

It gnawed in Luka like a canker that he had abandoned his father's body in the mountains. He would have had to search over every rock on the dark and stony battlefield, while the Imperials still ranged the place, killing and killing. Instead he had gathered the surviving men and led them back home. Now he should bring his father home also. Luka considered going into the defiles of the mountains looking for bones and his mind shrank from it. He should not turn from that: losing Reymarro was a chink in the family, through which hard winds could blow.

Jeon was leaning toward Luka again, his gaze aimed down the table. "Look at them, the swine. I cannot bear to see them here. Do you think they would show you such mercy, if they were in your place?"

"They are not in my place," Luka said. "Where I belong, I am immortal." He turned to Jeon and gripped his shoulder. "You have stood by me, Jeon. All through this. Trust me again."

Jeon said, "It was you who won the battle for us. But sometimes I think—"

"Trust me," Luka said, and cuffed Jeon's shoulder. Jeon fell still, his lips pressed together.

Mervaly was chattering away beside Luka to Casea, who was tilted slightly toward her, listening and sometimes laughing and sometimes saying a quick word that made Mervaly laugh uproariously. Luka said, "Where is Tirza?"

Casea faced him, her dark eyes wide in the perfect oval of her face. As always, she had her needlework, her hands moving in system. "She is not here in the castle. She's hiding. She's afraid of them, Luka." She was on Jeon's side, Luka thought, although not in the same way.

Luka leaned back, considering this. He did not think that Tirza was afraid. She had thrown the rock. He had heard this story now a dozen times, from several different people, how while he and the other men jabbered away in a back room Tirza started the war.

Mervaly said, "Let's not pick on each other. We should be glad now, and not worry about anything else."

Casea said, "I'm glad you're all right," and leaned over and kissed her. "Tirza was supposed to look after you."

"Maybe she did."

Jeon was frowning down the table toward the Erdhartssons. Luka remembered what his brother had said, back in the corridor, another glimpse of that black, cold streak in him. He could manage Jeon; he had seen how to get the best from Jeon. It was Tirza not being there that bothered him. He thought anyone who gave up such a gift as the power of language must have gotten something potent in return. He knew where she would be; he would find her.

OTO PICKED GLUMLY AT THE FISH BEFORE HIM; THE SOLDIERS were bringing in the meat, some huge roasts on platters, indifferently arranged. The soldiers were awkward servers and dropped knives and once even a platter full of juices. Oto kept on his calm, smiling face, nodded to others around the table, spoke occasionally. Broga sat like a lump, barely touching any of his food.

Luka, on the high seat, held everybody's attention. Time and again he lifted his cup and everybody roared his name and called him King and hero. Oto seethed at Broga for giving this bumpkin such a platform to perform on, a victory by a handful of fishwives over Imperial troops. If the Emperor found out about this, the Erdhartssons could be recalled. They could lose everything.

Also: the castle. In this room, where his father had fallen to his death, where half the people seemed not to notice Oto's existence, he felt the dread gather in him, some premonition he could not distill into any practical idea. He wanted to be gone from here. But this was where the struggle was. He fixed his gaze on Luka, up there exulting in his glory, and watched him for some weakness.

HERE AND THERE ALONG THE JAWBONE SOME LITTLE EVERgreen trees grew, like green whiskers, but the southernmost end was nothing but bare black rocks. Tirza sat on the highest, up above everything else. The surf boomed on one side of her, tossing its white froth into the wind; there was no beach on that side, only a long tumble of rocks down into the water, and then more big rocks offshore. On the biggest and flattest, sea cattle flopped and barked. Some pelicans sat on the choppy water, their heads cocked back on their long necks. The wind blew her hair back and she pulled her cloak up under her chin and looked east over the bay.

On that side of the spit, mild little waves slapped along a pale grey beach. In the tidal wash, green with rippling seaweed, starfish and anemones covered the rocks, barnacles as big as her fist. Crabs and tiny octopuses lived in the pools between them. The castle loomed up beyond it all, taller than anything else, a crown of spires.

Undercastle lay on her right hand, across the bay; sounds carried across the water, a calling voice, the rhythmic clanking of the forge. She saw some movement on the cliff and after watching awhile decided it was a woman sweeping off the trail to the top. The four fishing boats had gone out earlier, to winnow the passing streams, their red and yellow sails leaning on the wind. Midway across the bay, two naked boys with a raft were diving for oysters. Everything lay around her; everything went by her here. She could see it all from here.

She could see it all and yet no one could see her, and perhaps that was the way of this. Nobody ever really noticed her. Her mother had cursed her, and she was condemned, and everybody knew. Maybe there was a mark on her somewhere. Or just how she was, small and strange.

She remembered how after she escaped from the dragon, when she was lost in the wilderness, she would call for help and people would only drive her away. She remembered them calling her a witch, chasing her into a tree, and then trying to set the tree on fire.

In a fit of fury she made that into a story: she imagined that they made the fire, but it turned on them and burnt them up. Morosely she pulled the cloak tighter around her. She would do well enough by herself.

She dozed, and she dreamed. She was in the tree again, sitting on a branch looking down through the leaves, but the fire was gone. Instead the dragon was coming toward her, up the little gorge where the stream ran.

She huddled against the trunk behind her, afraid. He came up beneath her, and turned his huge red eyes on her.

He said, "I have done as you wished. They have suffered for what they meant to do to you."

She climbed up higher in the tree, out of his reach. "Go away," she said.

He gave one of his cold chuckles. "For now, I will. This is too far from the sea for my comfort, and I am not hungry anymore. I want to enjoy you on a clean palate." His eyes glittered. "In the meantime, wherever you are, wait for me." He turned and hauled himself back down the stream, crushing trees and bushes under his weight, leaving behind a long trail of broken things.

She woke. The dream faded. Back along the Jawbone, someone was walking toward her. She folded her knees to her chest and wrapped her arms around them, and watched: when this person saw her, he would turn away, too, and leave her alone.

But he did not, he came on toward her, leaping from rock to rock, and she saw that it was Luka. When he came up, she gave him a black scowl.

He sat down beside her. "I thought you might be hungry." From his belt pouch he took something wrapped in a white cloth.

Inside she found bread, cheese, a bit of fish. Suddenly she was overwhelmed with hunger and she gobbled it all up. He sat watching her. When she was done, he swung his arm around her and hugged her against him. "Mervaly says you're afraid of the Erdhartssons."

She exploded at him. "You let them in, after all we did—" She bit her lips that only spoke gibberish. She sank against him, her face against his shoulder, and cried.

He hugged her again. "I know. I understand."

She did not think he understood. She clung to him, saved. His arm gripped her fast. "I want you to come home."

She sat up straight, moving out of his arms, her gaze on his face. She wanted to tell him how wonderful he was, how he had defeated their enemies against all the odds; she wanted to tell him the story of himself, but she could not make the sounds.

"We should all be together. Jeon is turning very strange; he wants me to . . . to . . . What use would it be to win, if I must become like one of them to do it? And Casea is the one who is afraid." His hands kneaded together in front of him. She thought he talked to her as if to himself. "Mervaly I know I can depend on. And you, if you will come back." He smiled at her, his long face crinkling. "Besides, it's getting to be autumn now; you'll be cold."

She looked up at the castle, behind them and above them, dark with the sun behind it. He said, "Come in at least now and then."

She nodded uncertainly; when she thought about going into the castle again her skin crawled. Some evil harbored there, new, since her mother died.

She wondered if their mother had whispered some curse in Luka's ear, also, before she danced herself off the cliff. When he stood up, going, she stood, too, and followed him.

As they went along on the rocks he stopped and held out his hand to help her across. She took his hand, as if she needed help. They walked along the Jawbone toward the sea gate; she felt much better.

THE SERGEANT PAL DAWD MADE HIS ROUNDS, STARTING WITH the gatehouse and the yard. All the soldiers not in their camp out on the cliff top gathered here, sitting and standing around the paved yard; they would not willingly go into the castle. The gatehouse and the bridge and the yard had all been built much later than the rest of the castle, and Dawd wondered how anybody had gotten in before; maybe there had been an earlier entry, but he could see no sign of it, not on this side, where the gate opened on a sheer drop, which the bridge spanned, nor on any other side, which all went straight into the water.

Something nudged his mind; he remembered the passage he had gotten lost in, and shook that off; he didn't want to think about that. He spoke to this soldier and that one, and gave them their duties. Half of them he left there to mind the gatehouse.

Oto had ordered Dawd especially to secure the gate. Broga had ordered Dawd to mount a heavy guard on the tower where the brothers lived. Dawd could not do both at once, not with half the little army at work in the kitchens and around the castle.

Beneath the new tower was a rambling cave where they kept the kitchen. This also had been built by men, with brick walls, brick ovens. As he went in there he noticed that along the tables in the center of the room were many of the castle servants, the people from Undercastle. The middle table itself was heaped with fresh rounds of cheese and bread in stacks that still smelled warm from the oven. The soldier who had been the cook was gone and the old cook was back, haggling with a man over some mushrooms.

Dawd was relieved to see this; now maybe he would have enough men to do what both brothers wanted. He went through the new tower and made sure the brothers' doors shut and opened and that nobody lurked in the corners. Coming down that narrow stair, he crossed the center room to the hall, that cavern in the black rock.

He went through the broad space into the open sunlight, drawn to the stiff, salty wind and the sight of the sea. If the wind got any higher, they would have to rig up the storm wall. The whole wide ocean was bounding with waves, the wind spinning their tops off in flags of white foam. The top of the new wall was wet. As he came to the edge, a wave crashed below and threw up a spout of foam that rocketed along the whole wall before it sagged out of sight. Looking out at the ocean gave him the feeling sometimes that he was looking at the birth of the world. Then he noticed that at the far end some of the new wall had fallen down.

Casea, the King's beautiful sister, was standing there. In her plain dark gown she was slender as a flower stem.

Dawd said, "Now this will have to be mended."

"I don't think that's possible," she said. She turned the full, dark gaze of her eyes on him, her head slightly to one side, quizzical. Her curly red hair was like the roses of the south. He could not look away from her, even when another wave churned up the side of the sea cliff and a little more of the wall crumbled. He put out his hand to her.

"Come back; you will fall."

She laughed. She said, "May I help you? You seem troubled."

He blurted out, "I can't serve two officers."

"Serve yourself," she said, watching him, those wide, clear dark eyes.

"I need a master. How will I know what to do? I am not big enough to matter."

She put her hand on his arm, so light it felt like nothing. She was smiling, as if they shared some joke. She said, "Even so, you must serve yourself, you know." She went away. For a moment, as he turned his gaze to follow her, he thought the room behind them was full of people, but all he saw was the tall girl walking through the shadows.

* * *

AMILLEE SLAMMED THE CUPS DOWN ON THE COUNTER NEXT to the taps. Lumilla threw her a piercing look.

"Get to work, girl! What's wrong with you?"

Amillee muttered under her breath. Her mother made her furious; all this made her furious, this ordinary, boring, donkey life of work and custom. She filled the cups. Aken came up behind her, reaching for his special cup on the rack over her head, and brushed against her, and she dumped ale on him.

"Get away from me; I'm not my mother."

He goggled at her, startled, and looked down at his sodden apron. She went by him into the brewery public room, where every bench was full. They were roaring songs, calling insults and greetings, stamping their feet, all celebrating, while she had to scurry around giving them drink and carrying their dirty dishes. She wanted to kill them all. Her eyes stung.

The whole room erupted in cheers. Luka was coming in.

She drew back toward the taps, watching him plow through the room, where everybody wanted to shake his hand, to slap his back and call his name, so it took him moments to get to his chair. His face was bright as sunlight. His eyes snapped. Before he sat down, he waved to the room to be quiet. Nobody quieted. They screamed his name in a chant. They pounded on the floor with their feet.

He stopped, in the middle of the room, and held his hands up, and they hushed. He looked all around him. His voice rang out. "Remember," he said. "Some of us gave up everything to save Undercastle. Osa, poor thing, has died of her wounds. Leanara died in the first battle. Freo is dead."

In the silence Luka looked around him again, and he nodded. "Remember these. Remember that we suffered for this. Remember." He nodded. "That's all." He went off toward his place at the back of the room.

The others turned to one another, and the murmur of talk sprang up again. Amillee heard the names of the dead people, over and over, and they began to drink salutes. She brought Luka his cup, full of ale, and he smiled and reached out to pull her against him. "Well, pretty Amillee."

She recoiled out of his grip. She did not want that anymore. She wanted him to lead her into battle again; she wanted to be a hero again. She said, "What is this, you let them back into the castle? Did we fight so hard for nothing?"

Even through the noise in the room, people nearby heard that and listened, and a hush fell. Luka leaned back in his chair, not smiling anymore. Everybody was watching him and her.

He said, "I see how you feel. I honor you for your valor. But I am King and you are not."

A sigh went up from the others in the room. In a flash she saw that they wanted this from him, above all, this decision. Amillee looked him in the eyes, her back stiff. "Why are you the King, Luka?"

From the crowd a roar went up, angry. He was frowning at her, not angry, more quizzical, as if she had asked him something unexpected. She wanted him to say, Because of my people. I am King because of you. She wanted power over him. He watched her steadily, and he started to say something, and then a noise behind her pulled him that way, and he stood up.

Someone called, "The King—I need to find the King!"

She turned. In the doorway Aken was supporting a panting, ragged boy by one arm and pushed him toward Luka.

"There is the King."

The boy said, "I have a message . . . from inland—Terreon—" and slumped down onto his knees. "They need your help." Luka went to him, and the whole room's attention followed. Amillee sat down, her legs wobbly.

Luka said, "There's something happening over at Terreon, and I'm going out there. You"—he pointed to Oto, sitting behind the table—"are going with me."

The Erdhartssons had been playing chess. Broga sat stiff as a board now, staring at Luka, his hand fisted around a piece. Jeon came across the room from the terrace. "In Terreon? Nothing happens there. What is happening there?"

Oto stood, his face taut as old leather. Through the holes in this mask his eyes gleamed with some intent. "My lord, surely I am of more use to you here—"

Luka grunted at him. "No, you're not. You need better clothes." Luka turned to Jeon. "The boy was only the end of the relay; he didn't know anything, except they are in trouble there. While I'm doing this, I want you to keep my lord Broga company." He clapped Jeon on the shoulder: with Oto gone, Broga would be harmless.

His hand fisted on the table, Jeon growled at him. "I'll do what I can."

Broga's face was flushed; he had overheard this. He turned his murderous gaze on Jeon, and folded his arms over his chest.

Luka turned back to Oto. "Hurry. I have no idea what this is and it could be very dangerous. Get stout clothes. Order your horse brought around. I'll meet you at the gate." He bent, pushing his face into Oto's. "There are worse things, you know."

Oto smiled. "I am pleased to come, my lord." His voice grated. He cast a quick look at Broga, turned, and walked out. Luka smacked his brother again on the shoulder, and Jeon turned and saluted him. Luka went down into Undercastle, to find himself a horse.

OTO GRITTED HIS TEETH; LUKA'S LACK OF CEREMONY WAS picturesque but uncomfortable. He should have made a grand progress to this Terreon, as the Emperor would have, with heralds and solemn progress, proper food and drink, files of soldiers. That alone could have solved the problem, run off brigands, cowed local rebels, but here they were trotting hard along the high road, just the two of them, not even a banner.

The road carried them along the coast a way, by the edge of the sea cliff. Luka kept them moving fast through the flat winter-bound meadows, the rows of furrows still visible, sprinkled with chaff and stubble. At the far edge of the fields the trees began, thick and dark, and beyond them the first blue ridges of the mountains. Oto and Luka came to a gorge where a stream ran down to the sea and crossed by a narrow bridge of stone. On the far side, the road bent inward.

In the crook of the road was a fence; and inside the fence, a low-roofed house. As they rode up to the gate, Oto saw a boy hanging on the fence, gawking at them. Luka swept his hat off, and the boy yipped and bounded over the fence and inside.

An old man came quickly out the gate, bowing and rubbing his hands together. "Greetings, King Reymarro—"

"I am King Luka," Luka said mildly. "We need food and drink, and fresh horses."

"This way, this way." The old man led them toward the hut. Amazed, Oto saw he would be expected to enter this dwelling. Luka stooped to clear the lintel. Oto gathered up his cloak, the skirts of his doublet, his sleeves, and got through the door without touching anything.

Now they were in the dark, but then a lamp bloomed. In the dusky yellow light he saw a table, benches, a hearth. The floor was of dirt. Luka was already sitting down on the bench, and the old man was bringing wooden cups, a pitcher. Oto went carefully across the filthy floor. The bench was wood and did not look clean. He sat on it anyway, resigned. The bench was hard. The place smelled of mice. He leaned his forearms on the table, looking around, wondering how people could live in such a way.

Luka was watching him, smiling. "You think this is too mean for you."

Oto straightened, his hands on the table. "It is modest, certainly. You deserve more, sir. Being King, you should show more circumstance. The people expect it."

Luka's smile widened. He lifted his cup and took a sip of the ale. "I can move faster this way. Try the ale."

Oto took his cup, and put his nose over it: a fresh, bright tang greeted him. He sipped at the cool drink. "This is excellent." The old man came forward, to give Oto more, and he drank deeply.

Luka said, "Can't you make ale, in the Holy City?"

Oto grunted. The ale in the capital was notoriously bad. The old man went out and came back with a wooden tray with bread and a knife, a little pot of honey, some cheese. Oto wondered if he would have meat. He wondered briefly how he could get this ale back to the Holy City.

He said, "My lord, I have been thinking over our difficulty with the Emperor."

Luka made a sound like a choked-off laugh. "What do you take that to be?"

"We must make some bond with him. So that he recognizes you as King. Perhaps we could—" Almost breathless with the perfection of this, Oto leaned toward him. "Weave our families together. You could marry one of the Emperor's daughters, and I could marry your sister Mervaly."

Now Luka did not even try to keep from laughing. He leaned on his arm on the table, looking rudely into Oto's face, and after a while collected himself back to a mere smile. "Well, that's interesting. The Emperor has a lot of daughters? Could I have my choice?"

Oto sat rigid, the laugh ringing through his head. He forced his way forward with this, which did so much so well. "That would take some negotiating. But of course I could marry your sister at once." Again the excellence of this idea caught him up. "That would dissuade my uncle from any impulsive gestures. It would win us time."

"Ask her, if you want," Luka said, smiling wide.

"You could not . . . intervene for me?"

"My sister will do as she wishes. What have you heard—no message has come from the Emperor?"

Oto was still a moment. This was sliding from his grasp somehow. He drank more of the ale, the bitter and the sweet. He put the cup down.

"Since my father . . . died, there's hardly been time for a message to have reached the Holy City."

"So far," Luka said, his eyebrows raised. "Well."

The old man came back in again, carrying a platter with a heap of torn meat, and set it between them. Luka cut bread and piled the meat on it. Oto watched what he did, saw the utility in it, and they ate steadily for a while. The meal was simple but good, and Oto threw off his disappointed temper at his first failure. He had seen another way to move now.

Done, he drank more ale, and laying his hand flat on the tabletop, he turned toward Luka. "You have no idea of the reach of the Empire, Luka. You must tread carefully. My uncle the Emperor is busy with many matters, in all parts of the world, but he has powers you have not even dreamed of."

Luka's face settled. He pushed away the platter and mopped his chin and beard on a cloth. Unsmiling, he looked least like Mervaly. Was he afraid? Oto pressed on. "God gives all power to the Emperor, His chosen one on earth, to do His will." Oto touched his fingertips to his chest over his heart, the pledge of loyalty. "Resistance to him is a mortal crime."

Luka said, "Why does this god need to do that—make one man so great? Why does your god's will not simply happen? What else does it mean to be god?" His eyes glittered. He was only pretending to be simple.

Oto said, "God works His ways through us to lift us up from our base condition. He brings order, peace, justice, to those He favors and those who serve Him. The Emperor is the model of the ideal man, his life the ideal life."

Luka folded his arms over his chest, at ease again, smiling. "So. Of course, to stand against the tide, you need some actual place to put your feet. What will he say about the death of his brother here?"

Oto had been mulling that over; he knew of course that the Emperor would not care much about Erdhart but would care very much about getting justice for his death. How to say something useful about this to Luka was another matter. The answer rose readily to Oto. "Erdhart's murderer died with him. The Emperor will see that this is just." He brushed that out of his way. "Sir, I know you well now. I see your glory. The Emperor loves courage and strength—the warrior virtues. He loves honor. You could be among God's paladins. And should be. How can you flourish, here in this backwater?"

Luka reached for the cup. "Apparently, the ale here is a lot better."

"Your sisters are lovely. They would be ornaments at court. The Emperor would find them husbands to shower them with jewels."

"They don't want for jewels. I am King of Castle Ocean; what more could I be?" Luka nodded at him. "You go to court; you know the ways there. You know what I want. I'll stay here where I belong."

Oto said, "Only think, sir, of your own destiny."

Luka snorted at him. "Well, maybe. Let's get going; it's another whole day's hard ride to Terreon; we're wasting daylight."

THE RAW OCEAN WIND SWIRLED THROUGH THE CASTLE GATE yard, ruffling the horses' manes. Broga swung his arms to get his blood moving. The soldiers were all breathing white puffs and hunching into themselves. The sergeant came up to him and saluted him.

"My lord. Glory to the Empire."

Broga touched his chest over his heart. "And to the Emperor. You'll go along the coast, as far east as—" He glanced over his shoulder, toward the redheaded Prince watching him. Taking his brother at his word, Jeon had been dogging Broga steadily since Luka and Oto left, listening to everything Broga said. Broga faced the sergeant again.

"Go as far as the new fort. Which should be much advanced now. They'll need supplies; get a list from them; take a good look around." He should do this himself, he thought, but Jeon would insist on going along and he did not want Jeon seeing any more of the new fort than he already had. He lowered his voice to a murmur. "Find out if there's been any word of the fleet. This weather may be slowing them up." He didn't want Jeon to know anything about that, either. The fleet should have arrived by now, with more men and better weapons. "Return at once." He stepped back, and the sergeant saluted him again.

"Yes, my lord. Glory." He turned briskly and began giving orders to his men.

Broga went back up the stairs into the castle, his redheaded shadow traveling just behind him. He had nothing to do. He had just sent off the men he could have ordered around. He could not go to Undercastle, where everybody snickered at him, smiled, whispered behind his back.

The thought of that stoked a deep, dirty heat in him. He could not stop remembering being trapped in the sand, being dragged from the sand to lie at the feet of these villagers and fishermen. Their laughter still sounded in his ears, and would, until he had won back his honor.

Two flights up in the tower he shared with his brother, he had found a room to use for a chapel. It had no window and as yet no furniture, except a lamp in the niche. He lit the lamp and trimmed it, and knelt down to pray.

He offered his injuries to God, Who would redress them. He prayed for Oto to get what he deserved. For a while he thought over how he would furnish this room: he needed an altar; he needed hangings for the walls. He was aware constantly that Jeon waited just outside the door—that there was no being alone. He could not lose himself in prayer and after a while he went back down the stairs.

In the hall the storm wall had been raised across the open terrace and every hearth was blazing. The air was dim and warm and the light fluttered. Broga went to his usual place, at the end of the main table, several places down from the stone high seat. A servant came up at once with a cup and a jug; they had learned that much at least, not to make him notice them. The chessboard was there, and he picked up the black King, brooding on the crimes against him.

Jeon had gone around the table, to sit beside the high seat. Broga fingered the ebony King. "Do you play chess?"

The boy lifted his head. Even in this dim yellow light the red of his hair shone with a deep luster. The first silk of a beard fuzzed his cheeks. He said, "No."

"Come here. I shall teach you."

The boy studied him a moment; Broga drank ale, and Jeon left his seat, took one of the cups, and coming up to the other side of the table from Broga poured it full from the jug. "All right," he said. He sat down.

"You know the names of the pieces?"

"Nothing," Jeon said. "I have never even seen the game played."

"Well then. We shall start slowly."

He recited some names for the pieces, and then showed Jeon how each could move, and they began a game. The boy was witless, lost everything in a rush. Broga explained check and checkmate. They began another game. This time the boy risked nothing and Broga crowded him into a corner and won again.

Jeon sat back, his face red as his hair, his fists clenched; Broga knew how that felt, to lose, to be humiliated, and he smiled, laying his hands on the table.

"Well," he said, "you are a coward, Prince Jeon. I don't think you'll ever be good at this game, which requires courage."

Jeon was staring at the board, his body so stiff it seemed to vibrate. Broga said, "And wit, as well, another of your lacks." He reached for his cup.

Jeon's hand shot out and Broga jumped, but the boy was reaching for the chess pieces. He began to set them up again, never looking at Broga. He said, "You go white, this time," in a voice jagged as a ripsaw.

Broga grunted, surprised. He reached out and switched Jeon's King and Queen, lined up backward. "Well," he said. "I have nothing else to do, I suppose."

DAWD HAD LED THIS PATROL BEFORE, UP TO THE NEW FORT and back again, and always before he had taken the coast road, on top of the cliff, where there was more shelter from the weather. This time, on an impulse, he went along the beach way. He explained this to himself as a way to see more, but that wasn't the whole reason. The ocean drew him, the constant change and flux and color and smell and feel of the ocean.

He rode along beside his column, glad to get out of the castle. Oto had left him burdened with orders, and then Broga had sent him out here: he felt like something torn by dogs, the brothers fighting to control his time and his deeds.

But now surely this confusion would end, now that they both accepted that Luka was King. This felt good to Dawd. He had fought against Luka, and Luka had defeated him and then let him withdraw. In that, a sort of compact. Some common respect. Things were the way they should be. The Erdhartssons had accepted this. The business of the Empire was to keep order. Luka would give the orders henceforth, and Dawd would follow them.

His men marched along the sand. The surf and the rocks broke up their lines, but always they swung back straight and even, their pikes on their shoulders, all feet moving together.

He thought of the Princess Casea. The memory rose to the front of his mind, her wide dark eyes, fixed on him, saying, "Serve yourself." He had no notion how to do that and doubted he ever would, and now in Luka he had a King to follow who was worthy and he needed nothing more. He rode along beside his men, keeping a sharp eye on the beach ahead of them, picking a way through the rocks and driftwood, while the sea rolled its white edge beside him.

JEON SAID, "HE'S DOING NOTHING. EXCEPT PLAYING CHESS with me." He flopped back onto the softness of his sisters' bed, his arm over his face. Broga had beaten him and mocked him all afternoon. He would never win. He was too stupid and too dull. Checkmate.

"Why do you do that?" Casea asked. Beyond her, Tirza, helping Mervaly sweep up after the birds, turned her huge eyes on him with the same question.

He said, "It's an interesting game." He rolled over onto his stomach. "It's their game. It's how they think, lines and spaces, lots of rules, holding positions." He nodded at Tirza. "Remember that place we saw, up the coast, where they were building? Remember the wall across the terrace?"

"Which isn't there anymore, you know," Mervaly said sharply.

She laid the broom down, and spread her arms. From all around the room, the birds fluttered in around her, to perch on her shoulders, nestle in her hair, lean against her cheek, and she began to dance. The birds chirruped and sang and Mervaly danced slowly around the room with them.

"He says they'll fix it when the men come back. We'll wake up some morning," Jeon said, "and they'll have walled us up in a tomb."

Tirza gave a sudden explosion of laughter, looking around at them, as if to share some joke. Jeon buried his head in his arms.

The music of the birds trilled out. Mervaly swung slowly in circles toward the window, the birds all clinging to her like a mantle of feathers. "Luka will know what to do."

Casea said, "You said that same thing about Mother."

THE TABLE WAS SMALL BUT IMPOSSIBLY HEAVY. MARWIN WITH all his strength could not budge it, and when he brought in another man to help him still it would not move. It was as if the low black rock table was fastened to the floor. Marwin thought of telling Broga he could not do this, but Broga would be angry and Marwin could not think of a way to deflect his anger onto someone else.

The table looked like the common rock of the walls; long and narrow, it had a shallow well at either end, maybe to catch the blood of feasting or sacrifice. Marwin could see why Broga wanted it for an altar. He went out to the antechamber and brought in all the men he could find.

With a dozen hands lifting, the table rose off the floor enough that they could carry it away, through the hall and into the antechamber, where they had to set it down, and once again the table seemed to fasten itself to the floor. Grunting and groaning, they managed to hoist it up and then drag and heave and push it up the stair to Broga's chapel.

The redheaded Prince was sitting on the steps on the landing. A man with a torch stood by the door into the chapel and moved out of the way as they struggled in. The Archduke was pacing up and down the middle of the room, frowning, his hands behind his back. "What took so long?" He pointed. "That's the east wall, there."

They wrestled the table over against that wall and then he barked at them that it was too close and made them push it back a few feet.

"Now." Broga clapped his hands together. "Where's that priest? Where are my lamps?"

Marwin had not seen the priest since Erdhart danced off the terrace into the sea, but he himself was not a man to do much praying. He nodded to the man beside him. "Go bring the lamps from the hall, there." He sent away the rest of the soldiers, so that Broga would notice him more, and busied himself around the room, straightening and neatening as if it were not already straight and neat. He liked the greystone walls here, even if there was no window.

The soldier came back with two lamps, shaped like snail shells. Marwin took them, one in each hand, and set them on the altar. Broga said, "Nearer the ends. I need a striker." Marwin found his tinderbox in his belt and handed it to him, and Broga lit each lamp.

He stood back, smiling. The room brightened, warmer, even the black table shining. Marwin waved his hand, and the man with the torch went out, past the little priest coming in.

The priest crept in the side of the doorway, holding up the hem of his black robe, as if he dared let nothing but his feet touch the floor. His bald head shone. He bowed to Broga, at the same time making a blessing with his hand. Broga said, "You will consecrate this place."

The priest bobbed his head. "My lord, that may not be possible."

Broga flung his head back, scowling. "In the Empire nothing is impossible. Do as I say."

The little man before him shrugged, his face drawn. "Please, then, I need water. From outside the castle."

The Archduke shot a glance at Marwin. "Fetch water."

"My lord!" Marwin strode off.

The priest came out to the stair landing after him. The red-headed Prince was sitting on the stairstep, looking bored. The priest caught Marwin's sleeve.

"I need fresh, clean water, soldier."

Marwin smiled at him. He had no intention of going all the way outside the castle to get water. He knew where there was water much closer. He went down the stair, listening behind him to make sure the priest did not spy, and took his helmet and went across the antechamber into the great hall. The tide was high and the waves were crashing up over the edge of the terrace, throwing sweeps of water over the rock. At either end of the terrace the overflow streamed back toward the sea, and he went to the near end and filled the helmet. So they would think he had gone outside the castle, he lingered awhile in the hall.

He thought of Dawd, off on patrol. Things generally went better when Dawd was around, because he worked so hard. But now while Dawd was gone Marwin had some inside way to Broga, and he should use that, put himself forward, make sure he was there, ready, snappy with the salutes. Judging that he could have gone outside and back by now, he went on across the antechamber and up the stair to the chapel.

The priest was standing there wringing his hands. Broga said, "Good; that was quick." The Archduke had brought in a sword, not a soldier's sword but a ceremonial one with a gilded hilt and a sparkling blade. He kissed the blade and, going behind the altar, held the sword up against the wall.

The symbol of the Empire. Marwin signed himself, enjoying a warm, good feeling. Broga said, "Bring me the hammer. I shall place this with my own hands."

Marwin brought a hammer, and Broga drove a spike into the

chinks between the stones, high above the altar, and hung the sword, point down.

"Do it," he said to the priest.

The priest with the helmet full of water sprinkled the altar, and said some words in the old tongue. He went off around the room, dampening the corners and flicking droplets from his fingers into the air.

"That's enough," Broga said. "It is done now. Holy." Backing away, he folded his hands before him and lowered his head. "We shall think for a moment of the God-given mission of the Empire and the glory of the Imperial Family. We are called to purify the world. And now we have brought that mission into even this infernal place."

Marwin bowed his head. The silence stretched on; out on the landing, even the redheaded Prince made no sound. Finally Broga signed himself and straightened.

"I shall pray now. You may all be gone. Let no one disturb me." He nodded to Marwin. "You stand guard." Broga's gaze shifted; Marwin saw he was looking toward Prince Jeon, and took his meaning.

"Yes, my lord! Glory!"

"Glory," Broga said, and turned back to his altar.

Marwin went outside onto the landing. The Prince was slumped on the step, looking bored. The priest stood there staring down at his hands, and suddenly he licked his fingers. He turned abruptly to Marwin.

"That water. That water was salt." His voice squeaked. "That was seawater."

"Oh, well," Marwin said.

"You fool," the priest said. "You complete fool." He pattered away down the steps. On the steps, the Prince was still looking half-asleep, but he was smiling.

* * *

LUKA AND OTO REACHED TERREON TWO NIGHTS LATER, WITH
the rain pounding down on them. As they rode up, the gate in the
wall ahead of them brightened with torches; news of their
coming had gone on ahead of them, obviously, because fifteen
or twenty people waited and they cheered as the two men rode
up. Luka pushed his hood back, riding into the midst of the
light.

"I am King Luka."

In the crowd, suddenly, a voice rose. "It is Luka. My lord, remember me—" That man pushed forward to the front, talking
to the others. "I followed you back from the massacre— The King
is come! It is him! We have a King again!" He turned and thrust
his hands up over his head and everybody cheered and rushed
forward. Oto's horse shied back from the noise, and he let it carry
him off a little, out of the turmoil.

In the midst of it, Luka was reaching down to touch people,
to be touched. A single hand with a knife, Oto thought, and he
is gone.

There was no knife. Oto followed the crowd with their torches
and cheers, escorting Luka through the little town. Inside its
wooden palisade Terreon was no more than a dozen dwellings,
hardly more than huts, with walls of wood and plaster, blankets
of straw for roofs. In the steady hard rain they went on to a house
of some size, in the center of the town, and Luka dismounted and
went in, and Oto followed him, glad to be out of the slop.

Inside, the building was a long, low barn, the floor covered
with straw. The massive stone hearth in the center of the room
threw out billows of smoke. The man who had recognized Luka
ushered them to a table while as many of the people as could fit
crowded into the room facing them.

Luka sat on the bench, his hands in front of him on the table. "Tell me what is going on here."

Several voices all went up at once, but the first man, whose house this clearly was, turned and waved them quiet. He faced Luka again. He was a round man, with popping eyes and a gusty voice.

"My lord, it's pigs."

Oto almost laughed; he put his hand over his mouth. They had come all this way to save the place from swine. There was a fable, he thought, but he could not bring it right to mind.

Luka was not smiling. The fat man was rushing on. "They started showing up in the fall. From the beginning there were lots of them, more than most sounders. They ruined one of the orchards, first, and when we went out to drive them off—"

In the crowd a woman cried out, "They killed her!" The other people called out.

"There is a great boar leading them," the balding man said. "As big as a cow. It's not an ordinary pig, sir; it's a demon. It did kill old Mamy when she tried to drive it off, brave thing she was; everybody else ran."

A woman called, "They ate her!"

In the crowd, a man's voice rose. "It's a wer-boar, out of the mountains! It's a ghost!"

At that, Oto noticed, Luka gave a start. He said, "It came from the mountains?"

"Where else?" the fat man said. "We had gotten in the harvest, for which at the time, too soon, I thanked God. The boar means us ill. It led them to break into the storage barn and ruin half the barley. They went through the midden and scattered the refuse, and they attack anybody who goes outside. They are beginning to come through the fence." The balding man squeezed his hands together. "Help us. We thought you would bring soldiers."

Luka said, "You have able-bodied men here; we don't need soldiers." His voice rang, steely. "Where is this boar now?"

The fat man said, "Not in the rain, they won't come. But when the rain stops."

Luka nodded. "Very well. My companion and I have ridden far. I want something to eat, and something really good to drink. Tomorrow the day should be fine, and we'll get ready for your pigs."

LUKA MADE THREE SPEARS OUT OF FARM TOOLS, LONG, STOUT staffs tipped with iron, each one fitted with a stout crossbar a foot above the point. He knew the people here would do nothing until he showed the way.

He and Oto rode out in the afternoon to find the pigs and the whole village followed, but those people stayed well behind Luka. Oto rode at his stirrup, saying nothing.

Beyond the town fence, the fields spread out in broad skirts under a thin crust of snow, the furrows like pleats, the stubble of the cropped barley poking through. Up ahead, where the forest came down to the plowed ground, he could see something moving, and drawing closer he saw the pigs, ranging out of the trees onto the fringe of an old field, rooting at the snowy ground. Big black and brown sows with flopping ears, and little piglets, and scrawny half-grown shoats, they snorted and tore at the ground with their hooves, all the while the whole sounder moving steadily toward the little town behind its fence. Luka stuck two of the spears under his stirrup leather, and held the other in his left hand. As he rode toward them, the pigs all clustered together, their heads toward him.

Behind him, someone screamed, "There it is!"

The hackles rose on the back of his neck. Around the edge of the pig herd came the boar.

It was twice as big as any of the sows, black as a hole in the ground, covered with bristles like spines. Its head was like a plowshare, its tusks as long as Luka's forearm. When it saw him, it charged.

The horse jumped and twisted, but Luka forced it straight to meet the boar, hefted the spear in his hand, and as the beast rushed to him, he leaned out from the saddle, let the horse wheel out of the way, and drove the spear down at the boar as it turned to follow.

He felt the spear strike the boar, right down into its withers, and then the boar wrenched around and struck at the horse. Halfway out of the saddle, Luka leaned down on the spear, trying to drive it deeper. His horse screamed and reared and went over backward.

He leapt off, losing hold of the spear. The horse thrashed on the ground, and the boar drove its curved tusk into the upturned belly and tore it open with a single jerk of its head. Blood splattered across the dirt, the stench of spilled guts. As it did this the boar for an instant was broadside to Luka, the spear still jutting from its back, and Luka flung himself on it, hands on the haft, all his weight driving the spear deep.

The boar ramped up before him, lunging for him, its hind legs slipping in the uncoiling wreckage of the horse's guts. He could see the wiry hairs on its snout, the tiny eyes like an afterthought in the gross map of its face. He braced himself and drove the spear with the weight of his body, and with a grunting squeal the boar lunged and twisted back and away from him and the spear broke off in his hands and he tripped and sprawled on the bloody, slimy ground.

The boar charged him again, its jaws trailing rags of spittle.

Luka rolled away, taking his belt knife in his hand, and when the great snorting filthy head thrust toward him he slashed a red stripe across its muzzle. The blood leapt across its face. The boar backed up a step, and charged, swinging its head, hooking at Luca with its tusks. Luca jumped across the hurtling body. The other spears were still stuck under the saddle leather on the dead horse and he ran for them, the boar grunting and slavering after him. He tripped in the stinking mess on the ground and went flat, and the boar lunged full into him and a searing pain went through his side.

He rolled over onto his back and struck up with the knife, straight up over him into the gross dripping belly, and the blade bit deep. The boar recoiled. Luka bounded to his feet, his breath sawing in his throat, blood streaming down his left side. The dead horse was a yard away. He snatched a spear from the saddle. They faced each other, Luka and the boar, and the great beast bellowed and pawed at the ground. It shook its head, splattering blood around. Luka took the spear in both hands and ran straight at the boar, and it gave one last roar, turned, and ran away.

Behind Luka now he could hear the screams and howls of the people watching. He shouted, "Bring me a horse! Bring me a horse!" With one hand he pressed the long flap of skin back against his side.

All the pigs were running, squealing, a great bouncing noisy carpet of their bodies flowing back over the field toward the forest. Luka was breathless; he stumbled. It was hard to do anything with his side torn open. A horse came up beside him, and he turned to it, reaching for the reins. Oto was in the saddle. His mouth was open and he was bellowing, but Luka could not hear the words. He turned, to see the people of Terreon, suddenly brave, rushing out after the pigs, killing the laggards, dancing over the bodies. He felt the hot, sticky blood rushing down his side. His body trembled, very heavy. He leaned on Oto's horse, sobbing for breath.

THE BOAR HAD SLASHED LUKA'S SKIN OPEN FROM THE ARMPIT TO the hip but had hit nothing vital. A woman from the village made him lie down on a table, plastered something all over the wound, and wrapped him up in yards of bandages. Oto said, "My lord, surely—" And Luka went by him, putting on his shirt, and out to the street, where a fresh horse was waiting.

Oto said, "You think you can ride?"

"Come with me." Luka put his hands on the saddle and gathered himself; it took all his strength to lift his foot and put it into the stirrup. He crawled up onto the horse's back. The blood was leaking down his side again.

They rode out after the pigs, the townspeople following after in a mob, armed with sticks and knives. All the rest of the day they chased the pigs east, out of the fields and back through the forest, killing many. Luka questioned everybody as they came on them, but nobody had seen the black boar. With the sun going down and more rain coming, Luka called off the hunt and they rode back to the town.

Oto said, "I think you killed it." His voice quivered. "I have never seen such a fight. You must have killed it."

Luka knew the boar was not dead. He sat on his horse at the gate into Terreon as the people paraded through, carrying great bloody chunks of pig on their spears. Lifting his gaze, he looked back toward the forest.

Behind the forest, the mountains.

He remembered the tiny pig eyes, the bristles, the foul stench of the beast. It was not dead. He knew what this was. But his side hurt. He was hungry. He turned toward Oto, waiting there beside him, and nodded.

"Let's eat. Sleep. And then tomorrow go back to Castle Ocean." He would heal in Castle Ocean. Then he would hunt down the boar.

10

"YOU CHEAT!" BROGA CRIED, AND HAMMERED HIS FIST ON THE table.

"I didn't," Jeon said. He had.

"And you still lost." Broga swept his Queen across the board. "Checkmate."

Jeon was locked in his fury; his ears burnt. He thought he might kill Broga then and there and be done with it. Cram a chess piece down his throat. Broga was glaring at him, as usual. Jeon reached for the pieces, to set them up again.

Boots sounded in the doorway, and the corporal Marwin came in, who commanded the gate; he had been acting as the herald since the real herald died on the beach.

"Glory to the Empire." Marwin saluted. "The King and my lord Archduke Oto are here, my lord." His gaze veered to Jeon. "My lord."

"Well, then," Broga said, and pushed himself back from the

table. "It will be good to have the company of men again." His lip curled.

Jeon said nothing. His temper had cooled; he thought now of painting Broga's Queen with venom, so he died slowly.

In a burst of laughter Mervaly and Casea came into the hall, their arms linked. Several of the old people were appearing, as they would, now that Luka was back, and the servants began pouring wine. Luka strode through the door and everybody shouted and cheered for him. He came up to the high seat and greeted his sisters with kisses and gave Jeon his hand.

"Well met," he said. He glanced around toward the door, where Oto was standing on the threshold waiting to be recognized. "What happened while I wasn't here?" Only Broga was walking up to meet his brother.

Jeon said, "I hate him." He shook his head. "Nothing much. He sent some men down to the new fort." That reminded him, and he fixed Luka with a sharp look. "I overheard— They think some fleet is coming from the Empire, messengers, an army, something. It's supposed to have been here by now."

Luka grunted, and his face settled. "Did you find out anything else?"

"How to castle," Jeon said.

Luka glanced toward the end of the table, where the Imperial brothers were sitting down, and back to Jeon. "Did you beat him?"

"No."

"Ah, well," Luka said, and slapped his arm. "Someday."

Jeon set his teeth together. He said, "You're hurt. What happened with you?"

Luka shrugged. "There is a boar from the mountains, who has gathered up every pig in the country. They're tearing up the orchards and fields." He put his fingers to his side. "I'll mend, now that I'm here."

Down the table, Oto said, "Your mighty brother dealt them a fatal blow, I feel. Such a fight as he made against the boar should be sung in ballads, or figured in a great tapestry."

Jeon said, "Did you kill it?"

"No."

Down the table, Oto was talking low voiced to his brother but now lifted his head again. "My lord, we should make a great hunt for it. We need some dogs."

"It's out in broad daylight, and it's afraid of nothing." Luka rubbed his hands together. Jeon saw he was troubled, finding something deep in this. "It came out of the mountains."

Jeon lowered his eyes, understanding now what this was to Luka. The servants were bringing around the food. Trollo with his mouth harp had come up from Undercastle, bringing another boy to play the flute, and they were making music. Mervaly laughed.

Oto said, "My lord, you keep no dogs."

"No dog can tolerate the castle," Luka said. "Likely we can find dogs in the town. Some of my friends there hunt."

Jeon said, "Aken has a ratter."

Luka gave a laugh. Sprawled on the high seat, his feet up on the table, he was gnawing on a bone.

"We need more than a ratter," Oto said.

Broga said, "What does anyone hunt in this backwater?"

"Maybe a couple of ratters," Jeon said, talking to his hands. "What more do you need to catch pigs?" Luka gave him a hard look. Jeon said, "For instance, we could use a few ratters around here."

Broga said, "Watch your mouth, you stupid boy."

Jeon leapt to his feet, reaching for the knife on the table, and Luka caught him by the arm. "Sit."

Broga was on his feet. "I cannot bear anyone who cheats at chess." His voice quivered with fury.

"What are you all, but thieves and cheats?" Jeon cried.

Luka flung his bone across the room and leapt up. He thrust Jeon hard down onto his chair. "Sit." Facing the end of the table, Luka said, "My lord Broga, my brother is young. I don't think you have such an excuse."

Oto was hauling on Broga's sleeve. Broga and Jeon stared at each other; Jeon felt his ears heat. He still had the knife in his hand and he slicked it against his thigh. But Broga was sitting down again, under Oto's control. Jeon's sisters watched all this, rapt.

"My lord," Oto said, "let this go by. We must be friends. My brother will apologize."

Broga's jaw dropped and his face turned bright red. Luka said, "Nobody fights in this hall."

"Of course, my lord. But, see, nothing really happened." Oto spread his hands. "Let us have peace."

Mervaly was leaning forward, her head turning from one side to the other. She cocked an eyebrow at Jeon, who hunched down into his shoulders and directed his attention to his meat. A servant brought the jug with the ale. Mervaly said, "What did happen, Jeon?"

"Stay out of this, Mervaly," Luka said.

Casea said, "Which would be a shock." With a frown she lifted her hand with the needle, trailing purple thread.

Jeon met Mervaly's eyes, shiny with questions, and gave a little shake of his head. Somehow, he thought, he had let Luka down.

Abruptly Jeon realized all of this was a kind of giant chess game. He was young, as his brother said, and all this while he had seen this much too small. He put his arms on the table, staring off across the room, while everything he knew overturned itself and settled into another order.

* * *

LATER HE MET LUKA ON THE STAIR INTO THE KING'S TOWER and he pushed Jeon against the wall and spoke into his face.

"If you can't master yourself you can go where you'll do no damage. Take off. Sign on to a ship. Get a quest. Go on a pilgrimage. Grow up."

Jeon said, "Let me kill him. It will save us a lot of trouble."

"Why do you think you could?" Luka took a step backward. His stare drilled into Jeon's. "Stay away from them." He punched Jeon lightly in the chest. "Obey me." Two steps at a time he went up the stair.

"WHAT IS THIS?" OTO SAID, LOOKING INTO THE NEW CHAPEL.

Broga grunted. "It's that damned boy." On the wall the sword hung skewed, and the table he had brought in for an altar was pushed up against the wall under it; the lamps were broken. The oil had spilled down into the little wells on the altar. "Help me."

Oto came in after him and one at each end they tried to move the table, but it would not budge. Broga swore under his breath and signed himself. "I have guards on it, but somehow he comes in here and tosses things around."

Oto doubted Jeon tossed this table around, which was as heavy as if it had grown roots into the floor. He watched Broga straighten the sword and wipe it bright again with his sleeve. "I'll put more guards on it," Broga said. "The wretched brat. I need more lamps."

The pieces of the old lamps lay on the floor. Oto had thought at first it was the spilled oil that glistened on top of the table and filled the depression at this end. It did not look like oil. He dipped his finger into the well and touched it to his tongue.

It was salt. It was seawater. He turned to Broga, to ask him about this, but he was kneeling, was going into the locked room of his prayers. No talking to him in this state. Oto went out the door, where a guard leaned against the wall, half-asleep. He needed to think this all out, and he went up to his room at the top of the tower, and shut the door.

"I HAD HOPED TO SEE PRINCE JEON," OTO SAID, LOOKING around the hall. "To make amends between us."

Luka picked up his cup. "I sent him away." He had been passing judgments all morning; the most recent supplicant was just going out the door. Luka wondered what Oto had in mind here. Someone else already waited, out there; they had been a long while without a King.

"My lord," the Imperial man said, "my brother has admitted he was as much at fault as Prince Jeon, who is young, and untried in men's ways." Oto glanced back over his shoulder at Broga, standing stiffly behind him, for once keeping his mouth shut. "I pray you not to punish him. But we surely must separate them; my brother is rash also, and intemperate at times. Broga will take it on himself to go. He can carry messages, such as we discussed on our ride here. To Santomalo, maybe even on to the Holy City."

Luka said, "I don't think that's necessary." He gave Broga a sharp look. Oto moved, getting in his way, urgent with something else.

"My lord, in the messages, let me say that I may marry the Princess Mervaly."

Luka laughed at that. "Go ask her. That's hers to say, not mine."

"My lord."

"Ask her, not me."

"But I have your permission," Oto said doggedly.

"Yes, of course. Ask her all you wish." Luka pointed over to the doorway, where two townsmen loitered, waiting for his attention. "Now, if you will, get out of here. I have work to do."

* * *

OUTSIDE, IN THE ROOM WHERE ALL THE STAIRS BEGAN, Broga got up in front of Oto, angry. "What is this? I have no interest in going anywhere."

Oto pulled him into a corner. "Shut up and listen. You are not going to Santomalo. Listen to me. Here's where you will go, and this is what you will do."

"NO," MERVALY SAID, AND LAUGHED, AS IF HE HAD SAID something funny.

They were alone in the room, except for the shuffling, squawking birds. She stood in the middle of the floor, her hair fiery with the sunlight spilling through the window, more beautiful than he had ever seen her. His body rushed with furious heat. His hands groped in the air.

"Lady, consider the advantages. The King will thus be the Emperor's kinsman. He can stay here unchallenged as master of Castle Ocean."

She said, "He is King of Castle Ocean now."

"But if we married, we would guarantee that."

"Leave," she said. She was no longer laughing. "This will never happen."

"I beg you to reconsider."

"No."

"Then just keep your mind open to it." Her luscious flesh, veiled but not hidden by her clothes. As if she read his mind she lifted her hands and smoothed the front of the gown over her breasts.

"No," she said. "Leave. Please."

He turned and went out like a whipped dog. His heart thrashed in his chest. He would kill her. First he would slake his lust with her; then he would kill her. In his own chamber, he sank into a chair, ignoring the other men around, and locked his hands together and stared at the floor.

He was of the golden blood, heir in some degree to the crown of the world; she was a country girl, and yet she spurned him. Like everything else here, there was no order.

AT LOW TIDE, THE SEA POOLED IN THE BLACK ROCKS OFF THE very tip of Cape of the Winds, where her mother had fallen. There, with the sea constantly slapping and splashing in and out, a thousand little creatures lived, starfish bright as flowers stuck to the rocks, barnacles and limpets. Tirza sat on a flat rock watching the anemones sift the water through their delicate fingers. The sun on the water made wobbling arcs of light on the bottom. A long, dying wave rolled up, babbled into the pool at her feet, and dribbled away.

Behind, it left a tiny octopus, which scooted at once into a hole. Her mother had gathered those, and milked them for their poisons. With such a poison she had killed the first Imperial suitor. Tirza wrapped her arms around her knees, watching the constant surge and ebb. At a sound behind her she turned, and saw Jeon coming toward her.

She leapt up, glad, but he had such a long face she lost her smile and stood puzzled. He came down beside her on the rock and sat. He looked up at her. "Well, now both of us are exiled."

She sat down beside him, her knees drawn up, and he told her what had happened. He said, "And then I realized I had made a mistake. A stupid mistake."

She wrapped her arms around her knees, alarmed. Sometimes the mistake was in thinking too much. "Be careful," she said, a meaningless growl.

"Luka was right. I couldn't kill him; I have no power. I have no force." He said, "All this time I've been thinking that this with the Empire was so wrong, it could not be really happening, and it would go away, if I only hated it enough. But it won't go away. It's just getting worse. There's a lot more in this than I knew."

His face was taut. His eyebrows closed down over his nose. Through his pale eyes she saw the shifting in his mind. He said, "Luka knows."

She opened her mouth and shut it. She remembered Luka coming out here and talking to her, giving up his deepest thoughts to her, because she listened and said nothing. That was why Jeon was talking to her now, because she would say nothing, ever, to anybody. She was the Princess in the tower, locked away. A wave slopped into the tide pool, and carried off the little octopus.

"He told me to go away," Jeon said. "I'm not going anywhere. This is where I belong. If I belong anywhere it's Castle Ocean."

The tremble in his voice startled her; she saw he was crying. His grief flowed into her like a tide. She leaned toward him, put her arms around him, her head on his shoulder, the salt of the sea in her eyes.

SHE WANDERED THROUGH THE CASTLE, AND IN A LOWER chamber, in air rich from the surf, she finally found her mother.

Marioza was lying on her back on her ledge in the wall, bedded in seaweed, crowned with shells. She was smiling, like all the other dead, as if she knew something now that made everything Tirza knew unimportant. Marioza's eyes were open. Tirza leaned over her mother, to get in the way of her gaze, and her eyes met her daughter's a moment, and then looked somewhere else.

"Mama," Tirza said. "Tell me what to do."

On her mother's face the smile broadened, but Marioza said nothing. Tirza thought again, They know what to do, and I am what they are doing. I and Luka and all of us. That did not console her. She sat down on the floor, her arms around her knees.

She thought a curse should lift when the one who laid it died. She pressed the heels of her hands into her eyes. She remembered that other place, the sunlit cove, the dragon, who spoke to her, who listened and understood her, and a warm wash of longing broke over her, and she had to remind herself over and over why she had run away.

BROGA RODE OUT BY HIMSELF THE NEXT MORNING. JEON watched him go from the top of the cliff and, when he was sure he was gone, went down the path into Undercastle.

Everything had turned over in Jeon's mind. He saw what a child he had been, but he could not see the man he might become. Even the town suddenly looked strange to him, as if he saw it all new, and not as the one thing he always assumed it to be but as a million different pieces. As if for the first time he saw the rooms in the cliff face, how they bloomed into porches and doorways, the people going in and out. On the beach he had to tell himself to take each step as if he learned to walk all over again. In front of the domes of the bakery ovens two girls stooped to shovel in the wood. This should have been Leanara and he remembered why it was not and it was as if the whole world shook under him for the death of one old woman. In the sailmaker's shop the old man and his son were arguing, as usual, and Jeon felt that like some bedrock under his feet. All around him, the only world he knew, a boil of weightless incidentals. He walked on blindly through the town, enduring this.

LUKA HAD COLLECTED A LITTLE PACK OF DOGS FROM UNDER-castle, and Oto got one of his men to handle them. Luka intended to go back out to Terreon and pick up the trail there, but before this happened word came of the boar, only a day's ride away.

Luka had known this would happen. He thought, It is coming after me.

Oto's men were still out on patrol, and Jeon and Broga were gone; so only the two of them went off, with the handler leading the dogs on leashes. They rode steadily east, toward the vine country. The dogs tangled in the leashes, and went yortling off on every trail they crossed; Luka thought they were fairly useless.

He had brought half a dozen boar spears; remembering how the crossbar had stopped his thrust into the boar, the first time, he reset the crossbars on these much higher on the shafts. Oto was eager, this time, riding along beside Luka, his face intent. Once, Luka glanced at him and Oto gave him a huge, companionable smile.

They crossed the broad meadows. In a wood, well short of the vineyards, the dogs suddenly bunched together, nosed the ground, and began to bell. The soldier struggled with the leashes, and Oto said, "Sir, we should let them go."

"It's a hare," Luka said, but he nodded.

The soldier slipped the leashes and the dogs plunged away into the trees. Luka galloped after them down a short, steep slope. The thick wood hid the dogs from him, but ahead their savage bellowing rose to howls. They were on something, certainly. Oto had fallen behind him. The ground flattened out, the trees wider apart, old oaks, the space between them choked with brambles and vines, and he cut a game trail and followed that.

Ahead, the dogs suddenly began to yelp, rejoicing. They had cornered something. Luka took one of the boar spears in his left hand, and spurred the horse out into a clearing in the trees.

He skidded his horse to a stop. No boar, but a dozen men waited there, in a circle that now surrounded him. Leading them was Broga, a bow in his hands. Beyond, in the trees, Luka saw the dogs tearing at the carcass of a pig, which they had dragged to lead him here.

He yelled. He wrenched his horse around, and the horse went down like a rock, an arrow through its neck. Luka leapt to the ground, in their midst, and Oto galloped in behind him.

Broga said between his teeth, "I should make you eat sand," and nocked another arrow.

"Don't shoot him!" Oto cried. "They'll know an arrow hole. Kill him with your knives—"

Luka made no sound but launched himself straight at Oto. Oto's horse reared up, but he got both hands on Oto and dragged him down off the saddle and to the ground. The others closed on him. He ignored them. They would kill him, but he would kill Oto. Luka pounded down at the writhing body under him, smashing his fist into Oto's body, driving Oto's head against the ground. The others wrenched at him. Broga's voice was screaming, "Get him! Get him!" Their knives bit into him. He could hear nothing but an oceanic roar in his ears. He drove his knee into Oto, his elbows. A blade tore across Luka's face. His arm wouldn't work. His sight was dimming. He sobbed in a breath. His strength was gone, and he slumped down, the blood flowing out from him in a tide, Oto sprawled under him, and he gave up his last breath and was gone.

OTO LAY THERE, SOBBING WITH PAIN, AND SOMEBODY PULLED Luka's body off him. Broga said, "He's dead, now. You can get up."

Oto pushed himself up with his arms. His whole body ached and his nose pulsed a fiery throb. His doublet was drenched in blood. His hair dripped. The body sprawled beside him was slashed and ripped to shreds, even Luka's cheeks and nose and forehead. Still, Oto watched a moment, to make sure Luka was really dead.

"Not so big now," Oto said loudly, and locked his teeth against the pain, and wished he could kick the sprawled corpse beside him. "Help me rise."

CASEA LIFTED HER HEAD SUDDENLY AND SCREAMED. TIRZA, sitting on the bed, leapt up, and Mervaly rushed across the room and flung her arms around her. "What is it? What is it?"

"Something has happened. Something awful has happened." Casea clung tight to Mervaly, panting. Tirza leaned together with her, sobbing.

"Tell us—tell us—"

"I don't know. Something." Casea leaned her head against Mervaly's soft comfort; the fit had emptied her out. She never knew what it meant. She said, "We have to be together. Call Jeon. Find Jeon." She shut her eyes.

SO THEY WERE READY WHEN THE MEN CAME BACK, CARRYING Oto on a stretcher and Luka across a saddle. They stood in the gate yard, all four of them, all who were left, and they gathered together into one another's warmth and watched their brother come home.

Oto, on his stretcher, was babbling at the sight of them. A swelling bruise covered half his face. His nose was broken. "We caught the boar. He would go first, always—" Oto's bruised face worked into a grimace of pain. "I tried to help him and the beast turned on me—"

Broga stood beside him. "Thanks be to God we happened on them when we did."

Mervaly went up to the led horse, and laid her hand on Luka's hair. The voices of the brothers went on around her, like the chirping of birds.

"Luka died in my arms. I swear I will avenge him." Oto fell back on the litter, panting.

They laid Luka's body on the table in the great hall, where every King of Castle Ocean save Reymarro had lain. Tirza brought seawater in a basin and Casea held the towels and Jeon washed Luka's body, and Mervaly combed his hair.

The basin was heavy; the greenish water turned smoky with the blood. Tirza felt her hands shake. The body lay on the slab, white now, the wounds clean, and the wounds moved, and they whispered, Murder. Murder.

Casea whispered, "What do you think happened?"

Jeon stood back, dropping the last towel to the floor. "You saw their hurts. Luka's were all teeth. Oto's were all blows." He said, "And then there's Broga. How did he get there? They didn't even bother to cook up a good story."

Jeon was trembling. His face was rigid. Casea laid her hand on his arm, and he gave a violent shudder. Mervaly brought out a long green shirt, and they turned Luka faceup on the slab and dressed him. They drew the dark hose up over his legs and body, and Tirza cleaned his boots and put them on. They crossed his torn hands over his chest. All his blood was gone, and his face was white as the inside of a shell. One by one, they bent and kissed him.

Mervaly said, "Sleep, my brother. Sleep well."

Casea said, "Poor Luka, I shall miss you so much."

Tirza growled.

Jeon said nothing.

OTO WAS IN HIS CHAMBER, COVERED WITH BRUISES, UNABLE to walk. Out in the gate yard, in the gathering dark, the Imperials gathered in a clutch and Broga stood up before them and talked about the horrors of hell and the door of death, which once entered they could not come back from, and so they should consider their sins now, while they could still change their evil into goodness. Tirza stood just inside the wall, where she could listen to this, but her sisters went up into their tower.

JEON COULD NOT STAY IN THE CASTLE; HE KNEW THE BROTHERS would go after him next. He went down into Undercastle.

The beach was empty of people and the town was quiet. Even the dogs had stopped barking. The fishing boats were all still lying on the beach, their nets drooping. A woman with long brown hair stood to her ankles in the low surf, staring out over the water; she did not turn as he went by. The bakery's oven was shut down. He walked along the foot of the cliff, past the silent shops. Aken's butcher stall was empty but for the buzzing flies. At the weavery, the gate hung open and the women sat around the little yard talking, but as Jeon went up they fell still, their shoulders hunched, and pretended not to see him.

He came to the brewery. Here at least there were plenty of people. On the threshold he stood looking into the big drinking room, which was packed. As he came in, every eye turned toward him and seeing who he was then every eye looked away. He went up through the silent crowd to the tap at the front, where Amillee was sitting.

She said, "Is it true, then? He is dead?"

Jeon could not speak; he only nodded and passed his hand over his face. She turned away from him, tears glistening on her cheeks. "Oh," she said. "Oh. Then we are all lost, aren't we." She began to cry.

Jeon went out again, walking down toward the cypress. The women there might help him. There were far more women than men anyway. But the bench around the trunk of the tree was empty. He sat down there, pushing his feet out in front of him, and looked around.

Above the beach the lean-to roofs of the forge and the tannery poked up above the grass. No smoke rose from the forge. The stink from the tannery was stale. A dog came out of the forge and flopped down on the ground in front of it. At the little houses against the cliff a woman stood on the ledge, her broom in her hands but not moving. Two children dragged buckets of water up from the stream, stopping every few steps to rest and pant. Jeon heard someone call out, and another voice answered. Nobody came to him; nobody paid any heed to him.

He could not do what his brother did, his hero brother. He could not stir these people. The memory of Luka overwhelmed him again and he dug his fingernails into his palms and curled forward, forcing the grief back inside, raw, like something he could neither swallow nor throw up. He let himself hate these people who had failed him. He knew they were watching him. He could feel the pressure of their eyes. But they would not help him. He saw he would have to do this by himself. But first, he had to find some way to stay alive.

11

AT SUNDOWN AMILLEE WENT UP THE PATH TO THE TOP OF the cliff and along that way to the castle. She had a basket of bread, as her excuse to go in, and she took that down to the kitchen. The place seemed empty. A few soldiers sat around in the gate yard, but nobody challenged her. She went inside the big gate, where she had been only a few times before.

She saw none of the family. A guard dozed against the wall by the door into the great hall, and she slipped in past him, unseen.

The late sunlight washed in over the terrace, turning the air golden, the whole room full of shadows. The tide was out, the sea slumbering. On the table, Luka lay, his eyes shut and his hands on his chest. She went up to him, feeling as if she wended her way through a crowd, intending to kiss him, but she could not make herself touch him.

She went off to a corner, and sat down with her arms around her knees. She wept again, and wiped her eyes with her hair.

There was no hope for her anymore. She would never be happy again.

Nobody came into the room. The night deepened. The dark stirred and moved, and she thought she heard whispers, but it was only the wind. She grew cold; there were no fires.

She could not sleep for the cold, for the constant murmurings around her. In the middle of the night, then, she saw Luka rise up.

He sat up on the table, and swung his legs over the side. She stood, her heart pounding. He got to his feet and turned toward her—toward the wall. She stretched out her arms to him.

"Please. I love you. Take me with you."

He came up toward her, but not to her, to the wall. At the wall, he turned his head to her. Even in the dark she could see his face. The words came slowly from him, as if he were forgetting how to speak. He said, "Go home, Amillee. There is no place for you here." He went into the wall and was gone.

TIRZA LAY BUNDLED IN THE COVERS IN THE BIG BED, BUT Mervaly stood in the center of the room; she had not slept, she had not moved, all the night through. Her grief had swallowed up everything else and she had not sensed the time passing, so when the window paled she was surprised.

Casea came in, and walking up to Mervaly put an arm around her. "Luka—" Her voice stopped abruptly. She swallowed. "Is gone."

Mervaly heaved up a sigh. "Peace to him. Where is Jeon?"

"I don't know. Wandering around somewhere. Poor Jeon." Casea turned toward the bed where Tirza lay, cradled in blankets. "Mervaly, you should sleep."

"Don't tell me what I have to do."

Some edge in her voice caught Casea's attention, and she stepped away to look straight at her sister, wide-eyed. The dawn light through the window shone on half her face. Casea said, "What do you mean?"

"Just leave me alone, Casea."

"What do you intend to do?"

"I told you, leave that to me."

Casea said, "You said to leave it to Luka, remember? When will you learn?"

Mervaly frowned at her. "What have you learned? What would you do? Papa gone, Mama, now Luka—"

"So you would make it worse?"

"Before they kill us all!" Mervaly cocked up her arm. "I won't let you get in my way, Casea!"

Tirza had wakened, and now came in between them. With one hand she caught Mervaly by the arm, and with the other pushed Casea away. Mervaly took a step backward, suddenly cool. Tears spilled from her. She put her arms out and drew her little sister into her embrace, and in a moment Casea was throwing her arms around them both. They stood and wept, all together, Tirza clinging tight to Mervaly, and Casea whispering, "It's all right. It's all right."

AT MIDDAY DAWD LED HIS PATROL FINALLY INTO CASTLE OCEAN. His men were all worn to shades of themselves and he let them settle into the gate yard and went to find them food. The kitchen steps led him down into the long room. It was almost empty, all of the servants gone, no cooks, no scullions, only a few soldiers taking bread from a tray on the table. He took the rest of the bread back up the stair to the gate yard to feed his men.

He had half-expected someone to come down to meet him before this, but no one did. With his men camped, he went up the stairs from the gate yard, through the round room beyond, and into the great hall, before he even saw an officer.

This was Broga Erdhartsson, sitting on the carved stone seat behind the table. Startled, Dawd almost stopped in his tracks. Luka should have been there, oversprawling the seat as always. The sergeant was already edgy; he knew something was going wrong. Before the Imperial Prince he bowed.

"Glory to the Empire."

"Glory." Broga sat perched on the rim of the seat. The chessboard lay on the table before him. He said, "You were gone longer than I expected. What took you so long? Did you find trouble?"

Tired, and sick with this, Dawd fumbled over the words. "My lord, usually we only have to go half as far—we meet a patrol from the new fort, exchange messages, and then we come back." He drew in a deep breath. "This time no one met us. So we kept going east, three more days. I kept thinking—any moment—we would meet them—"

Broga snapped, "Get to the point."

But his head rose, looking toward the door. Dawd glanced around, and stepped aside. Oto was coming in, walking on his own feet, but supported by a man on either side. He was wrapped in blankets, and his face looked like a rack of meat.

The coiling worry in Dawd's belly turned into a full churn. He looked from one to the other, wondering where Luka was.

Oto hobbled up around the end of the table to the high seat; as he came Broga held his ground a moment and Oto's grim face writhed. Broga rose and moved aside and Oto sat down on the high seat.

"God's breath. Bring me cushions. What a hard place to sit."

Dawd gave a little shiver. He knew at once that Luka was dead. The Archduke's eyes turned toward him. "You've come back, at last."

Broga said, "Yes. Now. What's going on at the new fort? Why were you gone so long?"

"My lord, it's destroyed. The fort. It's been thrown down. There's nobody left."

Oto blinked at him; Broga's jaw dropped. Dawd looked from one to the other. "There were . . . remains. Burnt. The whole place—" His gorge rose again, as he remembered the stale reek of blood. The flocks of vultures sitting on the overhanging limbs of the trees on the cliff.

Broga said, "Burnt? What could have happened? How many men were there?" He turned to Oto.

The elder brother said, "We had over fifty men there." He put one hand on the table, his eyes blinking rapidly. "That was most of our army. They had the fort to protect them." He shook his head. "It can't be so. There isn't a force anywhere around here big enough to threaten an Imperial outpost."

He glared at Dawd as if he had done it all himself. "What happened? Who attacked them?" His voice rose. "There must be some indication! What brought them? Ships? Overland?"

Dawd licked his lips. "My lord, all I know is what I've told you. We buried those we found."

"Go." Oto thrust a hand at him. "Go; you're dismissed." Dawd went hastily out; at the door, looking back, he saw the brothers staring at each other, silent.

In the antechamber, he came on the corporal Marwin, at the foot of the stairs up to the new tower.

"What has happened?"

Marwin spread his lips in a smirk. "You're back. You missed the excitement. Come on; I'm supposed to be standing guard up here."

Dawd followed him up the steps. "What excitement?"

"Well, the boys went on a pig hunt, and poor Master Luka got himself killed."

Dawd had expected something like this. They had reached the landing; he turned, frowning. "He was killed by a pig?"

Marwin shrugged, his eyes narrow, the grin still on his face. "He was killed, anyway." Marwin leaned up against the wall beside the door there, all at ease, his pike beside him.

Dawd muttered under his breath. "What happened?"

"They brought him back ripped up and dead, and now King Oto sits on the high seat." Marwin settled his back against the wall by the door. "Never get in the way of golden blood and its ambitions, right?"

Dawd was silent. His mind went to the Princess Casea and a surge of guilty fear washed over him. She would hate him now. He swayed, turning away from Marwin, his insides tortured. "He was a good man."

"He was in the way," Marwin said. "Oto was too clever for him."

Dawd held himself still, fighting the urge to hit Marwin in the face. He swallowed. These were bad thoughts. Marwin was right; the golden blood was supreme. They were soldiers of the Empire. It wasn't up to him to decide who was right. He looked beyond Marwin, trying to gather himself, into the little lamplit room beyond.

"What's that?"

"The Lord Broga's chapel. Someone keeps going in and trashing it. Probably the boy, what's his name, Joon."

"Jeon," Dawd said, and went into the room.

He signed himself as he went in, because it was a chapel and there on the wall the emblem hung, the inverted sword, gleaming in the light of lamps. A massy black rock half-filled the room. "What's this?"

"It's supposed to be an altar." Marwin spoke from the doorway, his voice grating. "Come out of there. It's . . ."

"It doesn't look like an altar to me." The rock was an uneven lump. At either end a lamp rested precariously on the rough surface.

"The boy keeps messing it up. Nobody knows how. It's getting bigger. That's why I'm on guard, to see what's happening. Come on; let's get out of there."

Dawd went out again to the landing. Marwin was watching him, the smirk gone. "You went to the new fort? Look—" He leaned closer, his voice dropping to a murmur. "Get us transferred up there. This is . . . strange. Kind of."

"I can't," Dawd said. Perversely this made him glad. "There's nothing left up there. Something came in and wiped it out."

Marwin, for once, was silent; his lips parted. In the room behind them there was a sudden crash.

Dawd swung around, looking in through the door; one of the lamps had fallen from the altar and broken on the floor. He turned and went on down the stairs, eager to get out of the castle.

THERE WERE NO SERVANTS ANYWHERE. ONCE AGAIN THEY would have to use soldiers to do the work of the castle. Oto sent the men who had brought him down to the hall to fetch a mass of pillows and blankets, and when they had stacked them on the high seat hunched himself carefully down among them. His hurts were fading. He could walk better now. He thought he could sit upright for the whole afternoon. He gave Broga a hard look, in the place beside him; Broga was glowering off toward the terrace.

"We have to build a wall there," Broga said. "I thought that had been done."

"I am King here, I will decide what to do," Oto said. He remembered ordering the wall built and he even remembered seeing it there, but certainly it was gone now. He would have to straighten that out. But not now. Now this other thing.

"You must go to the new fort," he said. "We've been attacked. We need to take back that ground."

"We haven't got the men to hold it," Broga said between his teeth. Still not looking at Oto. "If fifty men couldn't hold it the first time."

"I am King," Oto said, "and you will—"

"My lords," said a new voice. "Glory to the Empire."

Oto veered around, startled. Prince Jeon came across the room toward them, bowed to him, bowed to Broga.

"Yes," Oto said. "What do you want?"

"I have heard about the . . . problem up the coast. I will go up to scout that for you. I know that area well."

Surprised, Oto stared at him. This sudden humility was of course utterly false. But perhaps his brother's fate had taught Jeon something. And Prince Jeon could be useful. The boy met Oto's gaze, patient.

Broga said, harsh, "Do you actually trust him?"

Oto smiled at that. Prince Jeon's eyes flicked sideways toward Broga and back to Oto on the high seat. "My lord," he said, "I shall go if you will or not; this is my kingdom."

"Well, then," Oto said. "I see no reason to stop you." He glanced at his brother beside him, cocked up on the edge of his seat, as if he would leap on Jeon. That might yet come. Oto smiled at both of them. "Go on, then."

"Glory to the Empire," said Jeon.

THE GROOM WAS BRINGING THE BIG GREY HORSE DOWN FROM the stable on the cliff. Tirza held on to Jeon's arm; she did not want him to leave. She shook her head at her brother, who kissed her and pushed her gently away.

"Let me go, Tirza. I have to think. And we should find out what happened up there, shouldn't we? Something went on up there, bad or good." He gathered up his reins, and leading the horse started off along the beach; the tide was out and the way open below the castle. She went along beside him, frowning.

He turned again to her, purposeful. "Spy on them. You can do this. Nobody heeds you. Find out what they know."

She gave him a sharp look from beneath her brows; it was true nobody noticed her, certainly not the Erdhartsson brothers. He said, "Spy on the soldiers then."

She took the bridle while he swung up into his saddle. Her face tipped toward his, her eyebrows knotted, and she said a stream of gibberish.

He said, "Keep watch on Mervaly and Casea." His throat tightened. Fewer of them all the time. Bending down, he put his arm around her and kissed her again. She ran beside his horse up the beach as far as the rocks below the castle. The tide was out, and he could skirt the foot of the castle without going up onto the cliff. When he looked back once, she was still standing there, watching him.

MERVALY STOOD IN THE CENTER OF THE ROOM, WEARING A LONG green gown; with the sunlit window behind her she seemed enveloped in a mist from the sea. With the constant fluttering and twittering of the birds the whole room was alive, moving. Her hair shone, red as sundown. Oto bowed.

"My lady princess. You have called me to you, and I am here."

She had a little speckled bird in her hands, and she turned and laid it on a shelf. Facing him again, unsmiling, she said, "I have given thought"—her gaze came straight to him, and locked—"to what you proposed, before. Now that my brother is . . . gone, that may be the best way, for us to marry."

A thrill ran through him; he had to keep his hands clenched together before him to keep from leaping at her and seizing her.

He said, "Princess, I share your grief for the young King, lost in the very prime of his youth." In spite of himself, his voice trembled. He moved a step closer. "Yet I find you noble, in your long sight."

She put out her hand to him. "Then we are agreed?"

"We must act swiftly," he said. "There will be . . . resistance." He took her hand in his.

Her fingers were warm and soft. He drew her closer to him; they were of a height. In her pale green eyes he could read nothing, no welcome and no warning, only distance. Then she kissed him.

The new tower, where the brothers lived, had no passageways through the walls. Tirza waited until some toiling soldiers, cursing under their breath, went up the stair with trays of food, and followed them quietly in. She stayed behind the wider of them and nobody noticed her. Oto and Broga sat at table, and the soldiers put down the trays before them and began to pour wine and cut meat and bread. She had never seen anyone eat so fussily, even the nuns at the convent in Santomalo. She slid into the dark side of the room and curled up in the corner behind a clothes chest.

"What do you think happened at the new fort?" Around the side of the chest she could just see the table. Broga was watching the servant put cheese on his bread. He was the one who had spoken.

"This whole coast crawls with pirates. Wait until the fleet arrives; we'll drive them off the seas."

Broga lifted his head and stared across the table. "Pirates? There were fifty soldiers in that fort."

"Obviously not good ones."

"They had some help," Broga said. "I think we did not kill Luka quickly enough."

Tirza jerked, her elbows pressing tight to her sides. She drew back deeper into the corner, until she could not see them, only hear. Broga's deep, raspy voice went on, "I think these people here did that, and we must find out who and punish this, or our power here is nothing. You shouldn't have let the boy go."

They had killed Luka. She squeezed her eyes shut, sick to her stomach, thinking how she might fling herself out there, seize a knife, and murder them.

Oto said, "You dream."

"They are all foul," Broga said. "But they're afraid of us now. The boy particularly: why do you think he was so willing to leave? And we have the upper hand and should use it. That's what it means, her begging you to marry her. Now we can redeem all that's gone before."

Oto's voice was keen. "I will manage this."

Broga spoke through his teeth. "We have limited time. Once Uncle decides we have failed he will move speedily to replace us. Father would have—"

"Father me no father! I rule now." A chair creaked. "Who has brought us this far? And who lost everything to them, in some ridiculous fight on the beach, which now I have at great cost to me regained? Do as I bid you."

Broga rasped, "I killed him. I avenged myself. Without me you would still be under his thumb."

"I was never under his thumb. You misunderstand everything." Oto fired out each word like a stone from a slingshot. Something hard hit the table; she heard the cups rattle. "When the fleet comes, we will wipe away the pirates, we will crush the local people into obedience, and Uncle will be very pleased."

"What about the boy?"

"He is nothing. We will dispose of him when it proves convenient."

"Then you are going to marry her."

"Oh, yes. Uncle will admire the legality. But I will be King here."

At that Tirza leapt up and shouted, "You will not! Never!"

The brothers wheeled around in their places; Broga's jaw dropped open, and Oto shouted, "Catch her!" Tirza bolted for the door.

From the hall a tall soldier blocked her way. She knew him: the big sergeant who was always looking at Casea. Tirza went toward one side and when he leaned to stop her she bounded through the space he made. His hand closed on her hair. She screeched, and he wrapped an arm around her and lifted her back into the room.

Broga sprang toward her, his jaw clenched, as if he would eat her. "Where was she? She heard everything we said. What did we say?"

Oto was still sitting. In his fist a knife, upright. "Enough. Not that she could tell anybody, but enough."

"Kill her." Broga held out his hand for a weapon. Tirza, clutched in the sergeant's grasp, let out a howl of rage and fear: Luka's face swam into her mind, and she forgot to be afraid.

"Murderers! Murderers!"

Oto rose, and pushed his brother's arm aside. "Not that way. They might find out. I don't want anything to interfere with the wedding." For an instant he looked into Tirza's eyes. His face was cold with calculation. His gaze lifted to the man holding her fast. "Throw her into the sea."

DAWD HAD THE GOBLIN GIRL BY THE ARM, THE FURIOUS COIL of her body straining against him, and he gripped her tight, pulling her up a little off the floor. His heart was thundering. He went quickly down the stair. Marwin started after him, and he turned and said, "Go back and stand guard. Remember your duty." The corporal went on back up to the landing and the door.

The goblin girl made no sound, all the while wresting and yanking at his grip on her. Finally he tucked her under his arm, pinning her elbows to her sides. At the foot of the stair, in the antechamber, two more soldiers were watching him, staring curiously at the girl; he could do nothing while they watched. He went on to the door into the great hall.

The bold light of the sun flooded it. All around were people making ready for the wedding. He turned back into the antechamber and beckoned over the two soldiers.

"You. Go in there; spur them. They're slacking." To the other, Dawd said, "Take my place upstairs with the Lord Oto while I attend to this."

One went in the hall, the other up the stairs. The Goblin whined, and twisted in his grip. He took her to the door into the hall again, and set her down.

"Run," he said. "I know you can find the way. Run."

Her eyes went round as stars, deep blue. She fled. He put his hand against the wall, leaning his weight against it, sick to his stomach, as if the floor under him tipped.

He did not want to face Oto, and as soon as Dawd could get away he went down into the town. The sun stood in the peak of the sky and a long line of women waited at the baker's, each carrying a dish in her hands to cook in the baker's oven. Dawd veered over toward the butcher's stall, where the man had a tray of meat pies, still steaming. The butcher, the size and shape of a keg, was in the back of the stall, hacking up a headless carcass hanging by its hind feet from the ceiling. When he saw Dawd he came spryly to the front. Most of the soldiers simply took what they wanted, but Dawd always paid, and the shopkeepers all knew him and liked him.

"That one," Dawd said, and pointed.

The butcher picked up the pie neatly with his tongs and wrapped it in a square of cloth. Dawd handed him a full Imperial. The butcher fumbled under the counter for his sack and spilled the contents onto the counter—several coins, some whole and some cut into quarters and halves—and after a moment took a half and a quarter and gave them to Dawd.

"Bring me back the napkin," the butcher said, and went back to his meat chopping. Dawd carried the pie off, taking a big bite as he did.

He went on through the town, stopped again to get a drink of ale at the brewery, but he could not sit. He took the cup and went along the beach, past the lapping edge of the quiet water.

The sea had infected him, he thought. He could not rest anymore. Everything orderly in his life was overturned. He was a soldier. He did as his officers told him. Now he hated his officers and he could not make himself obey them.

Far down the beach, well past the edge of the town, he saw a tall white figure walking, and all his body tingled. He went after her, long-striding to catch up with her, as he went making up some excuse to talk to her.

She stopped, and turned back toward him; she had seen him coming. She wore a common apron, the hem of her dress damp and bedraggled; her hair was knotted up on her head and her feet were bare, but she was a Princess born, and royal to her bones. He stopped and bowed to her.

He said, "My lady, you should not be out here alone, should you?"

She smiled at him, her eyes steady. "I am not alone now, though. What has brought you to me?"

"I have repaid," he said. This came out without thinking, and he put his hand over his mouth.

She said, "Tell me what you mean."

"I-I— Your sister. When you saved me." He licked his lips, coming suddenly to this and now uncertain. He blurted out, "I did not kill her."

She put out her hand and gripped the front of his doublet, her voice suddenly harsh. "What do you mean, soldier?"

"I let her go. They told me to—not, though. Only throw her into the sea, and I let her go." He clutched her hand; blinking his eyes, he felt blind, all he knew gone into a mist. "A helpless, invalid child. I could not."

He could not tell her that he knew the brothers had murdered Luka. He wanted to protect her, to encastle her in himself. Instead she took his hand and led him forward.

At her touch, his eyes cleared: before him the long bay lay like a glittering blue sheet. His heart ached. "I am a soldier. I obey orders. How can I—how can I—"

She led him down into the gentle breakers. Her voice was calm. "The sea washes everything away. All the needless things." He stood to his knees in the soft and endless sea, holding her hand, the sand crumbling beneath his feet.

 *12*

Tirza sat on the bed, and watched Mervaly put on her mother's jewels, the necklaces of coral and pearl, the earrings of chrysoprase like drops of green water, rings of serpentine, nacre carnelian. She said, again, "You mustn't do this." She gripped the bedclothes in both fists. "Why won't you understand me?"

Mervaly said, "I know you're upset, Tirza. Don't listen to Casea. She's a fool, Tirza. I know what I'm doing and she does not. Stay close by me, where I can protect you."

Tirza grunted. Mervaly could not protect her. But for that soldier she would be dead now and Mervaly likely would not even know. Tirza banged up and down on the bed. "They killed Luka. How can you do this? Please. Please." She sounded in her own ears like a twittering bird.

Her sister ignored her, part of a lifetime of ignoring her. Mervaly lifted the skirts of the pale green gown, so that the many layers of the skirts fluttered. On the windowsill, the seagull abruptly spread its wings and sailed off into the air. Mervaly moved around

the room, doing nothing except touching the furniture and looking out the window. The birds followed her with their small, bright
eyes. One of the swallows flew down suddenly and perched on her
shoulder.

"No, not now," Mervaly said, and touched it, and the bird flew
back to its nest. Tirza got up and went to her, and coiled her arm
through Mervaly's and leaned on her.

"Why can't you understand me? Change your mind!" That
came out all squeaks and whistles. She squeezed her eyes shut,
clogged with terror and sorrow.

Mervaly thrust her off. "Stop, Tirza! This must be done. Go
away, then, if you're just going to be cross. I don't like you
when you're cross." She did not smile. She had not smiled or
laughed since she told them she would marry Oto Erdhartsson.
She stood before the door a moment, and her hands moved
along her body, as if she encased herself in unseeable armor.
Then she left, to go down to the terrace to be married, but Tirza
went into the wall.

OTO STOOD BEFORE THE HIGH SEAT. HIS FACE STILL ACHED,
but he was walking well now, and he would not put this off.
A storm was coming in from the sea and so the barrier was up,
all the lamps and torches lit. The hall seemed bigger with so few
people in it—his brother, the priest, a dozen soldiers. None of
her family. That would not matter. This time, there would be no
dancing.

He saw no way he could not triumph now. He watched the
door across the way; she would come through that door, and bring
him a crown, a kingdom. Poor as it was, still a place to start from.
The Great Emperor had begun with less. Oto did not glance
toward Broga, beside him, not wanting to share this. Then the doors
opened.

At the sight of her he caught his breath. Jewels flickered at her throat, on her breast, her plump white arms and hands. Her dress floated around her, and her red hair was like a torch. His eye caught on the way she walked, every step precise, how she held her head, as if she wore a crown. For the first time, he thought how she might appear at court, among those languid ladies, and a warm, expectant pleasure filled him.

She knelt before him, and he took her hands. The priest came forward and spoke, and she and Oto recited their responses. All the while her eyes were raised to his, her hands tightened on his. He lifted her up to her feet, and bent to kiss her. At the moment their lips met he thought she glanced away, but then she shut her eyes, and when he straightened and looked back nobody was there except Broga.

MERVALY TOOK THE JEWELS FROM HER HAIR, AND LAID THEM on the table; she moved forward, toward the man sitting on the bed before her. She had sent away the others. She needed no one but him for this. She stood before him, just out of his reach, and bent and took off her shoes.

He watched, intent. His face was livid green with the fading bruises; it was like marrying a corpse. She lifted her hands to her hair, and let free the bindings, and shook her head so that her hair tumbled around her.

His fingers curled. She cocked an eyebrow at him, and put her hands on her breasts, lifting them, her thumbs on the nipples beneath the thin cloth. He swallowed.

She moved her hands behind her, unclasped the top of the gown, and began to peel it away from her. As she did, she began to sway, slowly, back and forth. She let the dress hang a moment on her breasts, as the cloth slid like water down her sides, and on the bed he started up. She shut her eyes. With her thumbs she twitched the cloth away, baring her whole body to him, and he was on her, dragging her to the bed, bearing her down beneath him.

 *13*

After he left Castle Ocean behind, Jeon let the horse carry him at its own pace up the beach. More than anything, he needed to get out of the thorny, overheated atmosphere in the castle so he could think.

He knew Oto and Broga had murdered his brother. Everything in him wanted to leap on them, kill them, too, even if it meant— as it likely did—that he would die. That was honorable, to die for justice, and Luka's wounds wept for justice. If Jeon stayed in the castle, he thought, the chance would come for his revenge, the opportunity overwhelming, and he would take it.

Part of him wanted to take it, to rise up with a sword like a flame and destroy them, whatever the outcome. Another part of him said, Wait.

Because he thought, now, there was something else. He thought now maybe he should be the King of Castle Ocean.

Which meant he should not die, even to avenge his brother.

He rode all the rest of the day along the shore, along the margin of the surf. The late sun blazed across the sea, but the sea-birds were flocking by him, moving steadily inland, and on the horizon dark clouds piled up. The wind rose. At night he lay down in a fisherman's hut made of driftwood and slept on the sand.

In the morning the storm was coming toward him, trailing its veils of rain, the lifting sea dark green. The heavy waves smashed and swept along the beach. He went along into the east; since he had left the castle, he had seen no other human being, and he did not expect to see one this day, either.

The storm roared onshore, pelting rain, and wind like fists. Swallowed up in the enormous tumult, he bundled himself in his cloak, the world all gone. This felt good to him, even the cold. He remembered all he could of Luka, every moment. What Luka would want him to do. In the afternoon the rain slackened and the bright sun shone, which he took for a sign.

He slept under the overhang of the cliff, shivering all night. The next day blazed bright and clean, and around noon he rode into a little cove where the tide was well out and found several people digging in the wet sand.

He waited on the beach and, when they came in, traded them bread and cheese for their clams. Being with other people now made him feel prickly, close, invaded. They talked readily enough about themselves; they came from a village inland, where the harvest would be lean this year, and so they were digging up clams.

He said, "Have you had any trouble with wild pigs?"

They only blinked at him.

"What about pirates? I have heard," he said, to jog them, "some place of soldiers was attacked, up the coast."

At that they began to nod and talk. They had heard something of that. Pirates it was, then. They'd thought so. "Yes, remember, I said so from the first. Brave ones, too, going after all those soldiers." The soldiers, it seemed, had thieved from the local people, raiding sometimes even as far as their village, and so the local people were on the side of the pirates.

Night came. He steamed his clams in seaweed with theirs and ate, and they fell quickly asleep. The wind laid the fire over. He sat staring into it, and Luka's face swam up into his memory again, vivid, laughing. He wept into his hands, hollow with loss.

Beyond the reach of the firelight the ceaseless wave rose up out of the sea and thumped onto the beach. His heart felt like a stone, dragging him down. Revenge. And yet that way they might lose everything. What use, if they all died? The wind blew the flames flat; the ocean roared, the voice of the world, too large for any human ear to hear.

He rode two more days, and in the next afternoon he came on the place where the new fort had been.

The sand had blown over a lot of the wreckage. There had been stones in rows, and some wooden walls above that, burnt down to the ground. The patrol that found the dead had done their work: on the higher ground lay mounds of sand in neat rows, each grave marked with rocks at head and foot. He counted fourteen. That did not seem enough.

The crabs and gulls and wolves had done their work also. Several of the graves were torn open, and bones spilled into the sand.

The pirates would have carried off anybody left alive, he thought. Maybe, therefore, they would have taken care to leave many alive. Dead bodies made bad slaves.

He went on past this graveyard. The fort had grown larger since he had last seen it; there had been three courses of stones at least, a square wall higher than his head. Now flat and blackened with fire. Burnt driftwood cluttered the beach. Higher, above the tide line, he left his horse and walked around kicking at the litter. He turned over helmets, scraps of black-and-white-striped fabric, more bones. The head of a pike. Dimples in the sand might have been footprints. He found, in the kelp strands, an odd little jewel, uncut and unpolished, a clear green stone.

Out of these pieces he could make no picture of what had happened. With the height of the cliff here nothing could have attacked from the land; whoever did this had to have come from the sea. He was exhausted now, but he could not bear to stay in this place, and he rode on.

HE STOPPED, SOME WAY DOWN THE BEACH, WHERE THE CLIFF sagged down and grass grew on an old landslide. Turning out his weary horse to crop this graze, he found a place out of the wind and lay down. Sleep overtook him. He woke deep in the night, caught the horse, and rode on toward the dawn edge of the world, chewing on the last of his bread. The seam of the world began to lighten, and far ahead, against the red smear of the sunrise, he saw the steep headland where to keep on eastward he would have to climb up the cliff and go inland.

With the sun halfway to the top of the sky, he rode up on two skiffs drawn onto the sand. The fishermen camped in the shelter of the cliff welcomed him for his red hair, glad to give him shelter and food. They had a brew with them, which made his head spin. When he asked about the new fort, they laughed, cheerful.

"Ah! We did that!"

Jeon sat straight up, startled. The man before him, one of a blurry cloud of faces, beamed at him. "We did it! The soldiers— they beat up Benes, and grabbed two of the women—so we prayed, and God sent us help."

Jeon grunted at him, almost relieved. "God didn't send any help anywhere else?"

They all shrugged, their eyes elsewhere. The jug came around again, fiery and sweet. He only took a sip of it, warned of the effects.

In the morning, when he saddled his horse, a young man came swiftly up to him.

"East," he said. "They're bad people, too." He thrust bread and a little jug into Jeon's hand, turned on his heel, and walked away.

So HE WENT ON TOWARD THE HEADLAND LOOMING IN THE DIStance. Fresh from the rain, streams came down into the sea, carving trenches through the sand, and the horse balked at crossing and Jeon got off and led it by the bridle. Once he had to ride far inland to find a place to cross. He began thinking he could turn back soon, that he had seen enough. Thinking so carried his mind, again, to Castle Ocean, where Oto and Broga would be waiting to kill him. He thought of Luka's shredded body and his gut tightened.

Maybe he was just a coward. Maybe he was making all this up, an excuse not to do what he should do.

Then on the beach ahead of him something was sticking up out of the sand, a raw, blackened arc.

This was the broken keel of a ship, half-burnt, lodged in the tidal wrack. He looked all around, seeing no sign of people, and then his memory jogged and he recognized this place. A narrow little stream came down through a gorge here, with a grassland just above the beach. He thought there should have been huts on the grassland, but there weren't. Inland, though, he knew there was a tree. This was where he had found Tirza, with the people getting ready to burn her.

He rode up toward the little meadow, the dead grass laid over like a brown blanket. Now he could make out shapes under the grass, a sunken fire pit, and an overgrown heap of something. His hair stood on end. He thought, if he kicked that open, it would be all burnt. He would find bones.

"Hey!"

He jumped, his hand flying toward the dagger in his belt. On the bank of the little stream a naked man was watching him.

"Hey! Leave them alone!"

"Leave who alone?" he said, and cleared his throat. The man was thin as a fishbone, his hair and beard ragged, his body bruised and scratched.

"Them that was there." The man began to sway back and forth on his widespread horny feet. "They was there, once. Leave 'em alone."

"What happened?"

"The devil came out of the sea." The man swaying, his eyes wild. "I saw it. I saw it."

"The devil." Jeon went closer. "What did he look like?"

"The devil. The terrible serpent, red as the fires of hell." The man moaned.

Jeon stood beside him, put a hand on him, and the man jumped. Jeon said, "I have some bread. Tell me what you saw. One man? Two? A dozen? What kind of ship?"

"The devil! I'm telling you—no man—give me something to eat."

"How did you escape?"

"I hid. Feed me."

Jeon gave him bread, but he got no more sense out of him. The old man curled up in the sand and slept, twitched and cried in his sleep. Jeon went up the little stream and came to the tree where Tirza had tried to hide.

He sat there at the foot of the tree, trying to piece this together. Somehow this all fit together, these attacks: the burning of Santomalo, the new fort, this place. Something tugged at his memory, whatever had happened when he and Tirza were shipwrecked. He wondered if those ships had burnt.

He thought, In all these places, Tirza was there, before they were attacked. The other places he had passed, other people, when Tirza had not been there they had seen nothing.

He thought then of the little green stone he had found and took it from his wallet. It felt warm in his hand. He turned it over in his fingers. The dark was coming. He should build a fire, eat something. His mind roiled, something struggling to form into an idea. All he could remember of the shipwreck was the monstrous seas, the horrible flashes of light.

That had not been pirates. Maybe it hadn't even been a storm.

Tirza knew. He remembered how upset she had become when he spoke of it. He had taken for granted then that it was just that she had suffered from it.

Now he saw something else in her distress. As if he was getting something wrong.

He rolled the green stone in his fingers. Now, at last, he had to decide what to do. He could ride away forever, keep on into the east, go on and on until his red hair made no difference. Or he could go back and try to make himself King.

He could not think how to do that. He had none of Luka's Kingcraft; he had no followers. He saw a dozen ways he could fail and die.

After a moment, he put the green stone back into his wallet and looked up into the branches above him, where Tirza had sheltered. He had saved her, then, when no one thought he could. Without thinking, he stood up, dusted his hands off, and rode back down the stream to the beach. There was no sign of the madman. He turned west, back toward Castle Ocean.

14

"No," Oto said. "You are Queen, a member of the Imperial Family now, and you must display yourself with the proper decorum. Obey me."

Mervaly glared at him, her hands clenched at her sides. The soldiers who had brought her and Oto's breakfast retreated to the door, their eyes downcast. She said, "My lord, I only want to care for my birds. I mean no disobedience." What she wanted was to pick up the ewer and smash it over his head.

He said, "And you must stop speaking up in council."

"Ah," she said, and paced two steps toward him, her back tingling. "That I will not do. I am Queen, as you said. I will have my rule here."

"You'll do as I say!"

"I'll do as I see proper," she said, and he lifted his hand and slapped her.

"Respect me!"

Her head had rocked under the blow; she straightened, coiled, and cocked her arm to hit him back, but then Broga came in. Outnumbered, she backed away, cooling down.

The King's brother stalked across the room, his coat disarranged, his hands dusty. His habitual look of scorn was on his face. He said, "The patrol we sent off yesterday to the south? Has not come back. That's two more men gone."

Oto sat down on the chair at the table. "Are they yet overdue? We may wait another day."

Mervaly stood back by the window, watching them. Broga, she knew, was more dangerous than Oto.

Broga said, "When will you waken to this? We are bleeding away our strength." His gaze shifted toward her. "They"—he laid weight on the word, staring at her—"are attacking us, and you, you fool, do nothing."

Oto glanced over his shoulder at her. His fingers tapped on his knee. "When the fleet comes we will have the men necessary to secure all the country. Until then—"

"The fleet!" Broga threw his hands up. "You talk of the fleet as if it were on our doorstep—it's been overdue for months." He cast a wicked glance at Mervaly. "And you should not speak of such things in front of spies."

"My lord, you overreach," Oto said. He leaned back and took her by the arm. She resisted the pull, but he wrenched her up by his side, and then clutching her hand, he brought her fingers to his cheek. "My beloved Queen is not a spy." He licked her wrist and she wrenched violently out of his grip.

Broga paced across the room. "They are all spies. They are plotting against us, all of them—the townspeople—all. We should never have let the boy go." He turned, brisk. "We should go after him, drag him back, find out what he knows."

"My lord," Mervaly said, "my brother knows nothing. There is nothing to know. I pray you, leave him alone."

Oto got her arm into his grasp again, and dragged her against him, groping at her with his fingers. But all his attention was turned on Broga. "I am the King, and will dispose. You will obey me, and my Queen—" He crushed her against him, smirking at Broga.

Broga stared at them a moment, his nostrils flared and his face harsh with contempt. Finally he said, "Just keep her away from the rest of them. We have to find out what's going on. Make her tell you."

Oto said, "Go. You must have important work to do."

Rigid with bad temper, Broga was silent a moment longer, and then he turned on his heel and walked out. Mervaly slipped from Oto's loosening grasp and went to the window. Slumping down in the chair, Oto seemed to shrink into himself, relieved.

He turned to his breakfast. "Mind me. You heard how he regards your brother."

She said, "Surely an honorable man of the most noble blood would not harm a child?"

Oto pulled a bright, false smile over his face. "Not if I restrain him." He gestured toward the table. "Be sweet, Wife. Come and cut my bread."

Truce, then. Time to think. She went to the table, and attended him.

GRUNTING, SOAKED WITH SWEAT, DAWD HEAVED HIS END OF the hod up the last step onto the landing. Marwin said, breathless, "Help me." Dawd went down and together they lifted the whole stack of stones up onto the flat. He straightened and wiped his face on the tail of his shirt. He had left his doublet and breastplate off when he got up that morning, knowing what was to come. With so many soldiers gone and no servants, they had to do this kind of work all day, and the uniform got in the way.

Marwin slacked against the wall. Stone dust smeared his face. He said, "Are we supposed to make this without mortar?"

Dawd looked around at the doorway they were supposed to seal. The square-cut stones they had just brought up were flat and even, and he thought they could set the stones dry. After that, maybe, plaster the whole thing. He faced front again, hearing feet on the stair from the top room of the tower, and Broga came rapidly down into sight, a guard behind him.

"Where is the priest? I'll drown him in his own holy water." The Archduke stopped on the landing, looking around. "Good; that seems like enough stone. Keep on." He went on down the steps, the guard following after.

"Now the priest is gone," Dawd said. He chose a stone and laid it into the doorway. He tried to keep from looking into the room beyond. It was dark, anyway, and the great lump of black stone filled it almost entirely. He stacked the stones carefully, lapping the chinks, like a puzzle he could put together. Bending over the hod, he sorted through the remaining stones for ones that fit best into the next row. "It's bad when we can't even hold the priests."

"Likely he's down in Undercastle," Marwin said. "How many men do we have left?"

Dawd had just counted; he said, "Nineteen."

Marwin jerked a little, all over. "Well, well."

"I want to bring them all in to camp in the gate yard. Inside the wall. No more patrols," Dawd said. "Double guards at night."

"Keep somebody out?" Marwin said. "Or keep them in?"

Dawd said, "You'd better get busy, or—"

Marwin knelt down and began laying stone. More steps sounded on the stair, this time Oto, who swung down onto the landing with several soldiers around him, all in their uniforms, their helmets on their heads, their pikes in their hands. Dawd and

Marwin snapped up straight, at attention, saluting. The King looked them quickly over, and then at the chapel door.

"What is this, now?" He wore a long, fine cloak with a fur hem, which he swung up over his arm. He laughed. "Well. The works of men." He went away down the stair with his guards.

Marwin stood back, dusting his hands off. "Tomorrow he'll order it all torn down again."

Dawd slid a stone into place in the doorway. He agreed with Marwin but did not say so. Dawd understood why the men were deserting. Although likely Marwin was right and they had just drifted down into the town. It was a long march home. Dawd's eyes stung with sweat and he swiped his forearm over his face and for a moment could not see. Then more footsteps pattered on the stair above.

This was the Queen, Mervaly, in slippers, holding up the hem of her gown with one hand. Her long, curly hair floated behind her. The two Imperials straightened, at attention, but she went softly by them without speaking. Dawd watched her go, faced the wall again, and pushed the last flat stone into place.

"IT'S ALL RITUAL," THE LITTLE EASTERNER SAID. "THE HEART of the Empire is ritual, and I do the rituals. Did." He nodded, or his head bobbed uncontrollably; Amillee could not tell. He was very drunk. She had only seen him before in his long pale robe and she had not recognized him when he first came into the brewery and insisted on sitting inside, away from the crowd.

"It doesn't work here," the little man said. "Nothing makes sense here." He gulped. He was going to be sick. Amillee went for the basin. He retched awhile, but nothing much came up, and he finally curled his arms on the table under his head and fell asleep. She took the basin off to the garbage.

Coming back into the room, she met her mother, hauling out a tray of cups. Lumilla said, "We have other custom, you know." She slapped the purse on her belt. More of the people were paying now in Imperial money, and Lumilla was very fond of it.

Amillee looked down the room toward the priest. "He's interesting. He grew up in the Holy City."

Lumilla harrumphed. "Well, this is Undercastle, where we are now standing, and trying to live. Take the pitcher out to the porch. What is going on in your head? Since the King died you never have both feet on the ground at the same time."

Amillee burst out, "What's there for me? To marry some poor lout—" Abruptly the whole emptiness appeared before her, the dull days of the rest of her life. "There must be more. I want more."

Lumilla shoved her. "Stop whining. Do your work; let that be enough."

"How can that be enough?" Amillee cried. "How can that ever be enough?" She stormed off out of the room, up the back stair, to get away from all this.

JEON CAME HOME BEFORE DAWN, PUT HIS HORSE UP IN THE stable without waking anyone, and found a passage there that went into the castle. He followed the narrow way up through the dark walls, one hand on the stone, which warmed at his touch. The passage crossed into the big burial chamber, and on the threshold he bowed before he went in. All around him in the silence and darkness he felt them watching him. He felt their charge upon him. At the far threshold he turned and bowed again, and went up.

In the hall, where the dawn light shone out beyond the terrace, a man wearing only the bottom half of a uniform was sweeping up. His doublet was a black and white heap by the far wall. He hardly glanced at Jeon; none of the Imperials thought much of him. He went back out to the antechamber and up the right-hand stair to his sisters' room.

There Casea was feeding the birds from a tray of seeds and fruit and bits of mice. When she saw him she dropped the tray onto the floor and rushed to meet him. "I'm so glad you're back." She began to cry, and he put his arms around her.

"Where is Tirza?"

"She is . . . out. On the Jawbone, likely. Mervaly—" Casea stepped back, her hands in his, and looked into his eyes. Tears ran down her cheeks. "Mervaly has married Oto."

"What?" He hurled himself away, turned around in the middle of the room, and faced her again. "What? Why?"

"I guess we are all a little mad, Jeon. She thinks she is protecting us. You and me, that is, since we must pretend that Tirza is dead." She wiped her eyes, which kept on leaking.

"Tirza dead?"

"No, no, she's lively as ever. Oto just thinks she is dead and so we must—he ordered her dead; it's a long story. What happened? Where did you go?"

"Up the coast." He did not want to tell her what he had learned, or what he was thinking. Instead he snarled, "Mervaly. She married him, and he is still alive?"

"Yes." Casea's voice went ragged. "He thinks he's King."

"What are you doing?" He gave her a suspicious look. She shrugged one shoulder. He thought, She is up to something. She too. With a grunt he went down the stair and into the hall.

The sea glittered, out there through the gap. He sat down at the table, in the place to the left of the high seat, and sat staring at his hands, lying on the table before him in the clear morning light, thinking about what to do next.

Broga came in, trailing one of his men, and crossed the room straight toward Jeon and said, "I sit there, boy."

Jeon gave him a long look, rose, and went on down to the end of the table. As he was settling himself again, there was a bustle in the doorway. Two soldiers marched in, swung to stand on either side of the door, saluted, and shouted, "Glory to the Empire!"

Oto walked down between them, with Mervaly beside him, holding his hand.

The muscles of Jeon's forearm twitched, as if he drove in a blade. He turned his head and looked toward the sun glistening on the sea, running wild all the way to the horizon.

With ceremony Oto and Mervaly came to the high seat and sat down together. Servants brought warmed spiced wine and fruit and bread. Jeon, through the corner of his eye, saw Oto turn to kiss his sister, paddling with his fingers in her neck, and Mervaly allowing this. Jeon took a chunk of the bread to calm his hands. In his mind he saw them locked together, naked, thrashing together, and his stomach turned.

He kept his gaze on the sea. He told himself, They think nothing of you. That helps.

Oto said, "Prince Jeon, now my brother. Welcome home."

He said, "I am happily home, my lord." He gave Oto a wide, empty look. Over the Archduke's shoulder Mervaly glanced at Jeon, and their looks crossed and he ripped the piece of bread in half.

"You went east along the coast? What did you find out?"

Now he could craft this. He said, "Somebody has been attacking along the coast. Pirates, likely slavers, they come in, burn everything, and take off everybody they don't kill."

"What did you find at the new fort?"

Jeon began eating the bread. "It's demolished, as your sergeant said. There were only a dozen graves. That means the rest left with the pirates."

"Where are they coming from?"

"Likely from the north seas. Another part of the world out of reach of your Emperor."

Oto said, "Keep your tongue polite, boy, or I'll twist it out of your head. You found other places they attacked?"

"A village, north of the new fort. On toward Santomalo, a cove full of wrecked ships." Looking at Oto, he could not help looking at Mervaly, and he blurted out, "I see you've found your place in this."

Unruffled, unsmiling, Mervaly said, "Someone had to act. Luka was gone. You ran away."

Oto gave a grunt of a laugh. Sitting on the high seat, he seemed different, his knees clutched, his head settled into his shoulders, his coat open: not the tidy courtier of old. He rubbed Mervaly's arm, and said, "You've proven useful to us, Prince Jeon. Keep on so, and you will prosper."

Jeon took his eyes from his sister, and lowered his head. "I am pleased to serve," he said. He put another piece of bread into his mouth.

CASEA HAD RUN OUT OF HER FAVORITE BRIGHT YELLOW thread, and she went down to the weavery, to get more. The woman behind the counter went to look, and came back shaking her head. "No, that's all gone. I have only a dark purple, and a very pretty lilac."

Casea had brought her work with her, as always. She had not looked at it as a piece in a long while; she had been rolling the finished part up to keep it out of the way, and giving herself over to the fresh new cloth. Now she spread the last several feet of it out on the counter. She was surprised how long it was; when she got to the end of the counter, she still had the roll in her hand, feeling as thick and heavy as ever.

She went along the piece she had spread out on the flat counter-top, stroking it with her hands, seeing the colors in their stitches and knots, swirls, satiny fills, intertwinings, and endings. Here was the dark red she had loved so much, wound with a thick black silk spangled in gold, and here she had run out of the red and the black silk had gone on alone, filled and tangled with the sun-bright yellow, the blue, the green, and the purple. And now the black silk had slipped away, and the yellow was gone also, and the other colors ran on in waves.

She saw what she had done, and coming to the unfinished edge, she looked on it with her eyes clear. She knew what she had in her basket, only a little blue left, only a few strands of the green. She looked up to see the weaver woman coming back, carrying a carved wooden box.

"Here is all I have," she said, and set the box on the table. "The ship from the south has not been here in a while; that's where I get most of these pretties."

The box was full of hanks of thread, some wool, some hemp, and some silk, but there was no yellow. No blue, either, and no green, only a dark purple and a lighter purple, lying there side by side.

Casea rolled up her work. Her fingertips felt frozen, as if she were touching death.

"There's this," the weaver woman said, and took another twist of thread from the box. "But it doesn't really match."

Casea said slowly, "Let me see."

She took the hank of hempen thread, which was a common brown, but heavy in her hands, and with a surprising feel: strong and smooth, like silk. She said, "I know what this is. I will take this."

"There will be more soon, maybe, though," the weaver woman said. "There's ships coming, I've heard."

"From the south?"

"No," the woman said, and waved east. "From east of Santo-malo. From the Empire."

TIRZA DREAMED, AND IN THE DREAM SHE WAS THE DRAGON. Or at least she was in his mind, looking out through the great red eyes, the sea vivid around her with his long, deep sight.

He was swimming south, past the sunken mountains of an older time, trailing a school of fish that stretched more than a mile through the cold streaming current. The sea was green and blue, constantly murmuring in its water voice, underneath the songs of dolphins and whales, the low conversations of the fish. She was cradled in the space behind his eyes; she could do nothing, but he could not see her there, or harm her, and so she waited.

Under him the seabed was rising, and the sunlight reached down into the water and touched him with its warmth. Then, ahead, there lay a clutter of floating trees.

Tucked behind his eyes, she felt his sudden rage, she felt them as invaders, the sense so strong she wrapped her arms tight around herself as if she would be blasted away. And under the fury, she knew that, in spite of being wood, the floating trees were packed with meat.

Her muscles gathered. The sun was rising, the tide running in, when he liked best to come near the land. The ships were teth-ered down, and rocked at the ends of their ropes. He went in among them and reared up beside the largest.

On the flat wooden surface a lone man gaped up at him, stunned, and the dragon blasted the ship with the firestream of his breath. The man leapt for the cool sea, and the dragon swung around to snap him up, and then the burning ship beside him erupted like a sea vent.

Helpless behind the dragon's eyes, Tirza screamed, enveloped in the blazing colors, the unendurable heat.

The enormous shock battered him almost unconscious. He tumbled over in the water, helpless, and the wash of heat drove him blindly down as far as he could go. The sea above him churned, stinking, some acrid smell like burnt flesh. His whole body hurt, as if he had been pounded all over. He swam up, and put just his head above the surface and drank of the cold dawn air.

Reeking of smoke. The sea before him foul with smoke and bits of the ship and bits of bodies, and the other ships suddenly were bustling with men, shouting, pointing. He sank into the water and swam to the nearest of the ships. This time he did not surface; he only drove his shoulder into the keel and broke it in half.

The other three ships were trying to scramble away, their wooden legs out clawing at the water. He stopped to eat up some men from the broken ship and then chased the next hull, the oars muddling the surface overhead into whorls of glowing light. Coming up from beneath, he closed his jaws on the very tail of it and dragged it under. Then there was more to eat. The last few ships were hurrying off, their yells and howls growing fainter. He busied himself hunting through the wreckage for meat.

Out on the Jawbone, Tirza stopped screaming and woke up.

JEON WALKED OUT ONTO THE TERRACE, LOOKING OUT TO SEA; A heavy morning fog was just lifting. Beneath the grey fuzz the sea lifted in a sullen swell among the rocks. In the hall, Broga was sitting at the table, playing chess with himself, and Jeon went up toward him.

"I'll play."

Broga said, "I find myself more challenging." He darted a look at Jeon, not even lifting his head. But he began to arrange the pieces, and Jeon sat down.

They played a game in silence and Broga won, as always; usually he concluded this with a summary of Jeon's faults, but this time he only said, "Tell me more about what you saw at the new fort."

Jeon reached for the black pieces. He had another kind of gambit to play and this was the opening. He said, "There was a survivor. A crazy man, living in the ruins. He saw what happened."

"Ah! You never told this to my brother."

"He never questioned me." Jeon kept his eyes on the pieces.

"One of our men? You should have brought him back."

"No, he was a local man. He was mad; he was living in the wild, eating leaves and mushrooms."

"But you spoke to him."

"Yes."

"Then what did he say? He witnessed it? Who did it?"

"It was some huge force, which came around sunrise. In three galleys, maybe more; it was hard to make sense of him. They carried off dozens of men, chained together."

"Slavers."

"Oh, certainly. The southern markets are always seeking slaves."

"Slavery is unheard of in the Empire," Broga said. "It is against God's will." Broga was staring at Jeon, a frown on his face. He picked up a pawn. "There's honor to be had here. God's work. Wiping these devils off the seas."

Jeon moved his men, wondering if Broga believed him or not. It didn't really matter, either way. He studied the board, seeing that Broga, as usual, was attacking him on the Queen side. He thought he should know by now how to take advantage of this. He moved up a horse, temporizing, to see if Broga would move his castle, as he usually did.

A sound drew his eyes toward the door; Mervaly was coming in, dressed in deep blue like the sky just after sundown.

Jeon turned his head toward her, seeing her much changed. She never laughed now and she wore dark gowns and she had her hair bound up. She ignored him and he made no greeting to her, but turned back to the game.

Broga had picked up his castle, but he did not put it down. He perched there on the bench, rigid, his body canted forward over the board, his eyes not on the board, but following Mervaly. His face was so stiff his cheeks pleated. Abruptly he tore his gaze from her and stared at the game, and he set the castle piece down.

Not in the usual place. Jeon moved up his bishop, seeing a hole in the array before him. Mervaly walked once around the room, stopping out on the terrace to watch the sea. The wind was frolicking in off the sea and she reached up suddenly and pulled loose the ribbon that bound her hair. The wind blew it wild around her; the sunlight glittered on it. She reached up both hands, twisted the long tresses together, and tied them up again. All that time, Broga moved his men, but he hardly looked at the board.

She went out, and he seemed to close in on himself. His shoulders moved. Jeon used his horse to take Broga's castle.

"Check," Jeon said.

Broga's face sharpened almost to a point, aimed at the board. His hand fisted.

Jeon said, "I think that's mate, isn't it?" And started gathering the pieces up for another game.

* * *

DAWD WENT INTO THE HALL, AND THERE WAS THE PRINCESS Casea, sitting by the terrace, with her sewing on her lap. He went to her, as he always did, drawn in. She looked up and smiled. On her knees the band of linen showed its many colors. In her hand a new color, a plain country brown, and unaccountably his heart leapt.

She looked up, tucking away the work into her basket, and she stood. "Are you ready?"

He knew this was the question she had begun to ask him, back in the dark passage, when she rescued him from the castle. Even then he had known the answer. He said, "Yes, I'm ready."

"Good," she said, and gave him the blessing of her beautiful smile.

"I AM LEAVING," CASEA SAID. THEY HAD MET AT THE SEA GATE and the castle loomed up over them. She took Tirza's hands between hers. "I can see what is going to happen and I will not stay here to witness it. The castle will have us all dead before this is over."

Tirza shook her head, so the tears flew. She put Casea's hands up to her face. Keep faith, she thought. She pressed her face into her sister's palms.

"I want you to go with me," Casea said.

Tirza shuddered.

"I know you," Casea said more gently. "And I know you will stay. You have your own thread to follow. You and Jeon." She kissed Tirza. "Not forever," she said. "I will not go forever." Her warm arms slipped away.

Tirza watched her go off down the beach, walking as she always did, as if she were going only to the cypress tree. She carried nothing; Tirza wondered what Casea would do to live, how she would fare, who had never been out of sight of the castle before. Pressing her fist to her chest, she watched her sister pass the foot of the way up to the cliff. At least she would stay by the sea.

Then, as Casea walked along, a man came from one side to meet her, and fell into step with her. He carried a basket in his hand and a pack on one shoulder. As they went along together she reached out and he shifted the basket to his other hand and took hold of hers.

Tirza thumped her fist on her chest, where her heart ached. Keep faith. But she would not go into the castle. Casea was right; it would consume all of them in the end: that was the curse. Tirza had nowhere to go; she walked out to the Jawbone.

"LISTEN TO ME," BROGA SAID. HE STALKED AFTER OTO across the room. "The boy told me a great fish story, that he saw someone at the new fort, who had witnessed what happened. He was lying. He was trying to divert me away from what really happened, somehow, which means he was in on it." Broga thrust his face toward his brother. "There are more of them, out there, on the sea, in the wild. We have to mount some kind of defense!"

Oto said, "Against who? A beardless boy with no army?" He turned toward Mervaly, standing in the window. "Does your brother have an army?"

She widened her eyes at Oto. She was sorting through this new talk, this new way of looking at Jeon, and she said finally, "My brother is a child."

Broga snapped, "He lied to me."

"A naughty child," she said. "He is harmless."

Oto barked a laugh. "Except to himself." He leaned against a table, his arms crossed over his chest. "Broga, stop making up trouble. They were pirates."

Mervaly said, "But Broga is right, my lord; that's a trouble." She cast Broga a sideways look. "It isn't my brother."

Broga said, "Why did he lie then?"

"He's a twisted little person. Somebody is attacking us." She fixed her gaze on Broga, trying to turn him to her thinking, away from Jeon. "You're right about that."

Oto stirred, noticing this exchange, and his voice turned harsh. "If he lied he made it all up." Oto's voice was clipped. He was ending this, or trying to. He looked from her to Broga, suspicious.

She said, "He did not make up all those dead and missing men, my lord."

Broga said, "That's the truth."

At that Oto flared, rounding on her. "I'll do this, woman. This is my work, not yours."

She wanted to roar at him. She flung another look at Broga, who at least saw beyond his nose, but Oto's brother was already striding out of the room, his stiff Imperial back to her. She glared once, furious, at Oto, and stalked off to the window. He would leave soon, and then she could steal away to her own room, to her birds.

WHEN SHE FINALLY MANAGED TO LEAVE THE NEW TOWER, SHE took a passage she thought would take her to her birds, but which instead led in a twisting way all around the castle. Around a bend, she came on Jeon, and she cornered him against the wall.

"You talk too much. They know you're lying. I can't protect you if you keep pushing yourself into his face all the time."

He kept the side of his head toward her. "I don't—"

"Yes, you do. My advice is to go find yourself a fool's cap, and sit in a corner and drool."

Now suddenly he wheeled on her. "So you can wallow in his arms—all Luka's blood on him—and you wallow in his arms—"

She slapped Jeon. That felt good, so she slapped him again.

He never moved, even to flinch. His cheek felt like wood. His eyes were dark as pitch. He turned on his heel and walked off.

She watched him go down the dark passage and into the wall at the end. He had been spying on her; she was almost sure of that. Wallowing. The little sneak, she thought, I'll pluck his eyes out. She wondered if he was up to something else, plotting something deeper. She felt the situation sliding out of her grip.

At last the passage took her upward and let her go to her room full of birds. She had been wandering around for a long while now, Oto would find her missing, would come here at once after her, and they would have a fight again, and this time maybe she would hit him.

The birds chattered happily at the sight of her. There were many of them, as often in the early summer, seagulls and the owl and the lazy old petrel. Three ravens were sitting on the ledge above the hearth, and the sparrows' nests were full of babies, so it was very loud. She sang back to them, getting their food out, and arranging it all for them. The room was a mess and she took the broom to it while they ate. Then she spread her arms, and they all rushed to find some place to perch on her, and she danced them around the room.

The door burst open. She turned, expecting Oto; in a feathery rush the birds all flew off to the walls or the window. Broga came in the door.

"So," he said. "This is part of it, isn't it."

She said, "Whatever do you mean, Broga?"

He strode up to her and caught her by the arm. "This is how you send word to your people, even when we never see you go— through the birds!"

She pulled away from him. "You're mad, Broga. The birds have nothing to do with you."

He drew the knife from his belt and held it up before her eyes.

"I'll make you tell me," he said, and pressed the tip of the blade under her jaw.

"Get away from me!" She recoiled from him.

He caught her by the wrist, and twisted her arm behind her back, and wound her up against him. She could not move. Their faces were inches apart. The knife jabbed at her neck. "Tell me. I'll have your evil heart out." A bolt of pain went up her arm and she whined between her teeth.

The birds exploded from the walls. They came at him in a mass, talons and beaks and blows of their wings, and under their attack he staggered. His grip on her slackened and she slipped and almost fell. Arms flailing, she caught her balance back, almost at his feet, and stood straight. The knife flashed wildly out. The tip of the blade caught her across the throat.

Now she did fall, blood pumping down the front of her dress, but she laughed at what she saw. The birds drove him down to the floor, the ravens on his head stabbing with their black beaks tore up gouts of watery jelly; the seagulls on his chest raked and gouged at his lips and then his tongue; the petrel sank its claws deep in his groin; the sparrows darted in and out above his blood-splattered hands. He sank down writhing under them, sending up desperate cries. She laughed, her hand to her throat where the blood streamed down. She would not live beyond this, but she rejoiced at it. The door crashed open, and now Oto came in, and his eyes popped and his jaw sagged. And she laughed.

OTO GOGGLED AT THE ROOM BEFORE HIM; HE SAW MERVALY first, slumped on the ground, covered with blood, and laughing. The feathery heap in front of her heaved and kicked and he saw Broga's hand and knew it was his brother. Oto started forward and the mass of feathers and eyes and claws rose up and attacked him.

He leapt backward through the door and slammed it. His breath came in sobs. He could not form sense out of what he had seen. He could still hear her laughing. He retreated to the far wall, needing the support.

Jeon came up the stair past him, gave him a hard look, and went on into the room; he did not open the door first. Oto blinked. His mind would not move. The door swung open from the inside, and Jeon stood there, his face frozen.

Behind him, Mervaly lay on the floor in a tide of her blood. The birds were settling around her, their piping like bells, their wings soft. They curled in her hair; they sang into her ears. Oto' went cautiously to the threshold. The slab of bitten meat on the floor, still wearing tatters of Broga's clothes, twitched here and there, but it was dead, too.

"My Queen," Oto said. His crown.

"Let the birds mourn her," Jeon said. "They loved her. She is where she belongs." He nudged Broga with his foot. "Get this out of here and bury it."

Oto was collecting himself, pieces sliding back into place in his mind, where this might lead, what he could make of it. He said, "I am King. I will give the orders."

Jeon came out onto the landing past him. "Whatever you say, Oto. Just do it. I'll send up the guards." He went on down the stairs. Without looking into the room, Oto reached out and drew the door shut.

OTO HAD THE MEN CARRY HIS BROTHER'S BODY OUT THE GATE and down the road to the little graveyard where the meadow widened. Erdhart was buried there, among a few older graves, and beside his place the soldiers began to dig another hole. Oto stood watching all this, pretending to pray.

The priest was gone. Oto himself would have to speak the necessary words, which was proper, anyway. He would say some-thing about this place now forever Imperial, because of the golden blood here buried. Castle Ocean would be saved yet.

Around him the soldiers in a line stood at attention. Two men laid Broga in the hole, on his back, his sword in his hands. Oto said his words and shoveled the dirt back into the grave; the sol-diers all shouted, "Glory! Glory! Glory!"

Oto rubbed his hands together. In spite of what he had said, he did not see any glory in this, and he did not want to look behind him at the castle. Instead, he turned, and stretched his gaze out over the edge of the cliff, out over the sea.

The fleet would come. Perhaps the winter storms had held it up. But this warm and gentle weather would surely bring the fleet here, and then he would have power again.

Someone was standing behind him, making subtle noises to draw his attention, and he glanced over his shoulder: it was one of the pikemen. With Oto's eyes on him, he saluted and said, "My lord. Glory to the Empire."

"Glory," Oto said. He flung a broad look over the other men, still gathered by the grave, not wanting to see how few there were: so few that now he saw them as separate men.

"My lord," said the soldier in front of him, "we've had some more desertions. Dawd is gone, sir."

Oto said, "Dawd? Who is Dawd?"

"The sergeant, my lord."

"The sergeant." Oto realized he had been looking for the ser-geant: the one he gave orders to. He said, "Where did he go?"

"He's just disappeared, my lord. Another five gone, too, my lord."

Oto swallowed; he wanted to walk into his chamber, shut the door, feel the solid walls around him. But to do that he would have to go back into the castle.

"Request permission, my lord, to speak."

Oto straightened, frowning. "Briefly. Yes."

"If Dawd is gone, am I the sergeant now?"

Oto grunted at him. "I now appoint you sergeant, Sergeant."

"Thank you, my lord." Marwin flexed in a deep bow, and saluted. "Waiting for orders, sir."

"THE BIRDS KILLED HIM. NOT BEFORE HE HAD KILLED HER, but she saw him die." Jeon sat down on a rock, looking out across the bay toward the town. The wind was blowing hard off the sea and the bay waters were choppy with whitecaps. "It was Broga who killed Luka. She got our revenge. Some of it, anyway."

Tirza had stopped crying. She folded up her legs to her chest and wrapped her arms around them, and scowled at him. The tears had streaked her dirty face and her eyes were startlingly blue. She let out a reel of noise, mostly clicks.

He could tell she was angry. He said, "This is how it's going to be, Tirza. There's nothing I can do to change it."

One hand lashed at him; she sputtered and looked away. Another grimy tear went down her face.

Jeon put his hand on her arm and shook her a little. "Don't put up your back at me, Tirza. You need me now. Everybody else is gone."

With the heel of her hand she scrubbed at her eyes. Stubbornly she refused to look at him. Still gripping her arm, he leaned in closer to her, his mouth to her ear.

"You know—they have an enemy. Somebody is attacking them. The pirates—whoever it is. Somebody is killing them."

In his grasp she stiffened. He reached into his wallet, and found the little green stone.

"What is this?"

She saw it, and she twitched all over. She struck at his hand, and the stone bounced away, but he did not need it anymore.

He said, "Everywhere, every attack, was a place you had been."

Slowly she brought her gaze around to meet his eyes. She growled at him.

He said, "I think you know who they are."

She shook her head.

"I think you do. Maybe you can even summon them."

She shook her head, over and over, and her eyes widened. She was afraid. He gripped her tight. She did know something, which frightened her, but which he could use. He let go of her with a little shove.

"Bring them here, Tirza. Whoever they are."

She shook her head. Her eyes were blazing blue, brighter than the sky.

"Bring them. I need them. I have no army. I need some force. Or Castle Ocean falls." He bent, and spoke into her face. "Keep faith with me, Tirza!"

She jumped, her mouth falling open. He got up. "Do as I say. I am head of the family now. Obey me." He walked off down the Jawbone.

CURLED IN HER HIDEAWAY BENEATH THE ROCK, SHE MADE herself dream of the dragon. Always, carefully, she remembered that she was dreaming.

With her sleeping eye she made the world around her, the beach, as she remembered it, the sheer cliff on one side and the blue-green purling water on the other; the memory swelled her heart, as if she had been happy there. And in front of her, sprawled out comfortably on the sand, was the dragon, red as sundown.

He turned his huge eyes on her. His voice rumbled like a rolling barrel. He said, "You ran away, coward."

She said, "You are only a dream; you can do nothing to me."

He gave his cold chuckle. His tongue flicked out. "I was always a dream. What do you want?"

"My brother needs your help."

The great red eye shimmered, fixed on her. "I have no interest in helping your brother." His voice lowered to a sensuous growl. "You know what I want. Tell me a story."

She sat down on the sand, her arms around her knees, and thought a moment. It was the Empire he needed to know about. "Once there was a man who refused to stop eating." She went on, describing how he ate up everything he had and then began eating everybody else's. The dragon listened, his reptile lips curved into a faint smile. She said, "He ate the beasts and the harvests and he ate the people and their houses and all they had, and after that, he went on to other places, and devoured them, too. Fatter and huger he became, but still he would not stop eating.

"At last in all the world there was nothing more, everywhere he looked. Then looking down he saw his own feet, and he ate them. And then he ate his legs, and then his body, until nothing was left but his head. And now the head rolls around the world, searching for anything else to eat, but there is nothing left."

When she was done the dragon said, "Whatever you mean by this, you do not need me to solve it."

"My brother—"

The dragon was rising to his feet. His great tail lashed once. The sun gleamed on his magnificence. He said, "I don't care about your brother. Listen to your own story."

"In my story," she said, "you do not eat me."

That made him laugh again. His eyes blazed. "Then, for once, you have lied. And I am very hungry, and you are here."

His head swiveled toward her, and he lunged, his jaws parting. She looked for an instant past his ivory white fangs, down into the red tunnel of his throat, to a darkness that went on forever. For an instant she teetered over that abyss. She turned and ran. He was behind her; terror consumed her; she flung herself on. She made the dream end. She was lying on the sand in her refuge, in the broad daylight, and she turned her face against the warm sand, so glad to be alive that she cried.

15

JEON KNEW OTO THOUGHT OF KILLING HIM. SO WHEN HE heard in Undercastle that the wild boar had come back to Terreon, he went out there.

He took his bow, and a vial he found in his mother's room, a little alabaster bottle in the shape of a twining octopus. When he got to Terreon, the people were disappointed he was not Luka and did not give him much of a welcome.

He found a townsman who had a sow in heat, and got some boys to coax and beat and push her out to the far edge of the barley fields. There they staked her out and Jeon climbed a tree.

The sow fretted, pulled on her rope, snorted, and soon a few pigs appeared at the edge of the trees. They crept up closer to her, grunted, and ripped at the ground with their front hooves, but they did not go to her. Even when she swung her backside to them and squatted down, her curly tail stiff above her back, they only called and panted and pawed.

More came, all through the day. Jeon sat out on a strong branch to watch. With each new boar he thought, Is this the one? But none went nearer to her than the edge of the trees, although she begged in her pig voice, showered them with scents, and winked at them with the eye under her tail. Where she walked back and forth at the end of her tether she wore a trench down into the loose dirt of the field. But none of them would approach.

At last, with the sun going down and the boars packed in shoulder to shoulder before the whining sow, the biggest boar Jeon had ever seen stalked up out of the woods.

All strut and bristle, its tusks like swords, the boar minced along on tiptoe past the others, out onto the flat field. Jeon dipped an arrow into the opening of the octopus vial, and laid the arrow to the string. Out there the sow crouched, her tail up, and the boar lowered its head and rushed her, and Jeon shot.

He missed, slightly; the arrow sank into the boar's side, and not its neck. The huge pig bellowed. It plowed to a stop and wheeled toward Jeon, and he scrambled back toward the trunk of the tree as the pig charged.

The arrow was stuck still in its side. Maybe its skin was too thick there. Maybe the vial was not full of poison. Maybe even poison couldn't kill it. Squealing, the boar hit the tree, and the trunk shook. Jeon lost his footing, and flung himself across a branch to keep from falling. The stench of the boar filled his nostrils. Kicking out frantically, he got himself up into the fork of the tree. He kept hold of the bow and the vial, but four of his five arrows slipped out of the case to the ground. Another terrific blow slammed into the trunk. He wrapped his arms around the tree and held on as the tree shuddered all over.

One arm still hooked around the tree, he opened the vial. Below him, the boar drew back just far enough for a good running start and launched itself at the tree again. Jeon tightened his grip on the trunk, holding the vial in that hand, the arrow in the other.

The tree jolted against him. A ringing crack went up through the trunk and the leaves above rustled. He held his last arrow out well away from him, and turned the vial over on the head.

Nothing. He drew a breath; the tree boomed under another crashing assault and he pressed himself against the trunk to stay on. Then on the lip of the vial a drop formed. He did not wait for it to fall but stroked the arrowhead through it. The tree was slowly tilting. He dropped the vial and unshouldered the bow, looking down.

Directly below him, the boar was looking back. Its enormous head tipped up, its damp snout twitching at the air, smelling Jeon. A deep rut of a scar crossed its snout like a new mouth. It pawed at the tree with one trotter, and then stood up against the tree, snuffling. Jeon drew the bow, and aimed at that old wound, only a few feet below him.

The arrow sank in to the feathers. The boar bellowed, and its tusks sliced the air just below Jeon's feet. The pig's hindquarters gave way and it struggled to push itself up again. With a long sigh, it fell over on its side.

Jeon went cautiously down, the tree groaning under his weight and sagging farther. The first thing he did was pick up his dropped arrows. The boar lay crumpled on the ground, its forked hooves still treading at the air. It was only a pig, after all. Jeon said, "That's how to do it, Luka." He felt a loose satisfaction, all over like a glow, and a sudden urge to piss. The vial shone at him from the grass, and he picked it up, and put it carefully into his belt pouch, went to his horse, and rode back to Castle Ocean.

OTO HAD DECIDED IT WAS BETTER TO COUNT EVERYTHING. That way he knew if anything changed. Coming down the steps to his chamber, he said the numbers under his breath. When he stopped, just for a moment, an uneasiness swept over him and he stepped back down again, counted, "Fourteen," and went on.

Where the door to Broga's chapel had been, which had been sealed up, the stones were falling out.

"You did a bad job of that," Oto said. "Make it stand."

The new sergeant said, "My lord, I live to obey."

"I will review the troops this afternoon, in the gate yard." They were walking across the round antechamber to the great hall.

The sunlight was pouring in across the terrace, hot and bright as molten metal. The sergeant paced along beside him, and Oto gave him orders, making a neat stack of words, dividing the day into work. "You will assign new guards, especially outside my chamber—"

Oto's eyes came to the high seat, on the side of the room, behind the black table. He stopped. Luka was sitting on the high seat.

Oto caught his breath, every hair stirring up. Luka was staring at him, not in anger: more puzzled, as if he was trying to remember who Oto was.

"My lord," the sergeant said, puzzled.

Oto jerked his attention back to the soldier. "Do you not see—" He flung his arm out, pointing, toward the high seat.

Luka was gone. Oto flexed his arm back to his chest. The sergeant was watching him sideways. "My lord?"

"I'm sorry. My brother's death. So distraught." Oto put his hand to his face and shook his head. "I shall go back to my chamber and pray for him." He turned his back on the high seat. He would never come into this hall again. "But first, come, and we shall set the day's watches."

THE SOLDIERS FILED STEADILY IN AND OUT OF OTO'S CHAMBER, saluted, took orders, and went out, and then more came, and he did this awhile. It was the same men who came in, over and over, but he pretended not, and gave them each detailed instructions, and sent them off. Whether they did what he commanded he did not see, or even care, so long as they took his orders.

Jeon came in. He had been gone, somewhere, his jacket dusty, his feet shod in riding boots. Oto remembered what Broga had said, that the boy conspired. Oto did not believe this; Mervaly had thought him something of a fool.

Now he had more pressing matters. He said, "I saw your brother."

Jeon stood there, in the middle of the room, and showed no surprise. "Luka. Yes. You will."

"Will he—does he—I did not kill him. I am innocent of his blood."

Jeon smiled. "Don't mind about him. They do no harm. They aren't much interested in us."

"I see your sister. The little one."

"Tirza." Jeon's smile widened. "Well, my lord, you are keen sighted."

"Broga. My brother." Oto came a step closer. Broga, for some reason, he dreaded most of all. "Will I—will he—come back?"

The boy shook his head. "No. Didn't you bury him in the land? No. The dirt gives up nothing."

"Aha," Oto said, and straightened, his hands at his sides. A sense of triumph filled him. He had forced valuable knowledge from the boy. A knock sounded on the door. "Wait!" Oto shouted. To Jeon, he said, "Can I not . . . drive them away? Some exorcism?"

"My lord, you are safe. Especially here." Jeon waved his hand at this room, with its walls of cut stone. The knock sounded again.

"My lord," came muffled through the door. "My lord—"

"Well, then, come in!" Oto shouted.

The new sergeant came in; he was more a snap-and-polish man than the old one had been, but he seemed to get less done. He did everything, though, with many flourishes, which Oto liked. Now the sergeant whirled his arm up in a broad salute.

"Glory to the Empire! My lord, there are ships coming in. Imperial ships. They're approaching the bay now; they've sent for pilots."

"The fleet," Oto said. "The fleet, at last."

He felt everything in him go slack; he had not realized until now how tight and close he was holding himself. He resisted the impulse to fling his arms into the air and cheer. Beaming, he nodded to Jeon. "Now we shall have troops. And arms. See? I told you the Empire would not forget us." He rushed to the door. "Come; we shall greet them." He pounded off down the stairs, free again.

JEON STOOD PLANTED WHERE HE WAS. HE HAD FORGOTTEN about the fleet. Now Oto had another army, bigger, probably better. The sea had betrayed Jeon; after all his work and planning, it was washing him off his feet. He thought, despairingly, he might not be able to do this.

Oto called, "Prince Jeon!"

Numbly he followed.

TIRZA WALKED DOWN INTO THE TOWN; FROM THE BUILDINGS along the cliff, a steady stream of the people was crowding toward the beach, where already half the town stood watching the mouth of the bay. She saw the flutter of a banner: Oto was there at the water's edge. She shaded her eyes with her hand, looking south toward the bay's entrance.

In between the tip of the Jawbone and the far beach, the thing was coming in. She had seen this before, the flat bulky front below the naked mast, the up and down of the oars on either side. Some deep memory rolled ominously in her stomach. A shout went up from the crowd. Everybody loved when a ship came.

She saw Aken the butcher's broad, tall back, down in the middle of a clump of watching people, and went up behind him. The galley was sliding in through the channel. Its red and blue awnings fluttered; men in striped doublets lined its sides, shoulder to shoulder, holding pikes, dozens of men. The galley's painted sides reflected on the water, and it stroked out onto the deep water of the harbor, hauled around bow to the beach, and with a clatter of chains and a splash lowered its anchor.

A little cheer went up along the beach, from Oto's soldiers and some of the townspeople. Next to Tirza, Aken did not cheer. He stood with his thumbs hooked on the strings of his apron, his face set.

She stared at him, putting all her mind into this, until at last he turned to her. His whiskered face was harsh. "What do you want, girl?" He spread his hands. Blood splattered his apron and blood encrusted his fingernails. "What do you think I can do?"

She went closer, half his height, looking straight up into his face, and poked him in the chest, scowling. She kept her lips together, for fear of barking at him. She pointed at the ship, now lowering a small boat over the side. She jabbed Aken again and drew her finger across her neck. Beyond Aken, Trollo was watching them.

Aken grunted at her. He gave a glance around, and frowned down at her. "Go away, girl. There's nothing left. Luka brought me back from the massacre in the mountains. I would have given my life for him. But he's gone and there's nothing left." Aken turned his back on her. Trollo met her gaze a moment, and looked away.

She went to Lumilla, the brewster, who was standing nearer

to the cypress tree among a bunch of other women. Lumilla gave
a little shake of her head.

"What is this, Tirza? What do you think we ought to do? Look,
there—another ship." Lumilla pointed down the bay. Another
great wooden whale was rowing up toward the entrance. "What
could we do against such as these?"

"Luka would have told you," Tirza burst out.

At the angry gush of noise the brewster recoiled, raising a hand
between them. "Go," she said. "Who can talk to you? Get Jeon.
Send Jeon to talk to me." She turned, and walked back into the
shelter of the other women.

Tirza stood where she was. The second galley was even more
splendid than the first, painted and gilded, its deck packed with
armed men, even in the cages on the masts, armed men. She
went on down toward the banner flopping and curling on its staff,
looking for her brother, and found him there, where Oto sat his
horse among his men on foot, Jeon standing at his stirrup, looking small.

AMILLEE LINGERED A MOMENT, HER EYES ON TIRZA. SHE FELT
sorry for the scrawny little creature, with her hair like wild rust,
her animal voice, now the last, almost, of her family.

Up there on its crag loomed Castle Ocean. Amillee thought of
Luka, and what he had said to her. But he was dead, and no one
was taking his place.

Her mother came to her. "I think," she said, "we are about to
make some money." She slapped Amillee on the arm. "Help me
bring out a keg."

Amillee said, "That's all you think about. I hate these people."
She stared down toward the galleys, messengers from another
world, where maybe they did things differently from here.

"Then don't help me," Lumilla said stiffly, and went on up the beach. Amillee folded her arms over her chest, waiting to see what happened next.

"TWO SHIPS," OTO SAID UNDER HIS BREATH. "TWO SHIPS."

Jeon glanced at him and turned back to the galleys. He wondered if he had lost the whole game now. If he had ever had a chance. He had forgotten how splendid an Imperial galley was, even these, battered from their passage, their paint worn. Lined up along the gunwales were a hundred men, heavily armed, against whom he had no force. He turned to look back toward the mouth of the bay, wondering if there were more coming, but out beyond the jagged tip of the Jawbone was only the dark blue sea beneath the pale blue sky.

From the nearer of the two big galleys a flat barge lowered down. A man as gaudy as the ship sat in the prow; four oars to a side, the crew rowed in toward Oto's banner. As it approached, the crowd on the beach gathered closer. The barge rammed into the beach halfway through the surf and its oarsmen leapt out and pulled it up to dry land. The officer stepped off and strode up toward Oto.

"My lord." A stout man in a red coat, gold buttons, gold strings of braid over the shoulders, his face leathery from the sun. He stopped before Oto and bowed.

"Glory to the Empire. Admiral Lord Count Unbard ip Stencop brings you the greetings of your Emperor!"

All around, the soldiers called out, "Glory! Glory!"

Oto did not bow. On the horse, he towered over everybody, which Jeon thought was the point. Oto said, "Is this is all? Two ships? We were promised a great fleet."

"Well, we are both disappointed, as I expected King Erdhart." The rolling voice clipped off the words. "I had five ships, several nights ago. We were attacked."

Jeon had been staring glumly at the ships; at this news, he took a step backward, startled. A buzz went up all around the crowd. Oto gave a quick look over his shoulder.

"We should go somewhere to talk. Do you have dispatches for me, Stencop?"

The admiral glanced over his shoulder; an officer stood there, who came forward with a leather case. He gave this to Stencop, who handed it up to Oto. Oto tucked it under his arm.

"We shall go to the castle, and there confer."

"I must settle my men," Stencop said.

"You have officers to do that," Oto said. "Follow me now."

He turned to Jeon. "You stay here. Learn a little." Oto turned his horse and rode off, and Stencop, with a frown, strode after him.

Jeon drifted off down the beach a little. He wanted to know what had happened to Stencop, but what Jeon saw before him he could not leave. The two ships were anchored close enough to see the men clambering over them; they had lowered another barge. Some bulk of wood cluttered the deck of the near ship. Jeon saw the soldier Marwin nearby and went to him.

"What's going on?"

Marwin was smiling across his whole face. "We've got it now, boy. They've brought us some kickers."

Jeon looked back toward the ship. "What?"

"On the deck there. Imperial War-bird Bomb-launchers. We call them kickers. Those are the Empire, right there. Wherever we put them, we rule."

Jeon grunted. "They were attacked. Something beat them." But left them their weapons. Nothing went perfectly.

Marwin shrugged. "Just a minor setback." His eyes slid toward the banner. "The Empire is here now."

Jeon pulled on his chin; his beard was growing out, and he

liked the feel of it under his fingers. Something warm touched his side. He started. But it was Tirza, wrapping her fingers around his, leaning on him. He slid an arm around her and hugged her. He wondered if Tirza had known about the fleet coming here or if the ships had simply fallen in the way of whatever it was out there. Now here the barges were beaching and he went over to watch them unload the weapons that were the Empire.

OTO KNEW STENCOP BY SIGHT AND BY NAME, AND DID NOT LIKE him; their families were rivals at court. His appearance here was a goad from Oto's uncle: "I have other men." Oto led the admiral into the castle and up the stairs to his chamber, the while counting under his breath. He did not let himself be drawn to notice the loose stones scattered on the chapel landing. Under his arm, the dispatch case felt like burning lead.

In his chamber, while a soldier brought Stencop a chair, Oto used a knife to slit open the case, and pulled out the thick paper with its seals and ribbon and ink.

The dispatch opened without the proper protocols, going straight to the evil. *I note with disapproval that this remote castle is not yet secured—*

He ripped the paper to shreds. The admiral stood by the chair, in the center of the room, scowling at him. "Sir. This is unusual."

Oto said, "He does not understand. He does not know what we're fighting against."

The soldier stood at Stencop's elbow with a cup of wine, but the admiral ignored him. He had a broad red face, and his ornamented collar always seemed too tight. Oto glared at him, who also knew nothing. "So: you were attacked. What happened?"

Stencop did not answer for a moment. His vanity left him. He glanced around, maybe looking for help, and facing Oto again straightened, his shoulders squared.

"We were anchored inshore for the night, in revet formation. I heard screams—it was near dawn. I got to the deck in time to see the ship at the other end of the revet on fire, and then everything in her blew up at once." Stencop's jaws moved under his beard, as if he bit down on something. "Then two more ships went down in just a few minutes. The first ship had half the bombs. The next two had all the soldiers." His jaw moved again, this time swallowing.

"This coast is infested with pirates. Who were they? What ships did they ply?"

"I never saw a ship," the admiral said. He seemed to notice the chair, now, for the first time, and he sat down. "Just my ships, burning and sinking. It was like something moving around under the water."

Oto guffawed. "What. Mermaids perhaps? You didn't fight back? You were attacked, but you did not fight back?" He thrust out his hand. "Amazing to me that you dare to wear the braid."

Stencop reached for the cup of wine the soldier had been trying for some time to give him. He said, "I am new come here and expected something of an Imperial welcome, the honor due a messenger from the Emperor. Instead I get this." He looked Oto up and down, and then pointedly turned his gaze around the room. "Where is your brother?"

"My brother is dead, sir. You deal with me alone. I rule here."

"The Empire rules here," Stencop said, and drank. "Or should. Which is the problem, is it not?"

Oto said, "Through me! Only through—"

A knock on the door jerked him around. When the soldier opened it, Jeon stood there.

"Well," Oto blurted out. "You waited, for once, to come in the proper way."

Stencop was frowning, puzzled, but Jeon smiled. He walked

into the room, tall, slender, his red hair hidden under a cap, his new beard a pale fuzz. Oto thought, Kill him. Soon.

Jeon said, "Sir, may I ask him a question?"

"Who is this?" Stencop said. "Who interrupts? Lord Oto, I insist—"

Oto rounded on the sailor again. "You'll obey me, Stencop. Me. Not whatever secret orders you have hidden in your sea chest."

They stared at each other a moment. Stencop was half out of the chair; finally, he settled back down into it.

"I assure you—"

"Later." Oto's hand chopped down, cutting Stencop off, and he turned back to Jeon. "Yes, yes. What is it?"

Jeon went up between them, Stencop in his chair and Oto standing by the table. "Sir, I think I know something important about the pirates."

Stencop said, "Who is this?"

"Prince Jeon, a son of the local house," Oto said. "What, Jeon? What is this?"

"Let me ask this of you." Jeon turned to the admiral. "Sir, when you were attacked, was it near dawn?"

Stencop scowled around the great greying shag of his beard. "Yes, it was." He glanced at Oto.

"And you were near to shore?" Jeon asked.

"We were at anchor, just offshore."

"And was the tide making?"

"Yes. We had to rake off the shore to get away. A strong tide."

Jeon turned back to Oto. "You know I found a witness, at the new fort. He said the pirates came in at dawn, with a making tide."

Oto thought, He is too slick; he is treacherous. But the logic drew Oto in. "Go on."

Jeon went to the table, where there were some pieces of dinnerware. "Let me show you. Last fall Santomalo burnt to the ground, no survivors." He put the saltcellar on the table. "At the beginning of winter, another village, here. Burnt. No survivors. In the midwinter, the New Fort. Burnt. No survivors." He set down the oil jar and the candlestick, a few inches apart, to the right of the salt. "Then, this attack on the fleet. Burnt." He stuck a knife into the tabletop to the right of that.

"Many survived," Stencop said hoarsely.

"The intent here maybe was different," Jeon said. "To disable the fleet, more than to take slaves." He reached across the table for Oto's cup. "So. Santomalo, the village, the new fort, the fleet. They are coming down the coast, harvesting people."

Stencop grunted. Oto locked his hands together behind his back. The line of objects on the table held his eyes.

Jeon looked from one to the other. "And here we are." He put the cup at the right end of the line. "And we are next."

Oto could not look away from this. His mind was churning. He was a King with no men. His only men were Stencop's men.

Stencop said, "They have been raiding up and down the coast and you have done nothing?"

Oto pulled his gaze to Jeon. "This is Castle Ocean. Who would dare attack?"

"They will go for Undercastle," Jeon said. "To do that, they must come into the bay." His eyes shone, and he leaned toward Oto a little, urgent. His voice dropped. He said, "But if we know they are coming, my lord, we can set a trap for them. You have wonderful new weapons. You can defeat them. And that will prove you King against anybody, my lord. Anybody."

Oto cleared his throat; he did not like Stencop hearing this, but Jeon made sense to him. He thought, Don't kill him yet.

Jeon said, "Right now, at sunrise the tide here is slack. But when the moon's full, ten days from now, it will be making. At dawn. And we should be ready."

Oto forced himself to laugh, careless. "Well, maybe. You have certainly thought this all out, haven't you. I'll take it under consideration." He nodded. He avoided looking at either of them; he needed to look sure of himself, the power firmly in his hands.

"If you are right, Prince Jeon, I will make you an Imperial Count."

Jeon bowed down before him. "Your servant, my lord."

STENCOP WENT BACK DOWN TO THE BEACH, TO SEE TO HIS men. Oto loitered awhile in the upper chamber. Jeon waited with him, and when he left followed him down the stair of the new tower. When they came down to the chapel landing, which was littered with broken stone, Oto stopped, one hand out to hold Jeon back. Jeon moved slightly out of reach: he hated Oto's touch. He saw that Oto wanted Stencop well out of earshot, and he guessed what Oto wanted to talk about.

"Why will they not do this properly?" He waved at the doorway into the chapel.

Jeon said, "Maybe they can't, sir." The doorway and the space beyond were packed solid with the black rock; that was what knocked the stones out of the wall, the rock pushing outward. It occurred to him it would push against any wall of quarried stone.

The possibilities in that flowered in his mind, so that for a moment he did not hear that Oto spoke to him, and he came back to himself only when Oto said sharply, "Are you listening to me?"

Jeon jerked his gaze to the Archduke's. "Yes, sir. I'm sorry."

"What will stop it?"

Nothing, Jeon almost said, and thoughtlessly he looked up the stairs, toward Oto's chambers.

At that, the Archduke hooted. "No need to speak. That says it all. I shall move myself out at once." He leveled a mirthful stare at Jeon. "You're not that clever, you know," he said, and went away.

Jeon followed him down into the antechamber. Somehow Jeon had not foreseen this: now Oto would choose to go somewhere else, perhaps out of reach. Jeon could not control this, only ride on it. In the center of the antechamber, the Archduke stood ordering around the three men posted there. Jeon glanced down at the foot of the stair he had just left. The gap between the living rock and the quarried stone had closed. Those stones along the edge were starting out of their places. The backs of his hands tingled. He went on, to go down to the beach, to see what was happening there.

 16

Marwin was saying, "This is why we're fighting in the south, see, to get this stuff."

With his foot he nudged a long, flat plank, not wood, which clinked when his boot struck it. There were three of these and they had been brought ashore like babies, each wrapped in its own coat of thick cloth and laid carefully down on blocks. The grunting soldiers were hauling a frame up from the grounded barge, an angular construction of wooden beams, taller than any of them, wider than three of them. The sun was bright and hot; Jeon was sweating, and he was doing little more than standing around watching. He unhooked the front of his coat and took it off.

Marwin said, "This stuff comes from some mine down south of the desert there. Look."

He stepped onto the plank with both boots. The plank was about as wide as his boots were long and he bounced once to make sure he had good footing. Reaching down, he got the near end of the plank and with a yank pulled it up toward him, and the plank bent like a bow. When he let go the plank slapped back down again into the sand with a thump.

"Hunh," Jeon said, mystified. But Marwin was beaming, his point made.

Another barge was heading in. This one had wheels on it, something at least recognizable. Jeon glanced around, wondering where Oto was. Stencop was off at the head of the beach, where his men were camping. Marwin called orders: the soldiers were rolling a wheel up to the wooden frame.

"We used these at the siege of Grom," Marwin said. "We tore those walls down in four weeks."

Jeon wondered what Grom was, and where. The Imperials laid the wheel down flat on the sand, called for help, and all together lifted the wooden frame and put it down on top.

Then it wasn't a wheel. Nothing in this was proving out as Jeon expected. He shook his head, to knock the old ideas loose. The Imperials were fixing the frame onto the flat wheel, tapping pins down through the wood with a mallet. One gave the frame a little push, and the whole apparatus swiveled smoothly around on the wheel.

"Ah," Jeon said.

Marwin gave orders in an important voice. The men working under him settled the wooden frame, peering at it from angles, sliding their hands under it. Someone brought a stick, well fashioned, some kind of tool, and they used that to level the frame. Now two of them went to the pile of planks Marwin had shown Jeon. Carrying the top plank, one at each end, they brought it to the frame, and tilted one end straight down into the center so the bottom of the plank rested on the frame's heavy footing and the top poked straight into the air.

Now it looked like a crouching animal, with a long neck, but no head. Jeon remembered that long neck flexing, and began to see what this was.

The soldiers busied themselves with straps and pins, fastening the neck part into the crouching body. No head appeared, but they fixed a cable to the top of the neck, and wound the loose end of the cable down around a spindle where the kicker's tail should have been. Jeon dropped his coat on the sand and moved off to the side, to see this better. A flicker of movement up the beach caught his eye, and he looked back that way.

Oto was riding down the path from the cliff, trailing a long line of men on foot, each carrying something. Jeon backed away from the kicker. He would figure this out later. For now, he wanted to see what Oto was going to do next.

AMILLEE STOOD ON THE PORCH OF THE BREWERY, LOOKING up the beach. The new camp was swarming with men. Behind her, Lumilla was bustling around, gathering cups; two fresh kegs sat on the open deck.

Lumilla said, "All these newcomers will be here as soon as they are let off duty. Now, listen to me. Serve them one cup at a time. Always take as much coin as they will give you. Nothing less than a whole. Don't keep broken coins with you; that way you can't give them anything smaller back. If they want to haggle, call me."

Amillee grunted. Usually ale went for a quarter Imperial a cup. She would certainly not ask the local people for a whole or give them only one cup at a time. Lumilla said, "They don't know the way here, yet, and until they figure it out, I mean to make money."

"Mother," Amillee said, "you are—" and stopped. The false King, Oto, was riding down the beach toward them. Amillee watched him keenly; he came here seldom. The few times she had seen him closely, his clothes had always drawn her, the sleek satins, the colors, but also the perfect way he wore them. Disappointed, she saw he was not keeping himself well. His coat was rumpled and his boots dirty. He was coming right toward her. Catching herself staring at him, she backed away, to get her mother to the front.

Lumilla had seen him also. She went to the porch rail, and gave him a fine salute. She had not been serving his men for so long without learning something. She called, "Glory to the King!"

He drew rein before the porch. "Indeed. And to you, also, glory, woman. I give you the honor of providing me your place here for my residence."

Lumilla coughed. "What?"

The false King said, "I require a dwelling here, and I will use this spacious and agreeable place."

People were coming up around them to listen. Amillee threw a glance at them all, and said, "Mother, don't let him do this."

Oto ignored Amillee. He said, "For this, of course, you will be recompensed." He held out his hand, and the man behind him put in it a purse, which clinked.

Lumilla's hand went out in front of her as if on a string. The crowd murmured, and Amillee cried, "Mother! No!"

"We can move into the caves," Lumilla said, and the purse was in her hand.

"Mother! Why—" Amillee turned, and looked up at the castle. "Why is he doing this? What's going on?" She thrust one arm out, pointing. "Look!"

Everybody swung around that way, toward the castle, its thorny spires black against the sky. As she watched, a speck fell from the side of the farthest, and then another.

"Birds," someone said. No one else spoke, and no one looked

away. Amillee could feel her heart beating faster. A shower of little black bits fell from the tower. Not birds.

Her mother said, "Yes," to the false King. She tucked the purse into her apron. "We will move into the caves."

TIRZA WAS STANDING AT THE EDGE OF THE WATER, WHERE the shadow of the cliff began. The sun was behind the castle now. In the space before her, at the foot of the cliff, the soldiers had made a camp. All those men had come ashore, made cloth huts, dug fire pits, set around lines of stones to mark their places. Scattered among these they did not look so many. She could see Jeon there, among them, doing little. A horn blew, and the Imperials lined up before their officer. Now she could see how many there were, more than all the people in Undercastle. They wore the striped doublets, but no iron hats, and they did not carry pikes, but knives with wide, blunt blades: ship knives.

Jeon was walking along the tidewrack, toward her.

Suddenly with a great yell all the Imperials went rushing away past her, down the beach into the town. She waited until Jeon reached her, his face bound up with thinking, and took his hand and pulled.

Deep in his mind, he went tamely along with her. She led him on toward the town, now full of soldiers calling and waving their arms and looking around. At Aken's stall a crowd hid the big butcher from her sight. As men came away munching down on beef pies, more gathered there, the pack of bodies constantly growing.

Trollo walked by, playing his harp, and gave her a quick smile. Several children trailed him. In front of the brewery cave, Lumilla was stacking up furniture from her house.

The porch of the brewery was full of soldiers. At the weavery, more Imperials leaned on the counters, flirting with the weaver sisters. Tirza led Jeon to the cypress tree and sat on the bench, and he sat beside her. She gripped his hand still. She turned, and said, "There is nobody but us now, Jeon."

His hand tightened around hers, but he was looking back up toward the beach, toward the big, ugly frames on the beach, where Oto rode his prancing horse up and down. She tugged at Jeon. With one hand she pointed down toward the Imperial man.

She said, "Jeon, don't do this. Don't be one of them. Luka told me, once—what use—" Now she was going to cry, thinking of Luka. She scrubbed her eyes with her hand. "Don't," she said. "He'll kill you. He hates you."

Now, at last, he faced her. He had that new smile on his face. He said, "You don't trust Oto. I understand that."

Once he had almost known what she was saying, but now he didn't. A tear leaked down her face.

He said, "But he loves me, he says. He's promised to make me a Count, Tirza. Isn't that wonderful?" He laughed.

She shrieked at him, loud enough that out in the sunlight people turned to look. He put an arm around her and hugged her, pinning her to him. "You think he's lying."

She nodded, helpless.

"Well, don't worry," he said, and laughed again. "I'm lying, too." He rose, and walked away, back up the beach, back toward Oto.

NIGHT CAME. THE SOLDIERS ROAMED THROUGH UNDERCAStle, drinking and eating and watching the women. Oto had settled himself in at the brewery, which blazed with lamps. Jeon went up the beach, to get back into the castle, and the Admiral of the Fleet walked out in front of him on the path and stopped. Two of Stencop's officers waited a little way off.

Stencop said, "An excellent evening, my lord," and bowed.

Jeon bowed back, very dignified, as if he understood what was happening. He said, "So it is, my lord. I invite you to walk with me."

"I will, thank you." Stencop turned to pace along beside him. Now Jeon could not go into the castle, and so he made a way toward the camp, along the foot of the rock. The ensigns trailed them. Stencop walked along in silence for a while. He was a bushy man, with swathes of hair coming out from under his hat, and great caterpillar eyebrows and a beard like a nest.

He said, "My lord, I am curious. You seem to be one who understands this place."

Jeon said, "I am a son of the castle, my lord."

"I have many questions."

"Perhaps I can answer them."

They were coming to the tents, laid out in rows; this reminded Jeon suddenly of the graves at the new fort. The rows of pawns in chess. Stencop said, "My tent is nearby. We can sit down and talk."

They went side by side down a lane between the hovels of cloth, to a bigger hovel, close under the beetling rock of the cliff. Inside were small cloth chairs and a table and a ewer of wine. A lamp suspended from the peak of the tent lit the place, and the air was close and smoky.

An ensign had followed them in, and poured two cups of the wine. Stencop said, "I found this in the town. It is acceptable." He settled himself down on one of the flimsy cloth chairs and waved Jeon to the other. "Drink with me." With his eyes and a nod, he sent the ensign away.

Jeon drank the country wine. Stencop poured both their cups full again.

"This—the tower seems to be losing some of its stones."

"Yes," Jeon said.

The admiral blinked. "This does not excite you?"

"The tower is very new," Jeon said. "Perhaps it was not built properly."

"Ah." Stencop's face cleared. He drank more of the wine. The chair beneath him, too small for him, wobbled whenever he moved.

He said, "I came expecting the Lord Erdhart to be King here. All my dispatches were for King Erdhart. Halfway here, in the town they are building where the port of Santomalo was, I heard that Erdhart was dead, perhaps at the hands of local people. I was waiting for new instructions from the Holy City when another dispatch came that his sons Oto and Broga ruled in his place and I should proceed. Now arriving here I find the Lord Broga dead also, and the place in an uproar."

Jeon said, "It was a bad winter."

Stencop said, "So I have given the messages and my remaining cargo to King Oto." He shifted on the chair, which groaned under his weight. One beefy forearm rested on the table, and his voice quieted. "He tells me that his father died in a coup attempt, which he suppressed. Broga in an accident, a fall or something, he is unclear. He says the castle is treacherous and we should not go there and he will live there no more." Stencop's jaw worked beneath the thickets of whiskers. "But in the town I have heard other stories. That Broga was murdered, by—in revenge. By local—I know not what to think." Beneath the bushy brows his eyes poked at Jeon.

Jeon said, "My lord, I am the King's servant."

"Be candid with me."

"Sir, I am." Jeon spread his hands. The little tabletop between them had a pattern of inlaid squares, like a chessboard. "Do you play chess, sir?"

"No."

"A pity. Nobody will play with me anymore, and I was just getting the feel of it."

Stencop's big hand gripped the edge of the table. His body shifted on the chair. "You think these pirates will attack here."

"The full moon is a week away. If not then, the next time the tide will be high at sunrise. They will come. Nothing has stopped them yet. Undercastle is full of things they want."

"My lord Oto seems unconvinced."

Jeon said, "My lord Oto does not believe anything he hasn't thought of first himself." He traced the squares of the tabletop with his forefinger. "It's a poor realm where the King is his own courtier."

"Hunh." The admiral's eyebrows moved up and down. "Perhaps."

"But we should at least prepare," Jeon said. "You have all the men and all the weapons. Who is in command here?"

Stencop was frowning. "Well, the King, surely, the local man is always . . . unless . . ." His thick lips pushed out thoughtfully. "At least that's something to be done."

His head turned; in the distance, there was a long, muffled crash. Jeon leapt up, and went outside, Stencop on his heels.

THE WAXING MOON HUNG OVER THE BAY. ALL THE LIGHTS OF Undercastle shone, even up on the cliff, but brightest around the brewery. Tirza lurked by the way that led onto the Jawbone, watching the uproar on the beach. They were singing, out there, and dancing, very badly; they were all drunk. She wanted to go out onto the Jawbone, but she wanted to see Jeon also, and he was in the camp, off to her left.

Her ears filled, and then the sound swelled in them, a thunder of falling stone. Under her feet, the ground shook a moment.

She ran up the moonlit beach, to where she could see all the castle. In Undercastle people were screaming. At the edge of the shadow of the castle, Tirza stopped on the sand, and looking back she saw just beyond the four straight old towers the new tower tilting over.

One side of it was gone already, as if something had gnawed it, the little cap of its roof sliding sideways over the fallen stone. She caught her breath. As the tower leaned, it shed more stones, until in a hail of pieces it all disappeared.

She gave a yell, triumphant, but behind her, in Undercastle, a howl of terror went up.

"The castle is falling!"

"No!" she called. "No, it is the new tower—" and stopped. The mob was packed there on the moonlit beach, immobile, a single swarm, paying heed only to what they saw, and she knew they did not understand.

THE MOON WAS BRIGHT AS A THOUSAND LAMPS. WITH THE others Amillee stood, trembling, her gaze on the dark shape of the castle, waiting for the next tower to fall—for everything up there to crumble into dust, what had been there all the long ages.

Nothing happened. Only the one tower had come down. The great crown of spires stood against the sky, solid as the rock beneath it. The crowd sighed, giving up some of its watchfulness, and began to move around.

Beside her, the priest said, "This is evil."

"Well," Amillee said. She had seen the castle every day of her life, but she could not really tell which of the towers was gone. In daylight maybe she would. That might help her understand what this meant. The priest swayed, holding her with one hand to keep his feet. In the other he had a jug.

"Nothing like this happens without some sign," the priest said. "It's not ordinary. It's just once. Means something. Evil."

It meant, Amillee thought, that she should act, and not wait to be led. She backed away, looking around, wondering what she should do. The priest staggered away from her. The jug was empty and he dropped it, and his voice rang out, surprisingly loud.

"Listen to me. This is the end of the world. We must pray—"

Amillee muttered, "Damn you, fool," and started after him. The crowd was turning toward him, and he wandered into the light of the brewery.

"I call to you, I say, I say, we must give ourselves to repentance, renounce the evils, and go back to the old ways, or—or—"

On the porch of the brewery somebody shouted, "Get him! That's a deserter!"

The priest staggered backward, his voice failing, as a flood of striped doublets poured down from the porch. Amillee bounded up to his side and pushed him behind her. Locking arms with Trollo on her right and on the left a girl from the weavery, Amillee took her place in a wall of bodies. Behind her, people clustered around the priest, protecting him. A voice rose in a confident whoop. "We beat them before— Remind them who we are, hey!"

Amillee faced the Imperials, who came straight at her. They had no pikes, only their short knives, which didn't even have points. For a moment, as they came, she imagined they would reach her and bounce harmlessly away, but then they smashed into her, and she was thrown down, and they trampled over her, and something struck her on the side of the head.

She lay there, dizzy, her hand aching, and a hurt jabbing her ribs when she breathed. Somebody had stepped on her hand. She tasted dust in her mouth. Painfully she stood up, looking down the beach.

The Imperials had rushed on after the priest, and the crowd was bundling him away toward the ale caves. The mass of people pushed back at the soldiers, jeering, at first still making a game of this.

The Imperials waded into them, clubbing with the flats of their knives, hacking with the blades. More soldiers rushed up through the dark. Outnumbered, the crowd began to scatter. The last few, backing away, launched a hail of stones at the soldiers. Amillee looked around for a weapon. In the deceptive clarity of the moonlight the fighting was a dark rumbling mass on the beach. She could not tell one from the other, which she loved and which she hated. Then she saw, nearer, a body crumpled on the ground.

She knew at once it was Trollo, by the cap, and she went and knelt down beside him. He had locked arms with her, when this all started. They had stood together against the Imperials. He was still alive, and she slid her arm around his shoulders and lifted him. He turned his head slowly toward her. His face was split in half like a melon, blood spurting from his forehead, his nose and mouth. His eyes met hers, clear, wide blue eyes, seeing her, and then he was not there anymore, his eyes open, but seeing nothing.

Amillee held him still, unable to make herself move. On the beach there was no more fighting, only screams, and the savage, triumphant yells of the soldiers. More bodies on the ground. Somebody tugged on her.

"Come on, girl," her mother said. "Hurry. Come on. Leave him, poor Trollo. Come." Amillee stood up, and Lumilla put an arm around her and pulled her away, toward the ale caves.

In the back of the caves, where the wall had been tunneled through to make one big room, half the town were hiding, crowded in the dark. Somewhere the priest's voice was sounding, "It is the end. We have failed. We have lost our way." Nobody seemed to be listening. Amillee sat down by the wall, beside her mother.

"Repent," the priest said in the dark.

"Oh, shut up, you old fool!" Amillee cried. She drew her knees to her chest, folded her arms on them, and laid her head down and shut her eyes.

THE SUN WAS JUST RISING; UP THERE, THE CASTLE'S NEW OUTline stood against the pallor of the sky. Where the new tower had been was empty. Jeon folded his arms over his chest. The fight had been bad; a lot of people had died, all of them people from Undercastle. Now the Imperials were herding the rest of them down onto the beach, just above where the kicker stood.

On his far side, Stencop was saying, "You don't even have control of this village." Jeon turned toward him.

There, just above the high-tide line, Oto sat on his horse, looking around. He wore a broad hat against the sun. Finally he brought his lofty gaze to the admiral, standing on the sand below him. Oto said, "Last night seems to have proven different." He looked toward Jeon, off to the side. "Prince, what do you say?"

Jeon made a meaningless noise in his throat. The townspeople were lining up higher on the beach, the soldiers nudging them, ordering them. Aken and Lumilla were standing at the front. Stencop was unyielding, his body braced, his head back to glare up at Oto.

"Because of my men, only! You have bungled this, my lord. Admit it!"

Oto said, "I think they only need a demonstration." He gave another look at Jeon, and swung around toward the kicker, slightly down the beach. The officer there came smartly toward Oto, snapping out a salute.

"Sergeant," Oto said, "prepare a live fire."

Jeon drifted back up the beach, to where Lumilla and Aken stood. All around the outside of the massed townspeople, Imperial soldiers formed a line, shoulder to shoulder, fencing them in, far more now than the local people.

On the beach, several men worked busily over the kicker. The sergeant strutted around giving them orders. One soldier wound the wheel on the bottom of the frame, and the flat plank of the neck bent backward, backward, until it curved almost double, head to heels.

With that in place, Marwin marched up to Oto. "Glory to the Empire! What am I to kill, sir?"

Jeon started. Smiling, Oto looked across the beach at the townspeople. Aken was staring at the kicker, his mouth lost in the greying thicket of his beard. Lumilla glanced at Oto and turned a look of fear on Jeon. "What are they doing?"

"Proving something to us," Jeon said.

Oto said, "Sergeant, show these people what we can do." He pointed down the beach. "That tree."

Lumilla cried out, "No!" Aken ground his jaw. Oto was pointing at the cypress, far down the beach, the meeting center of the town.

Aken said under his breath, "Do something." Jeon did not move.

He was watching Marwin, who was standing there staring at the tree, holding out his hands in front of him, up and down, side to side, as if he measured it. At last he crouched behind the kicker and said more orders. The men pushed the frame smoothly along on its base until it faced down the beach toward the cypress. Now they slotted a head onto the neck, a kind of basket. Jeon muttered. It was all coming together now, what this was. Marwin leaned over the winch that held the head down to the frame's heels.

The townspeople said nothing. It was quiet enough that Jeon could hear the wind sifting through the grass at the top of the cliff. Marwin's voice giving more orders was thin as a reed. The

Imperials opened the box they had brought so carefully up from their ship. Inside Jeon saw three big, round balls, each the size of a man's head, made of something hard and shining, each one packed well in a grainy white stuff. Salt, he realized. And probably the box itself was heavily muffled. Any jar might set them off. The Imperials lifted one of these balls, carried it gently up to the plank, and fit it into the basket at the end.

"Stand back!" Marwin cried. "At arms!"

A soldier stepped smartly to the back of the frame, and put his hand on the winch. "Ready!"

"Ready!"

"Ready!"

"Kill!"

The soldier yanked at the winch handle. The cable flew loose, and the neck straightened out so hard the whole frame bounced off the ground. The round ball hurtled up into the air; as it flew it gave a thin, shrill shriek. It rose in a high, powerful arc, and fell, and crashed down into the cypress tree.

The birds scattered squawking up into the air; for a moment there was nothing, and Marwin said, disappointed, "It didn't hit anything hard enough to crack"—and the cypress went up with a roar that shook the beach.

The crowd screamed, and ran. The whole tree blazed like a bolt of fire, twice as tall as it had been alive. Bits of char and ash showered down out of the air; Jeon saw part of a dead bird drop into the bay. Lumilla went down on her knees. Aken swore.

Oto was smiling wide. He said, "I think that's enough. Admiral Stencop, you will attend me in my summer palace. Prince Jeon, you as well. Come along." Oto turned his horse and rode toward the path.

Jeon was still staring at the kicker. He wondered what its range was, if the cypress was as far as it could reach. He walked around it, looking at every side of it, seeing how every part of it was fixed to its purpose. It was all power, the rigid triangles of the frame, the simple, mechanical motion, the one predictable action, over and over. Marwin was right. This was the emblem of the Empire, this death mill.

Something curled softly around Jeon's ankles; he looked down and saw the rim of the surf foaming around his boots. The Imperial men were hastily packing away the box of fireballs, drawing it up farther on the beach, away from the wet. The edge of the surf at his feet slipped round and soft back down the damp sand, in under the rise of the next uncoiling wave. And that was the answer, Jeon thought. Chaos was pregnant. Order was dead. He glanced around; Oto was already gone into the brewery.

Jeon wondered where Tirza was. He missed her; he missed all of them, but her most, of course. He knew she was angry with him, that she thought he had gone over to the enemy. In the end, he hoped, she would see otherwise. He would make her see otherwise. She loved him; she had to believe him.

Or he would be dead, and it wouldn't matter. He went on up the beach, after Oto.

WHERE THE CYPRESS HAD BEEN WAS A WIDE SMOKING PIT gouged out of the beach. Tirza stood on the edge, looking into the space where Mervaly and Casea had sat, where they had heard songs and stories and arguments and news. Where poor Trollo had played. The crater was still burning, here and there, in its black deeps. All around, the filthy crust glittered with tiny droplets of melted sand.

Her brother had done this. Was doing this. Was helping Oto do this, her own brother.

She looked back over her shoulder. The town was packed with soldiers. Only the brewery was open. In front of Aken's stall his old horse slouched in its patched harness. Aken came out with a box to put in the wagon.

As Tirza stood there, Lumilla came by, with Amillee a step behind her, both carrying bundles and packs. Amillee paused to look at Tirza, but she said nothing. Her face was deeply lined, like a much older woman's. After a moment she turned and went on, going away with her mother.

At the end of the beach, the castle loomed up its crown against the sky. The new tower's squat pale shape was gone, but where it had been a black nub rose: perhaps that would grow larger. Tirza shivered. If she went in there, she would walk inside those walls. She would find the passageways, the chambers, new and old. She would find her mother, sit with her brother, her sister. That must be where she belonged, part of the seamless web. Yet she dreaded to go there. The feeling overcame her that she belonged nowhere anymore. She stood a long while, looking up at the castle on its cliff top. But then she went out onto the Jawbone.

REMEMBERING WHAT JEON HAD SAID, OTO WENT BY THE graveyard, and while pretending to pray dug up a handful of the dirt from his brother's grave. This Oto put into a pouch and hung on his belt. In the brewery he sprinkled some all around the room where he slept and the chair where he liked to sit on the porch, and now and then he touched his fingertips to his tongue, tasting the comfort of the earth on them. It occurred to him he should put some into his boots, also. That would require another visit to the grave.

Now at midmorning he sat on the porch, a table between him and Stencop, and said, "It is to happen tomorrow, then? If it happens? This supposed pirate attack?"

"Yes," Stencop said. "The bay mouth forces the tide here; I imagine it will be very high tomorrow at sunrise."

Oto shrugged, looking off toward the beach. "I am not utterly convinced of Prince Jeon's theory, but we must deploy the kickers in any case." Things like this bored him. He wound his hands together, soothed by his own touch. "I shall rely on your experience for that. Of course if anything goes wrong, you are responsible."

The admiral gave him a stiff nod. "I want it no other way, my lord. And there is the issue of my men."

His men, Oto heard. He thought, My men. He said, "Which is?"

"The townspeople will not serve them. They can get no bread or ale or meat."

"Take it, then," Oto said, and laughed. "Give them the King's leave." He waved at Stencop. "Go do your work, sir. Do it well."

Stencop got heavily up from the chair. "I shall. And to you, the same." He turned on his heel and tramped across the porch and down the steps to the beach. Oto watched him go. He could hardly bear the admiral's constant attacks, veiled even as they were as defenses. Oto knew Stencop was only waiting for his chance to seize the crown.

As Jeon also was, of course. Jeon was not a good liar; Oto read him to the last word. But Jeon had no power and Stencop had an army.

Which was Oto's army, properly. He had only to watch for the chance to eliminate Stencop. And Jeon too. Maybe there was some way to get Stencop to do that. Accomplish both ends in one stroke. Oto liked the artistry of that. Arrange it so no one would blame him.

His cup was empty. He looked around for the big tawny girl who had always served him, and she was gone. He looked wider, and saw, among the several men lounging on the porch, no one but soldiers. He sat for a while, waiting to be served, but no one came. Finally he caught the eye of the new sergeant, lounging by the steps to the beach, and sent him for more ale.

STENCOP SAID, "AH, PRINCE JEON. I AM GLAD TO SEE YOU." He laid a heavy arm over Jeon's shoulders. "We are about to position the engines."

Jeon was staring at the three kickers lined up on the beach. "Is this all you have?"

Stencop grunted, mirthful. "This will be enough against such a force as might come here."

"What does the King say?"

"The King has wisely left it to me. I am the more senior at this."

Jeon slid his hands behind his back. He did not believe Oto would leave this force to Stencop for long; he flung a quick glance up the beach toward the brewery. He said, "Can we move them?"

Stencop said, "Easily enough, if we must. But I am minded to leave them here, where they have an excellent command of the whole bay."

Jeon stepped to one side, to look across the water. He wondered again where his sister was. "Can they hit the Jawbone from here? That spit, over there, the far edge."

"No, hardly," Stencop said with a disbelieving laugh. He was relaxed, confident, sure of himself: Jeon realized Stencop still trusted Oto.

He said, "Well, then, why not put one of these out there?" He pointed across the shining water. "Put one out there, one here, and one up there, at the deepwater end of the bay."

Stencop folded his arms over his chest, frowning. "Why separate them? They're stronger together."

"For one thing," Jeon said, "you can cover more."

"They'll come to this beach; that's all I need to cover."

"Yes, they'll try to overwhelm you all at once."

"And we'll beat them, all at once."

Jeon said, "You have already lost to these same people. It will not be like the fight against the locals, simple people with no weapons, a few quick blows and over. Now, look." He pointed Stencop down toward the mouth of the bay. "That's the place to get them. They have to come down the channel, whatever kinds of boats they have. The channel is narrow, and the tide runs fast through it. Once they're into the channel they cannot go backward. If you attack them, they can't scatter, and they can't run away: all they can do is keep coming up the channel, right into your shot. But from here, you can't completely cover the channel. Put one kicker here, and one here, and one over on the far side of the bay, where you can pound him all the way."

Stencop was staring down the bay; he said, "Very clever, Prince Jeon." Now for the first time Stencop looked back over his shoulder, toward the brewery. "However, I believe we also need to cover the town. After the other night. And we only have enough bombs for each kicker to shoot twice."

Jeon said, "The town is empty. The people are leaving."

Stencop said, "That doesn't mean they won't come back. They're treacherous."

Jeon said, "If you divide the kickers, also, no one will be able to command all of them at once. No matter what happens, you will have charge of something."

Stencop gave him a startled look. "The King has said that I command all."

"For now," Jeon said.

Stencop had lost his ease; his mouth sucked thin, he stood staring a moment at Jeon, and finally said, "I shall have to give this careful thought."

Jeon bowed. "As you will, my lord admiral. I only serve."

* * *

FROM THE TOWN SIDE THE BIG BARGE WAS PLOWING THROUGH the bay toward the Jawbone. Tirza walked down along the spit, keeping to the rocks, and stopped on the top of the slope, with the fringe of stunted cypress behind her. The barge pushed into the curve of beach below her. The eight men sculling it along leapt over the side, hauled the barge up onto the sand above the water's edge, and began unloading stacks of wood.

She knew what this was. She had seen the cypress tree burn; now they were going to plant the same thing that had done that on the Jawbone. She hated these people. She hated her brother for helping them.

The men went around the top of the beach with some boards of wood, scraping away rocks and sea drift down to the hard ground, clawing and gouging at the ground to flatten it out. Around this clearing they stacked the pieces of their monster. She gathered up stones, filling her skirt with them, and circled back to the slope between the beach and the scraggly trees.

Down there, they had the boxy frame halfway up, like a wooden mouth yawning at the sky, and they were carrying over the long tongue. She dumped the rocks at her feet and began to throw.

The first one missed, and plopped into the bay. The working-men below all turned toward that sound, and the next stone hit the one nearest her on the neck. He yowled. The third stone bounced off the frame but struck somebody on the rebound so hard he sat down. Pointing up at her, they rushed at her, and she darted off into the rocks.

Almost at once they went back to their work, and she crept around to another place on the rise, and threw more rocks.

They chased her again, shouting. She leapt nimbly along ahead of them, leading them after her up the rocky slope, and scrambled in under the low branches of the cypress thickets at the top. In there she had a favorite place, a crevice deep under the rocks, and she ducked into it. For a while they looked for her. Curled in the damp hollow of the earth, she looked and saw their boots tramp past. Then their voices faded and they went away.

She crawled back up to the sunlight, thinking she would keep at this and slow them down, at least, but when she walked out of the cypress a man in a striped doublet sprang on her.

With a yell of triumph he knocked her down. For a moment, he kicked and struck at her, bellowing. She rolled onto her back, with him above her, between her and the sky, and she drove both her feet up into his crotch. His bellow of delight turned into a screech. She sprang up and raced away down the Jawbone. The other men were running from the beach after her. Her knee hurt; she had banged it on the rocks when she fell. Her elbow hurt. She ran on, dodging in among the rocks, looking for another hideaway.

OTO SAID, "YOU SEE THEY RESPECT ME NOW. I SHOULD HAVE done that sooner." He rode along the beach, smiling. Beside him, Jeon said nothing. As they approached, the scattered midday crowd scattered, shrinking away, and nobody would look him in the face. The shutter was drawn across the front of the bakery.

"There were more people than this," Oto said presently. They were halfway down the beach to the charred stump of the cypress tree, where the first of the kickers stood, with soldiers all around it. "Are they hiding?"

"They probably went away inland," Jeon said. "They will come back. They belong here. They're only frightened. But they live here." As he spoke, a raw heat brightened in him, for their sake, a rage at what had happened here.

Oto laughed. "I did. I frightened them, burning their tree. Yet I miss the meat pies."

"Easy enough to make. Come down here and let me show you something."

They rode up to the kicker by the cypress stump. The soldiers at once bowed and swung their hats, and Oto gave them a few salutes. Jeon dismounted from his horse and let the reins trail. Glancing out across the bay, he looked to see if the third kicker was in place, and saw the men there all running up the ridge at once.

Oto said, "Yes, get on with it."

Jeon faced him. "Stencop came to me yesterday and got me down here to help him set up the kickers. He agrees with me that we have a high chance of seeing the pirates soon, and he put the kickers around so." Jeon pointed to this one, and then down the beach to the next, and then across the bay to the one on the opposite shore.

"This was his idea, setting them up this way. I thought it odd not to put all the kickers together at the best place to defend the channel. But look." He moved behind the one and sighted down the long horizontal side of the kicker toward the castle.

Oto said, "I think you're mad, anyway. The pirates will not attack such a strong position as this." He swung down from his horse. "Especially with a fleet here."

"What fleet? Two ships?" Jeon stood back, and Oto stooped to look along the side of the kicker.

"And?"

Jeon pushed the little brake lever, and the big machine turned of its own weight. The far corner of the long edge, like a sight, slid across the surf, then the sand, and finally came to rest aimed directly at the brewery.

Oto straightened, his face rigid. "What are you trying to say, Prince?"

Jeon shrugged. "You mentioned secret orders?"

Oto glared at him. His beard was scraggly and his coat hung

open and as he stood there he lifted one arm and flapped the coat to cool himself. He said, slowly, as if he thought it all out as he spoke, "Well, then, I think it's time for me to take command, isn't it."

"My lord," Jeon said, and bowed.

"Call Stencop to me," Oto said. "We shall hold council." He mounted his horse, and rode slowly away down the beach toward the brewery. Halfway there, he turned and looked back at the kicker. His hand went to his belt. Jeon went off to find Stencop.

OTO KNEW HOW TO MANAGE THIS: HE FISTED HIS HANDS TO-gether on the table, and stared across at Stencop. "I am the King. You deployed the kickers in an odd way, and I feel the need to take control."

"That was—" Stencop shut his mouth. His gaze licked side-ways, toward Prince Jeon sitting off behind Oto. His eyes on Oto again, Stencop said, "As you wish. My lord. Do you want to move them?"

Oto paused only a moment, thinking this over. He said, "This supposed attack will occur tomorrow. If it fails to appear we shall move them, yes. But for now. I will command. You, my lord," Oto said, nodding at Stencop, "will command the position down the beach. The kicker on the far side of the bay—"

"Not him," Stencop said, clipped. He gave another fierce stare down at Jeon, who obviously had advised him on the placement of the kickers. Oto sat back, smiling. He had seen through the boy's designs again. Oto resisted the urge to throw a look of tri-umph over his shoulder.

He said, "Prince Jeon will attend you. I'll put the company sergeant in charge of the kicker across the bay. The army can remain in camp, so close on the beach as they are, summoned as needed. We'll post a sentry at the mouth of the bay."

"Very well," Stencop said, and rose, ponderous. He swept the whole beach with his look."Where have all the people gone?"

"Out of reach of the pirates," Oto said. "They'll come back." He reached for his cup, but it was empty. Stencop was moving away, Jeon after him, but staying a good way behind. Oto almost laughed. He had made enemies of his enemies. Yet his cup was still empty. In the midst of his triumphs it was galling that he suffered such a constant want of service. He put the cup down with a thud.

STENCOP SAID, "I WOULD CHAIN YOU TO THE KICKER, IF YOU would not get in the way."

Jeon avoided Stencop's eyes, and looked instead out across the mild waters of the bay. Nothing in this was going as he wished. He moved down toward the beach a few steps and Stencop said sharply, "Stand." With a crook of his finger he beckoned one of his ensigns. "Watch him." Stencop gave Jeon another fierce glare and turned to another waiting officer.

"Send the second watch officer down to the end of the beach, where he can see anything that approaches—give him a good horn. Tell him on his life to stay awake."

"Yes, sir! Glory!"

"Glory. Send me the troop commander."

"Glory!"

Stencop grunted, and tramped up behind Jeon again, and shouted, "You will stay here, guarded, until this is over! Then we—the King and I—shall discuss how to deal with you." Stencop fell still, his breath harsh. "I am going to my quarters. Watch him." Stencop stalked off down the beach. The ensign beside Jeon crossed his arms over his chest. Jeon sat down on the sand, watching the sea.

* * *

Tirza woke just before dawn, when the sound of the water changed.

She was curled up below the overhang of the dune, ten feet above the edge of the bay, across the water from the stump of the cypress tree. All night, the waves, broken to chop as they fought their way through the narrows, had slapped and rippled along the pebble beach, but now the water was rising in long swells that dropped hard on the sand. Something big was moving into the bay.

She sprang up. Beyond the cliff the eastern sky shone pale as shell. In the blackness overhead the stars were going out. She ran down to the beach, and out there, on the flat, dark water, she saw the darker shape moving down the channel.

At the tip of the Jawbone, a horn blared.

She saw his head rise up into the air, the great, flared lizard head, and she screamed. "It's a trap! Go back! Go back!"

He heard her; his head turned, and the horn blared again. From down the Jawbone, where the kicker was, came shouting. The horn was blasting, over and over. A thin whistle cut through the metallic shriek, coming closer. "Go back!" she screamed, again, and out there he sank beneath the water, and suddenly an enormous rolling ball of flame burst like a little sun in the center of the channel.

The boom rolled toward her, and the shock blew her backward hard onto her bottom on the sand. She flung herself facedown. Another thunderous crash, and then another almost at once, and a wash of heat blew across her back. A stench like dead things. Suddenly she was being pelted with falling ash and burning things and water, pounding on her like hail. She leapt up, her arms over her head, looking toward the channel.

The air was thick with smoke and dirt. Huge surf was smashing up on the beach and slopping up around her feet. A long, hollow crash still resounded, on and on, echoing off the cliff. The sun was tipping over the edge of the land, and the sky turning white, but the bay was a cauldron of dark rolling smoke and sound.

She ran down the beach, her teeth gritted together. Ahead, she saw the men at the kicker there, busy cranking the tongue backward, two of them carrying up the ball, to load it again, to shoot again. The sergeant stood there, watching. She stopped and got a rock and hurled it. Ran on. The sergeant heard her coming, and he shouted. The others stopped, twisting around to look. She stopped and scrabbled for rocks on the beach and, finding nothing but weed, bits of wood, threw that, shrieking in rage and terror. The sergeant was racing toward her, two of the others a step behind. She cocked back her arm to throw a handful of sea drift, and then, behind them, out of the bay just below the kicker, the head of the dragon rose, blazing red in the glare of the new sun.

OTO'S HORSE REARED, AND HE FOUGHT IT TO A STANDSTILL, his gaze directed across the water. The horn had brought him out of the brewery, and he had seen nothing, only the crew working the kicker, and then the wonderful explosions. Roiling black smoke hid the water from him, but he knew nothing could have endured that. He bellowed, "Victory!" The horse bounded again, its neck black with sweat. Bits of dirt and embers still floated in the air. The men around him were cheering and clapping themselves on the back.

He turned down the beach, toward Stencop's place. "Victory!" he roared again, and galloped down the beach, to make sure Stencop recognized whose victory this was.

THE ARMY WAS STILL RUSHING OUT OF ITS CAMP, GATHERING IN ranks along the high side of the beach. Stencop stalked around yelling orders. Jeon had not moved all night, the ensign stoically standing guard all the while, but now the ensign was shouting and throwing his fists in the air like everybody else. Jeon went down to the edge of the surf, where the black wave beat hard on the sand, and stared down toward the channel.

He thought, What was that? What was that?

Under the seething cloud of steam and smoke the surface of the bay still quaked; all around him steaming drops of water rained down. Behind him the cheering went on, and down where the cypress had been those men were whooping and celebrating also. Oto on his horse was galloping toward them along the beach. The sun was coming over the cliff top, the air suddenly warm. Jeon stared across the water, trying to make out what it was he had just seen.

Just behind him, Stencop said, "Well, you were right about that, anyway." He lifted his voice, heavy with command. "Good kill. Reload."

Jeon did not move. He did not think this was over. He had seen something out there, before the first bombs struck. Something not a ship. He strained his eyes for signs of wreckage in the rocking, empty water.

Then from across the bay, over on the Jawbone, where that third kicker was, a blinding light flashed, a rumbling explosion rose to a thunder, and another fireball billowed up into the air.

The Imperials' buoyant cheering died away. Stencop turned his head. "What is happening?"

This explosion had raised more dust and smoke, a great cloud that rolled across the bay toward them, hiding the Jawbone from sight. Jeon gawked at it. He thought suddenly of Tirza, out there somewhere.

Then through the masking cloud a dark mass appeared, hurtling toward him.

He went rapidly backward, up beside the kicker. The sun was

full risen now. The surf began to roll up hard on the beach. The wind harshened. Out of the cloud before Jeon charged something red as a fire and bigger than a house. It had horns, it had enormous eyes, and it was coming straight at him.

Stencop was roaring, "Stand! Stand! Glory to the Empire! Kill!" He drew the saber from his belt and thrust it overhead, and from all the army came a single scream.

"Glory!"

The men by the kicker had winched the neck back double. Pacing up and down beside them, Stencop waved his sword. "Point-blank! Straight ahead!" Two soldiers hauled up the round bomb, glistening, while two others worked to aim it.

Jeon thought nothing: as they slid the bomb into the basket, he took one step forward and kicked the winch handle.

The winch spun. The kicker's neck snapped straight up, and the whole frame bucked, knocking the soldiers there flying. Stencop bellowed, furious. The screeching bomb flew off into the air, far out over the bay. The monster had reached the shallows, was charging in sheets of spray up toward the beach. It opened its jaws and blasted out a long flame, bright green even in the daylight. Jeon threw his arm up to shield his face. Around him, the soldiers were rushing up into a rank along the beach, their knives in their hands. Off in the middle of the bay, the last bomb exploded, harmless.

Closer, Stencop roared in Jeon's ears. Stencop's hand fisted in Jeon's hair, and Stencop shoved his sword into Jeon's face.

"So! So, all along! Die, then— Down there—" Stencop propelled Jeon forward toward the bay, ahead of all the screaming soldiers, toward the beast wading up through the surf. "You first!"

Jeon resisted, his arms out, his head tipped back; the dragon swung toward him. Even in his terror, he saw it was magnificent. Stencop's sword jabbed him in the back. "Death— Glory—" Jeon had nowhere to go but forward and he ran forward, out of Stencop's grip, up beneath the eyes of the dragon.

It crouched above him, massive and glistening. One eye fixed on him. He saw his face mirrored in the enormous curve. Then the dragon opened its jaws again and lunged, and its teeth fastened on Stencop.

Jeon backpedaled, away, back into the midst of the soldiers. Howling, they were rushing in to hack at the great scaled shoulders of the beast, and behind them all, safe up at the top of the beach, Oto galloped up and down, waving his sword over his head and bellowing, "Fight! Fight!" The dragon struck again, taking a mouthful of Imperials. Its neck was bleeding. Jeon worked his way steadily through the pack of men up the beach toward Oto. As Jeon passed, some of the soldiers were slacking off, looking around, their hands with their knives falling to their sides.

"Get the eyes!" Oto screamed. "Attack its eyes!"

The fiery blast licked out again, and the kicker burst into flame. With a sweep of its head the dragon knocked a dozen burning soldiers across the beach. The rest were shrinking back, their voices wailing now, not cheering. Oto spurred his horse up to rally them. "Glory, you fools, you cowards! Glory!" That brought him within reach and Jeon sprang.

He got Oto by one arm, and swung his weight against him, trying to drag him out of the saddle; the horse lurched. Oto wrenched it back on its hocks, brought his sword around, and struck Jeon across the head with the hilt. Dizzy, Jeon lost his grip and fell on his back. The tip of the sword sliced at his head, and above him Oto reined his horse around to trample him.

Jeon rolled to his knees, dodging the blade; his head was still muzzy, but he saw Oto before him. With all his weight Jeon lunged against the horse's shoulder. Flailing out with one hand, he caught and gripped a rein. Oto slashed down the blade and

Jeon leapt back again, yanking on the rein, and that brought the horse's head around and the sword bit deep into its neck.

The horse reared up, screaming, spraying blood through the air. The sword sailed off. Jeon ran to pick it up. All around him the Imperials were running back up the beach, headed for the cliff, turning their backs on the dragon. The horse crumpled to its knees, Oto still in the saddle, there right before Jeon, and he drew the sword back and ran it into Oto's body.

Jeon had never killed anyone before. He was surprised at how easy it was. The soldiers had fled away, back into the shelter of the cliff, but there were bodies and bits of bodies all over the sand, and now one of them was Oto's.

The beach trembled under the footsteps of the dragon. Jeon stood where he was, unafraid. The great beast stalked past him, gave him a single gleaming look, and dragged itself down toward the bay. Its shoulders and sides were slashed, its long neck torn, there were long slick wounds like burns on its back, and even so it was splendid.

Then Jeon saw his sister running around the rim of beach that led from the Jawbone.

Her red hair flew. She was tattered and barefoot, her arm bruised, her face dirty. He shouted her name, and her head turned toward him, but she ran straight on, up toward where the dragon slouched, alone on the wide beach, bleeding from a hundred wounds.

The dragon swung its great head toward her; where its blood pooled on the sand it burned like coal fire. Tirza went right up before it, and it lowered its face to her. Jeon realized that she was speaking to it. He went up close enough to hear her voice, and then the beast answered her.

A shudder of despair went through Jeon. He stood watching

his sister and the creature she had conjured from the sea, and wondered what he could do now.

Tirza said, "You came."

The dragon said, "I have searched for you since you left. I meant to devour you, because you abandoned me. But you saved me. If you had not warned me I would have died. And I remember the stories."

"I have more stories," she said. "And you are hurt. Let me help you."

"I am grievous hurt. I don't think you can help me." He was turning back toward the sea, his gaze leaving her. She put her arms out to him.

"Take me with you."

He turned his enormous eyes on her again. "I do not know where these wounds and the sea will take me."

"Tirza," her brother said.

She twisted her head toward him; he had come down close behind her. He stood there, his arms at his sides and his eyes blazing.

"Tirza, see? I've won. Oto is dead. Stencop is dead. I've avenged everybody. I have taken Castle Ocean back." He put out his hand, and his fingers closed on her wrist. His hand was slick with blood. He said, "I have done everything for your sake."

She shook her head. If this was even true it made no difference. Yet her heart quaked, and his bloody hand held her fast.

His gaze burnt into her. He said, "Keep faith with me, Tirza."

That broke the spell, and she laughed. "That's a curse, Jeon. Not a blessing." He did not understand what she said. He would never understand her. But she had defied one curse and she could defy another. She drew her wrist out of his grip and turned back to the dragon.

"I want to go with you, whatever happens."

He lowered his head; his tongue licked over her feet. She climbed onto his back, up onto his shoulder. On the beach, Jeon stood alone, watching her, above him Castle Ocean like a broken hand against the sky, and then the dragon carried her into the sea.

About the Author

CECELIA HOLLAND is widely acknowledged as one of the finest historical novelists of our time. She is the author of more than thirty novels, including *The Angel and the Sword* and *The Kings in Winter*. Holland lives in Humboldt County, in Northern California, where she teaches creative writing.

About the Author

CECELIA HOLLAND is widely acknowledged as one of the finest historical novelists of our time. She is the author of more than thirty novels, including *The Angel and the Sword* and *The Kings in Winter*. Holland lives in Humboldt County, in Northern California, where she teaches creative writing.